"I can't imagine b
anything when I l
lumberjack at my side," Keena said.

"Not even jumping possums or whatever?" Travis asked as they sat in the bed of his truck, their legs dangling over the tailgate. The way her giggles floated away in the night was sweet and satisfying.

He watched her face. "What can you see?"

Keena tilted her head back. "So many stars. A brilliant slice of the moon. The warm glow of the lights in the house. The outline of the mountains rising up. There are a lot of shades of dark out here, I guess."

"And what do you hear?" Travis asked as she relaxed next to him.

"Rustles that may or may not be steers intent on revenge," Keena said with a smile in her voice, "but they aren't nearby. I can hear your breaths."

Travis was certain she could also hear his loudly beating heart when she said that.

Dear Reader,

Starting over can be scary, can't it? When I write, I sometimes begin in the wrong place, too early or too late in the characters' stories. Only extensive rewriting powered by Diet Coke can fix this problem! Life presents us all with occasional blank pages—career changes, new relationships, empty nests—that require some hard work as we find our way, but they're also full of possibility.

In *The Cowboy's Second Chance*, Travis Armstrong and Dr. Keena Murphy are both caught in this mix of fear and anticipation of big change. Travis has retired from the army and returned to Prospect to fulfill his purpose in the Armstrong family—fostering teens who need a safe space as much as he did as a boy. Keena's in town to help a friend, but while she's there, she finds that her career and the life she's built around it could be so much bigger. Travis and Keena learn that leaping into their new beginnings, even if they're nervous at first, leads to a bigger and better story together.

I've enjoyed getting to know the Armstrongs and their neighbors. Thank you for joining me in Prospect. To find out more about my books and what's coming next, visit me at cherylharperbooks.com.

Cheryl

HEARTWARMING

The Cowboy's Second Chance

—

Cheryl Harper

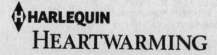

HARLEQUIN
HEARTWARMING

H HARLEQUIN®
HEARTWARMING™

Recycling programs
for this product may
not exist in your area

ISBN-13: 978-1-335-47564-0

The Cowboy's Second Chance

Copyright © 2024 by Cheryl Harper

For questions and comments about the quality of this book, please contact us at CustomerService@Harlequin.com.

Harlequin Enterprises ULC
22 Adelaide St. West, 41st Floor
Toronto, Ontario M5H 4E3, Canada
www.Harlequin.com

Printed in U.S.A.

Cheryl Harper discovered her love for books and words as a little girl, thanks to a mother who made countless library trips and an introduction to Laura Ingalls Wilder's Little House books. Whether the stories she reads are set in the prairie, the American West, Regency England or earth a hundred years in the future, Cheryl enjoys strong characters who make her laugh. Now Cheryl spends her days searching for the right words while she stares out the window and her dog, Jack, snoozes beside her. And she considers herself very lucky to do so.

For more information about Cheryl's books, visit her online at cherylharperbooks.com or follow her on Twitter, @cherylharperbks.

Books by Cheryl Harper

Harlequin Heartwarming

The Fortunes of Prospect

Her Cowboy's Promise
The Cowboy Next Door

Veterans' Road

Winning the Veteran's Heart
Second Chance Love
Her Holiday Reunion
The Doctor and the Matchmaker
The Dalmatian Dilemma
A Soldier Saved

Visit the Author Profile page
at Harlequin.com for more titles.

CHAPTER ONE

DR. KEENA MURPHY sat on the metal bench bisecting the long, narrow locker room and inhaled slowly. She held that breath for an exact count of ten. Tap by tap, one trembling finger at a time on her knees, she counted down. Exhaling lowered her racing pulse.

The paper gown covering her blue scrubs crinkled with each small movement. Whatever industrial cleaner the hospital's janitorial crew used on the floor smelled so familiar. Muffled chaos in Denver Medical Center's Emergency Department registered faintly, so Keena strained to differentiate the voices of her coworkers, the doctors and nurses still out on the floor.

Her sticky, dry mouth was a reminder that her twelve-hour shift had not included any time for food or water.

The doctor in her knew that was a terrible

way to care for herself, even as she also understood how it continued to happen.

She'd met every single demand of the job tonight, and that was all that mattered.

"What a day." Angie Washington yanked the surgical cap off her head and balled it up in the gown she had crumpled in one hand. "You okay, Dr. Murphy? You don't look so good. Cheeks are pale." The bench jolted as she dropped down next to Keena and wrapped her fingers around Keena's wrist to take her pulse. "Bet you were hoping for a nice, quiet shift tonight, lots of time to make your goodbyes. That's the kind of shift *I* wanted tonight. We don't get too many of those, do we?"

Keena appreciated Angie's brisk delivery, as if there was nothing out of the ordinary about Keena's end-of-the-shift routine. The nurse was right. The shift had gone as most of them did, but this wasn't like her. She never let her ER team see her sweat. It had become Keena's way of life. The fact that she'd been counting down the minutes until she could slowly fall apart tonight worried her the most.

"What will I do without you, Angie?" she

murmured and pulled her arm back. Whatever her pulse was doing, it was okay now.

This leave of absence was coming at exactly the right time. Keena's reputation as
Steady Murphy, the nickname the nurses
had given her early on for her calm response
to pressure, was spotless. The fewer people
who witnessed her control being as shaky as
her grip as she opened her locker, the better.

"I was definitely not prepared to see a
woman with multiple gunshot wounds."
Keena dealt with trauma regularly but sta-
bilizing the woman who'd been hurt by her
angry ex-husband had required every bit of
Keena's experience and most of the faith she
possessed.

"What you did was amazing. She was
lucky you were on duty." Angie waved a
hand. "Any hesitation might have killed her."

Keena frowned as she studied her neatly
folded jeans. "What *we* did, Angie. You didn't
leave me alone for a second, and she needed
all of us."

"She sure did and a few angels besides.
The fact that she made it through surgery
is proof miracles still happen around here.
Honestly, that was plenty for one night."

Angie sighed. "Following it up with the victims of a multicar accident on I-25 was…" Her voice trailed off as if it was impossible to find the right word.

"Yeah." Keena stood and pulled her clothes out of the locker. Tonight, a shower would absolutely be required before she could drive home. Fatigue made it too difficult to carry on polite conversation, so she gave up and started for the shower. When steam emerged, Keena gritted her teeth and stepped under the water. The fiery spray burned away the brain fog and made it easier to consider getting home. Her skin was a bright pink when she returned to her locker. No more pale cheeks.

Angie was still there, reapplying her lipstick.

"I'm leaving you in charge until I get back. Don't let anyone make a mess of my department." Keena was pleased at her stronger tone. Steady. That's what her team expected.

"Hope that wide spot in the road knows how lucky they are to get you, Dr. Murphy." Angie finished tying her shoes. "Three months and you'll be back? Is that what I heard?"

"That's the plan." Keena shoved her scrubs

in the bin to be laundered. "Dr. Singh is traveling to Haiti to assist with the medical mission there, and Prospect…" Keena ran her hands through her wet hair and twisted it into a knot on top of her head. "That's the name of the wide spot. Prospect doesn't have another doctor, so Dr. Singh asked for help finding a temporary replacement." She'd been lucky enough to work with Dr. Singh while she was still a resident, before he'd left for the slower lane of small-town doctor.

"Think you'll be…bored? The head nurse here when I started told me that working Emergency changes a person. Rewires your brain. Tonight, we did the impossible. May have to do it all over again tomorrow, too." Angie raised her eyebrows. Her opinion was clear. Colds and vaccinations would be quite the change from shifts in Denver's only Level 1 trauma center. The worst cases were transferred here, and the challenge had been invigorating for most of Keena's career. Here she accomplished feats few people could manage. That had been what drew her to medicine all along, the chance to perform at a high level and stand out in the crowd. She had been lucky to work with the best of the best, from the administration on the corporate-level floor all the way down to the security guards who stood at the door each night.

If Keena and her team thought of themselves as braver than the rest, they had plenty of opportunity to prove that. Angie's question prodded one of Keena's own doubts about spending months away from her hospital. Being bored might sound lovely, but Keena wasn't convinced, either.

"Angie, when was the last time you took a vacation?"

The RN peered into the distance as she considered the question. "Well, my husband and I took the kids to Disneyland over the summer." She shook her head. "Honestly, getting two teenagers there and safely home was more stressful than some shifts here at the hospital. I don't know how two children can fight like cats in a gunny sack and still agree to conspire against their parents the way these two do. Next time I get a break, we're leaving those children with my husband's mother. A vacation sounds nice, Dr. Murphy. You deserve to rest a little."

Keena was hoping for just that. The wear

and tear of Emergency added up. Slowing down in Prospect would be as nice as a vacation, leaving her refreshed and ready to take on nights like tonight without faltering. If the fear that she would lose her edge if she stepped out of the emergency department for too long floated through her mind now, Keena brushed it away.

It was a silly fear. Keena had been at her best under pressure before. That's all she wanted, a return to her old self. Her life was good; her work here had purpose. All she needed was a little R and R, and the adrenaline rush of shifts like this one would be exciting again.

"Boredom is going to be a blessing." Keena flexed her fingers, relieved to find them steady again. Returning to reality thanks to a mindfulness routine she'd learned out of self-preservation was good medicine, but only a bit of peace could restore her energy. That was the prescription she'd written for herself.

Keena double-checked the shelf in her locker to make sure she'd collected all the items she'd kept on hand to make hospital life more convenient—deodorant, toothpaste, toothbrush, floss, hairbrush—all the little things that could make difficult shifts bearable. Satisfied that everything was packed away in the box she'd been filling all week and her large bag, she was ready to leave.

"You know you aren't getting out of here without some kind of farewell from us, right?" Angie was leaning against the door to the hallway. "We're going to miss you too much around here for that."

Keena straightened her shoulders, determined to leave on a high note. "Since you've all been running this race right beside me tonight, I expect us all to keep this short and sweet."

Angie saluted.

"As a nurse, I try to never say 'the doctor knows best' too loudly. Bad for your egos." Angie held the door open. "But I hope you enjoy your break. When you're ready to come home, we'll be here." As Angie and Keena passed the large front desk, everyone seemed to be holding their breath.

A box of cookies sat on the nurses' station, decorated and arranged to spell out *We will miss you!* in hot-pink letters. Angie handed her one. "Your favorite color."

Touched that Angie would remember

something like that, Keena ate two cookies and read the comments on the enormous card signed by everyone in the department. Leaving was bittersweet.

She stopped to carefully survey all the faces, returning each person's smile with one of her own. "Thank you for all you've done tonight. I'll see you in a few months."

"See you soon" was much more accurate than "goodbye."

As she headed for the sliding doors, the security guard there tipped an imaginary hat, so Keena returned the favor before stepping out into the early-morning sunshine.

The reminder of the world outside the hospital and that it kept turning, no matter how frenetic the hours inside had been, was welcome. With each step she took, breathing became easier, and by the time she slid behind the steering wheel, Keena had evaluated her plans for the day and knew they were sound. In the heat of a crisis, Keena never hesitated. Decisions came easy.

Second-guessing herself was annoying and something she wanted to eliminate, especially since it had gotten worse as her mental energy flagged. Moving temporarily to Prospect, an old mining town way up in the mountains, presented an overwhelming list of unknowns, starting with whether or not Keena would excel at a family practice, especially without a partner nearby like Dr. Singh.

Having more time for her medical diagnoses didn't change the fact that people were depending on her to get them right.

"The answers to questions you haven't been asked yet aren't in this parking lot, Keena," she muttered to herself in the exasperated, pragmatic tone her mother always used. It was the same voice that told her to get a grip in the middle of any new crisis. Growing up, Keena had learned her mother was more about practical solutions than nurturing care. Whenever she needed to check herself, her mother's voice was always there to help out. After she settled into her rental house in Prospect, she'd give her mother a call.

The short drive to her apartment took no time. Everything she'd need to take to Prospect was packed in two suitcases and a small stack of boxes near the door. Years of discipline kicked in, and Keena moved to her bedroom. No matter how alert she felt after the relief of successfully completing a busy shift at the hospital, the lack of sleep would eventually catch up to her. She didn't want that to occur on winding mountain roads and she'd arranged to meet Dr. Singh at his office that afternoon, leaving sufficient time for a nap.

Sleep came easily enough, but Keena was wide-awake before her alarm beeped and she hit the road.

Keena drove south out of Denver before turning west and starting to climb. The Iowa girl in her gripped the steering wheel tightly as each curve took her higher and closer to narrow shoulders. The signs of an urban community faded, replaced with scrubby grass, tall trees and even taller mountains in the distance, but following Dr. Singh's clear instructions was simple enough.

Eventually, a two-lane highway led straight into the middle of the historic district of Prospect. Keena studied the raised wood boardwalk that fronted the facades of the town's Old West businesses, including a livery stable, a barbershop and a bank. Other modern businesses had taken over some of the space. An old movie theater, the Prospect Picture Show, was showing *Rio Bravo*, and the large, two-story building called the Mercantile caught her attention.

That was Dr. Singh's landmark, the easy-to-see spot marking the hard-to-see medical office nestled behind it. Making a quick turn on the small street on the other side of the Mercantile brought her right to Prospect Family Practice. This structure was smooth plaster with a large glass wall that made it easy to see the office's reception desk and seating area.

Parking was simple. Keena pulled into one of the empty spots lining the fence of a large park that covered the block behind the Mercantile. There were two kids chasing a ball right down the center of the grassy area while two women chatted at a picnic table. The playground at the opposite end was empty.

When Keena turned off the ignition, silence settled over the car immediately. There was no traffic noise, just sunshine, mature evergreens, a street giving way to an old neighborhood, and small-town quiet. The difference between where she'd been at sunrise and her present circumstances was overwhelming. Her temporary home presented a postcard-perfect image in the late-afternoon golden light.

Keena knew better than to romanticize the situation, but still, she wanted to savor the scene.

"It's as important to be in the present in good times as it is in bad," she reminded herself. Anxiety could still catch her off guard, even here in this setting, but she didn't have time to consider what that might look like because Dr. Singh stepped out of the medical office, waving wildly.

The familiar sight amused her. PJ Singh was a man who'd never met a stranger, and his friends received his wholehearted enthusiasm at all times. The residents who'd worked with him were lucky. But patients had always been his biggest fans. Keena had never met another doctor who connected with the patient, young or old, as well as he did.

He'd explained to her over and over how important that was when she was a young doctor. Keena learned quickly, had steady hands, and handled the rush of medicine well. She had been made for the ER. Family medicine required different skills and an understanding of how to treat the person, not only the injury.

That had been her biggest concern about this move to Prospect. Could she execute this type of medicine to the standards she'd set for herself and her emergency department?

Keena was determined to do good medicine here. Dr. Singh knew her and trusted her to take care of his town.

And Keena trusted herself not to let him down.

She might have her own doubts, but no one else would.

Steady Murphy was prepared to tackle the challenge of life in Prospect.

CHAPTER TWO

TRAVIS ARMSTRONG GLANCED at his watch as
the sun dipped behind the ridge of the mountains that surrounded the valley leading up
to Larkspur Pass. He'd been dispatched to
Sharita Cooper's place by his brother half
an hour ago to greet the new doctor who
was scheduled to arrive since Wes was involved in something at the Majestic Prospect
Lodge. Given every one of his four brothers
had rearranged their lives to return home
to the Rocking A at Travis's request, it was
easy enough to make the short drive over
from the ranch house and hunker down on
the porch steps.

But the doctor was late.

And his nerves didn't handle waiting well.

Worse, he'd finished the book he left in the
truck for times like this, so he didn't have
anything to read while he waited.

He pulled out the house key Wes had sent

him to deliver. His orders had been to make sure the doctor had all the necessities for the night, so that Wes could follow up in the morning. As the property manager for Sharita Cooper, their neighbor to the south who had turned a visit to Florida into a semipermanent lifestyle, Wes was responsible for renting the place to the new doctor in town. He had also been managing the Majestic, their neighbor to the north, but the Hearsts had decided to reopen the place instead of selling it. Wes was committed to helping them any way he could. As Prospect's only lawyer, Wes ended up with a lot of different responsibilities, so it was nice to have a chance to help him out. Travis was still fighting the urge to apologize for getting in Wes's way around the ranch since he'd retired and come home.

After years of having sole responsibility for the Rocking A's operations, Wes should have had a harder time adjusting to being crowded by the rest of them. Instead, as soon as Travis had mentioned the renovations needed to meet the foster home requirements, the Rocking A ranch house was bursting at the seams, filled with Armstrong men.

Hanging out in the silence of Sharita's

empty house wasn't such a bad assignment after all.

Travis did a quick walk-through in the kitchen. Wes had brought in some staples, milk and bread, things like that. Electricity was on. Heat was running. November nights weren't terrible and the first snow was still weeks away, but the chill in the air would only grow sharper until springtime.

He propped his hands on his hips as he considered what else might be needed for immediate comfort. Utilities. Food. Toilet paper? He stuck his head into the bathroom to see that was also covered.

"Well, that took up ten minutes or so," he muttered as he moved over to the single, long window that looked out over the front yard. Nothing. No sign of the doctor. Sharita's house was comfortable, as lived-in as the Rocking A ranch house had been before their recent renovations, but there wasn't a lot of space to explore.

Travis pocketed the key and went outside. Nerves were always better handled outdoors.

The woodpile was low, so he grabbed the axe from his truck bed and moved toward the scrub of pines that formed a barrier between Sharita's house and the Rocking A fence line. Ever since the Rocking A's ambitious renovation and expansion had ramped up a month ago, Travis had escaped the noise and mess by riding the fence early in the morning. Was that necessary? Not really. Wes could do it all and had kept the whole place in good shape, but Travis insisted on taking the parts he could manage. If he recalled, there was a dead pine that needed to come down before it wrecked the fence.

Wes negotiated with the bank, talked to the accountant, buyers, suppliers and who knows who else.

Travis? He was all about the hard labor. Repairing fence. Putting out feed. Corralling stock.

Travis liked to work. Particularly jobs that required a strong back…that was his lane. The army had deployed him as an infantry soldier, a type of work that had been a challenge every single day. Coming home was a relief. He'd struggled to find his place in the Armstrong family in the early days, but staying in his lane now was fine.

He'd even found a way to broaden it and on the Rocking A, too. Thanks to him, there was a new crop of foster kids headed to the ranch. Why now?

Ever since the snowball of the foster home application process had started rolling down the hill, gathering speed, he'd been asking himself that.

"You pushed for this. Don't chicken out now," he snapped as he stepped up to the dying pine and swung with a satisfying whack. Each swing was accompanied by one of the thoughts he couldn't escape.

Why you?

Why would anyone entrust kids to you?

What makes you think you can do this?

What if they don't like where you came from?

What will happen to these kids when you mess up?

Travis shook his arms out as the pine fell. After dragging it near the chopping stump, he broke the tree down with more swings.

At this point, none of the doubts mattered. He'd started the process of becoming an approved foster home months ago, taking the lead, meeting with the caseworker and reviewing her comments on the improvements that would need to be done to the ranch to offer the best home possible for those teenage boys who might have nowhere else to go.

His brothers had pitched in to meet the caseworker's demands. They all understood. This place, Walt and Prue, had saved them all in one way or another. Continuing that was important.

Wes found the money.

Clay led the renovation.

Grant worked long days on any task necessary.

Even Matt was sleeping on a lumpy couch in town to make room for more kids who needed the Rocking A.

And Travis...

Well, he'd put in a full shift, day after day, but he'd also spent more time "checking fences" than strictly necessary.

The guilt receded a bit as he swung the axe.

When he noticed the shadows lengthening from the pines, he stopped to look at his watch. If the doctor didn't show soon, he was going to be late for the big celebration dinner his mother was preparing to mark the completion of the house renovations. Ducking the noisy, crowded event was tempting, but he knew it would cause an epic storm of disappointment.

Meeting his family's proud and expectant faces head-on opened up the dark gulf inside.

But disappointing his mother on purpose might kill him.

"Um, hi," a soft voice said from behind his left shoulder.

Travis twisted to see a petite redhead, one hand raised in an awkward wave. He made the connection from "beautiful woman" to "doctor he was waiting to meet" quickly but his mouth took a minute to catch up.

Speaking to beautiful women was one of the skills he'd always hoped to refine but never had.

"I didn't want to interrupt you midswing or startle you," she said as she took a hesitant step closer. "Are you Wes?"

Travis shook his head. "No."

When she glanced uneasily over her shoulder, Travis realized that might not have been the best answer. "I'm Travis. Armstrong. Wes is my brother." He set the axe down in case identifying himself wasn't enough to eliminate her concern. Facing a tall stranger with an axe might set him back on his heels, too.

She immediately clasped a hand over her chest. "Oh, good. No one warned me about any dangerous rugged lumberjacks and I was afraid it had slipped Dr. Singh's mind." Her smile was as bright as her long red hair as she moved forward. "I'm Keena."

Rugged.

Travis ran a hand over his beard as he contemplated that. Was rugged good?

Her hand was strong as they shook. Travis appreciated that.

"I'm Travis," he said before he could stop and closed his eyes at her amused smile. They both already knew his name. "And I'm very good in social situations."

Her amused laugh eased some of his disgust at his eternal awkwardness. "What a relief, as I am also wonderful with introductions, Travis."

Did he believe that? No way, but he appreciated the effort to make him comfortable.

"Wes was tied up with other business, so he asked me to bring your key over and make sure you were set up for the night." He pointed down at the axe as he picked it up. "I chop wood in my spare time."

He was relieved when she fell into step beside him.

Apparently it took more than a weird guy with a sharp tool to scare her away.

Then he realized that was definitely the kind of thought to keep locked up deep inside his own head.

"So, not a professional lumberjack." Keena shoved her hands in the puffy jacket she was wearing. It was bright pink instead of black or drab green. He liked that, too.

"Strictly amateur. Hobby. Part-time?" he asked in a weak attempt at a joke. Her bright smile was the payoff, so he kept talking. "Live next door. At the Rocking A. Wes also lives there. You can't see it from here." He motioned over his shoulder. "House is a couple miles that way, but you can see our cattle now and then."

Not the most exciting conversation, but he was proud of himself for stringing that many words together in succession. His family would be impressed.

"That may take some getting used to. In Denver, my next-door neighbors are so much closer." Her lips curled. "Still cows, though, thank goodness."

Travis frowned as he made sense of her answer. When her joke landed, his laugh sounded more like a grunt but that pleased her. Her giggles floated over their heads.

"I don't know what has come over me." Keena covered her cheeks with both hands. "I've never made a cow joke in my life." She touched his sleeve. "And I grew up in Iowa." Keena raised her eyebrows as if to communicate to him how long she'd successfully avoided making random cow jokes.

Since most women thought he was as dull as he was quiet, it was nice to be included in her amusement.

When they stepped up on the porch, Travis dropped the axe against the wall. "Lean into it. You have come to the right place. A good cow joke always goes over well around here." Then he opened the door and waved her inside. "Take a look and then I'll help you carry your stuff inside."

"Oh, you don't have to do that. My packing was pretty minimal." Her voice trailed away as she inspected the kitchen, flipping the light switch on and off, before opening the refrigerator. "Oh, someone left groceries?" The question showed in her confused frown. "Was that you or Dr. Singh?"

Travis cleared his throat. "Not me. Wes was my first guess. He's good with this kind of stuff. Thinking ahead." He was good at everything.

Keena sniffed. "Not quite as impressive as chopping firewood though, right?" She pointed at him, then turned down the hallway toward the bedrooms and the bathroom.

Every step she took was determined, as if she couldn't waste the energy. Efficiency seemed important to her.

When Travis realized his hands were dangling like dead fish, he gripped them together in front of him and tried to relax his stance. Years in the army meant he stood at attention without even realizing it more often than not.

"This place is perfect. I saw the Homestead Market in town." Keena tugged off her coat. Jeans and an electric-blue sweater fit her and her surroundings perfectly. "Is that a grocery store?"

"Everything." Travis cleared his throat and tried again. "It's Prospect's one-stop shop.

There's a hardware store in the Mercantile, but Homestead has groceries and an assortment of everything else under the sun."

She crossed her arms. "Can't wait to explore."

Travis met her stare. The silence stretched between them until he realized she was waiting for him to leave. "Please let me help you unpack your car. My mother would be ashamed if she found out I didn't."

Keena nodded. "Okay, you're proving chivalry isn't dead." Then she led the way outside.

"More like being a good neighbor. She'd insist we unload the car, no matter age or weather. That may be a Prospect kind of thing." Travis tested the suitcases and boxes in her trunk before lifting both suitcases with one arm and the heaviest box with the other.

"Okay, Mr. Universe. Why didn't you make it easy on yourself and carry the whole car inside? We could have unpacked the trunk in the living room." Her teasing was warm, amused.

That made it easy for Travis to laugh.

"I'll try that next time." He waited for her

to open the door and then set everything down in the living room. "Unpacking in the living room will still work."

She nodded. "Definitely. I have plenty of time to unpack this weekend before I start in Dr. Singh's clinic on Monday, but I'm going to need a good night's sleep before I tackle all this. Food, sleep, then settling in."

Travis shoved his empty hands in his pockets.

Keena smiled politely at him, waiting again.

"At least I can make toast for dinner. Where should I eat in town when I need a real meal?" she asked, shifting slightly toward the door. Was that a hint?

"No 'welcome to Prospect' dinner planned?" Travis asked. That surprised him.

"I was originally planning to drive to town tomorrow. Dr. Singh and his wife had agreed to meet friends for dinner in Fairplay tonight. I had a long shift at the hospital last night, so I thought I might wait until tomorrow but…" Keena sighed. "Obviously, I'm here now and that answer should have been much shorter. Good example of my own smooth social skills. I blame fatigue.

I'm having dinner at their place tomorrow night."

Travis pursed his lips as he considered that. "I have good news and I have bad news."

She wrinkled her nose. "Hit me with the bad first."

"There's only one full-service restaurant in town, the Ace High."

She frowned. "That's a poker hand, right?"

"Kinda." Travis shrugged. "It's also the restaurant in the building that used to be the finest saloon in Prospect's old town, home of expensive poker games during the silver boom."

"Okay. One restaurant. That makes the decision easier, I guess?" she said slowly, confusion wrinkling her forehead as if she had no concept how any place could function with only one restaurant.

Travis understood that. He'd grown up in Prospect, but living all over the world had taught him the power of restaurant choices. It would be good to have more options.

He decided not to explain that the decision would be even more basic when she made it into the Ace. There was no menu. Her options were this meal or that meal. The end.

"Good news is that the food there is very good. All of it." Travis stepped closer to the door. The discussion of food reminded him that his mother was cooking and she would not appreciate it if he was too late. He might not get dessert.

The idea that sparked immediately...his mother would be ecstatic if he brought their new neighbor home.

Keena nodded. "That is excellent news. I can eat my own cooking sometimes, but no one wants to suffer that fate every night. I'll have some time to expand my skills now that I'm in Prospect for a bit."

This time, when their eyes met, they were both smiling.

As the awkward one in every group, Travis didn't experience that connection often. He realized he was having a hard time breaking it now.

Then, before he knew what he was doing, he said, "If you're up for it, I know a place a little closer where you can get a delicious meal. There's a celebration planned tonight. You won't even have to do dishes this time, since it will be your first visit."

She tilted her head to the side, waiting for more information.

"Come to the Rocking A. You need to know where the house is in case you have any emergencies. I'll introduce you to Wes, and my mother is making pasta." Travis realized that might not be the draw for Keena, but he loved his mother's red sauce.

"Come on. Being neighborly. That's a big thing in Prospect." Travis had never tried to wheedle a woman into coming to dinner in his life. He wasn't sure whether he was succeeding or failing until she smiled.

"Meeting the neighbors is important when you're new in town, right?" Keena picked up her coat. "Should I follow you? Are you sure your mother won't mind another person for dinner?"

"There'll be so many of us there, she likely won't notice another person at the table." Stuck, because he hadn't thought any of this through and he'd certainly never expected her to say yes, Travis stopped in the doorway. He wanted to sweep open his truck door in a courtly gesture, but he was sure the floorboard was littered with twine and wire and no telling what else he'd picked up working on the ranch, so he nodded. "Follow me. I want you to know how to find me."

The urge to smack his forehead was so strong that he almost followed through. Fighting it meant he missed the opportunity to stammer and stutter and explain that he'd intended to say that she needed to be able to find Wes just in case.

But that was a blessing, too.

Spending time with Keena Murphy was fast becoming exactly what he wanted to do.

CHAPTER THREE

KEENA WAS SURPRISED to be climbing up the ranch house steps behind Travis Armstrong on their way to meet his family for dinner. He'd seemed surprised to be issuing the invitation. How he'd frozen in place had been sweet and funny at the same time. She recognized the reaction even if she never let herself visibly hesitate under similar circumstances. Acting confident even when she didn't feel it had been critical to success in the ER.

It had also gotten her through countless confusing, loud family gatherings when her divorced parents' always changing "yours, mine, and ours" had threatened to swamp Keena growing up.

Faking it until she made it had become Keena's chief coping mechanism. It never failed.

Her plans for the night had been boring and entirely sensible: unpack, investigate her new place, and sleep until she couldn't sleep any longer.

But then Travis had invited her to dinner, his boots shuffling as nervously as a boy asking a girl he admired out on a first date. She'd been too charmed to say no, so now she had no choice but to make her best first impression on the Armstrongs.

She'd taken half a minute to smooth her hair and run her fingers under her eyes to eliminate any mascara smudges before getting out of the car, but there was no way she was prepared to wow her first new acquaintances in her temporary hometown.

Travis stopped before opening the door and glanced over his shoulder at her. "I can't decide if it's kinder to warn you about my family or let you experience them naturally." Since he appeared more apologetic than honestly concerned, she had a feeling Travis was trying for humor again.

She got the idea that he didn't show that to many people.

Keena pursed her lips. "Do I need weaponry? Can I borrow your axe?"

His shoulders eased a fraction. "Nah.

They're more likely to smother you with affection than make you fight your way out."

"The axe might still come in handy." Keena put her hand on his arm and squeezed. That was one of the tips Dr. Singh had passed along to her to deal with anxious patients. Touching them got their attention, broke the cycle of anxious thoughts, and provided more comfort than words alone.

This time, it helped her, too.

Also, his arm was…hard. Muscle-y. Covered in plaid flannel. All in all, pleasant.

Then Travis reached for her hand and tangled their fingers together. "I'm glad you're here. You're helping me, causing a diversion, and I…" He closed his mouth firmly, obviously reconsidering whatever it was that followed. Keena was immediately interested in whatever required a distraction but now was not the time to dig for more info. "Let me walk you out when you go."

Keena blinked. "Urging me back to my house already?" She had so many questions. That was true always, but she was doing her best to contain them here.

He sighed. "Nope, but this will be the last time we speak together without interruptions and curious glances for the rest of the night. Gotta make it count." Then he squeezed her hand, pushed open the door and led her inside.

Keena craned her head side to side as she followed him, curious about how her new ranch neighbors lived. The hall opened into a spacious living room. She could smell fresh paint and varnish, so the current-but-still-classic style made perfect sense. Comfortable, old furniture lined the walls, but the place was modern without being trendy. Everything was clean and bright.

Then an older woman popped her head through an open doorway ahead. "My boy brought a friend!" she exclaimed. "I never thought I'd see this day." Her emphasis on *friend* suggested she was more interested in romantic friendships than run-of-the-mill neighborly kinds.

"I texted my mother to warn her I had a guest. I regret that decision," Travis murmured next to her ear. "I don't know if you've ever been measured for a wedding dress by a stranger, but…" He shook his head.

Keena stretched up on her toes so he could hear her. "If we were in Iowa right now, my father would be staring you down just like at all first-time introductions to possible boyfriends. I like your mother's way better."

Travis's eyes were warm. "Big family?"

Keena shrugged. "When you add in all the half-this and step-that, yes. My dad doesn't discriminate, though. Any girl who brings in a boy gets to see the same show."

They'd argued enough over that when she was still at home that she'd had time to perfect it.

"Everyone is welcome here," Travis said, "but my mother might give your father a run for his money." He squeezed her shoulder. "She doesn't do double standards, though. If she's ever lucky enough to have daughters-in-law, she'll be as ready to protect them as she is her sons."

Keena liked that. Having a father who treated his daughters differently than his sons was wrong and annoying, but a protective mother who would battle for all of her family equally was sweet.

When they were quiet, they could hear the rumble of hushed conversation coming from the kitchen.

His lips thinned. "I could make you a to-go

plate and some excuse about being worn out by the day if you'd rather."

Keena tilted her head to the side. This was her best "patiently waiting" pose.

Travis sighed. "Okay, would you make one for me, then?"

Keena moved around him and pulled him along to the kitchen where she halted, surprised by the sheer number of people watching her. She hadn't expected the size of the crowd.

"Trav, make introductions," his mother said as she stirred an enormous pot on the stove. If the living room had been comfortably updated, the kitchen had been fully modernized. It was still beautiful, in a modified farmhouse style, but the enormous stainless steel refrigerator was impressive, the center island gleamed with some shiny stone surface, and the cook was moving as if she was orchestrating a symphony of pots on a large stovetop. Wood floors and the butcher-block countertop lining three walls added warmth.

"At the table, we have," Travis said as he pointed and each person waved, "Wes, Matt and Grant." They were seated next to each other on a long bench at the large table. "On this end, we have Clay and his friend, Jordan Hearst." Keena smiled at the other woman, glad to see her. "Jordan and her sisters are reopening the Majestic Prospect Lodge, our neighbors on the other side. Jordan and Sarah are moving here from LA. Keep on going past the turnoff for the Rocking A and you'll see the sign."

Travis studied her face and waited for her to nod.

He understood how interested she was in getting to know another woman who was also new in town. The way Jordan patted the seat next to her made Keena think she was just as anxious.

"Sarah's still in LA, but she'll be here before Thanksgiving," Wes added.

"And then we'll all be hearing wedding bells, no doubt," Grant muttered under his breath.

"Now, now, you'll find a lady who can overlook that attitude someday," Matt said as he clapped a hand on Grant's back. "Maybe start looking across the street? Trav, Wes and Clay seem to have a lock on the neighbors to the right and left." Then he stood and took

Keena's hand. "It's nice to meet you, Keena. You're a brave woman."

Keena smiled into his deep brown eyes, immediately caught by how warm they were.

"With Dr. Singh's leave of absence, I sure am happy to have another doctor in town." Matt pressed his hands to his chest. "I don't like treating humans. Cows and horses complain so much less than people."

She couldn't look away from his face, but eventually she realized he must be a veterinarian and smiled at his joke. Travis waved his hand in front of her to break Matt's hold on her as his brothers laughed. Keena expected she'd see a dazed expression if she glanced in a mirror now, but it was the correct reaction. Five men, all handsome, all wearing some version of a plaid button-down and jeans, but she couldn't decide where Travis fell in the lineup. Who was the oldest? Youngest?

"My dad, Walt, and my mom, Prue."

Keena shook his father's hand first and realized it might be the first time she'd ever actually seen a twinkle in anyone's eye. Walt's lopsided grin was welcoming and she understood that whatever it was that charmed her in Travis could also be found in Walt.

When she turned to offer Prue her hand, the older woman surprised her by hugging her tightly. Since none of her family had been big huggers, it took a minute to adjust but she eventually squeezed lightly and stepped back. Seeing how stylish Prue Armstrong was in her beautiful sweater with some kind of diagonal hem and large pin on the shoulder made Keena wish she had taken more time to put herself together before she'd walked in.

It was too late to worry about that now, so Keena moved to sit in the chair Travis pulled out next to Jordan. Comforted a bit that Jordan was wearing a sweatshirt that appeared to have sawdust on the shoulder, Keena told herself to pretend she was confident and completely comfortable there.

Eventually it might come true.

"Where are the eatin' irons, Prue? Let's get this party started." Walt clapped his hands.

"Soon as you come get the *silverware* to finish setting the table like you were supposed to, we'll be ready." Prue's sweet smile didn't quite reach her eyes. "We're eating family style, so everyone bring your plates over to the stove and fill them up while your father finishes setting the table." Prue and Walt held a silent staring competition in front of the stove before he winked and her lips curled. Keena wanted to know what that was all about.

Travis led Keena to the stove first, an obvious honor reserved for the guest.

"Your parents are cute. How long have they been married?" Keena asked as she dished out spaghetti from the large pot.

"Forever, but they're divorced, have been for years. They never quite split up for good." Travis shook his head. Now she had more questions. She'd ask later.

"Make sure you get some of that garlic bread. I made it from scratch for the occasion," Prue Armstrong said as she hovered near the stove, like a proud mama bird over her nest. "Keena, look at this backsplash." She motioned regally at the gray-and-white tiles. "Didn't my sons do excellent work?"

Keena nodded. "And this pot filler. I've only seen them on TV shows. I can tell you love to cook, Ms. Armstrong. It must be wonderful to have all this space to do it." It was an impressive setup for someone who enjoyed cooking.

"Oh, call me Prue, but yes, ma'am, that pot filler was my special surprise from my ex-husband. Turns out, he was listening all those years when I thought I was talking to myself." Prue grinned. "Were there easier ways to get my attention rather than ignoring me, refusing to do any updates until we were divorced and living in separate houses, and then surprising me with a somewhat impractical but sweet gift like this in the kitchen in a house I don't even live in?"

Keena assumed the question was rhetorical and waited.

Prue scooped a large helping of salad onto Keena's plate. "Absolutely, but with an Armstrong man, you can count on hardheadedness."

Walt grunted. "Only way to love a woman who holds a grudge for decades." He dodged the dish towel Prue lobbed at his head before winking at Keena.

Keena bit her lip and turned to Travis for help.

"Step away from the stove," Clay said, "you're scaring the visitor, Mama."

The rest of the table cleared their throats and made conversation about the weather to fill in the silence.

Travis leaned over her shoulder to say, "Should I have warned you? They love each other…we think. They'll get back together… we hope, but…"

"Starting to believe arguing is their love language and one disagreement got too far out of hand," Wes murmured from across the table as they sat down. "Eventually the fireworks stop, Keena."

Clay cupped his hand over his mouth. "We need a matchmaker to take control of the situation."

"Only problem is finding one better than our mother. She'll be a tough cookie to crumble," Grant added.

"They never actually stop sparking, Keena, but both parties retreat for breathing room." Jordan patted her hand. "I'll give you the whole scoop."

Surprised and pleased at how easily the entire family had rolled her into the fold, Keena nodded. "I'd love that."

Keena made friends for life, but she'd never made easy friendships or acquaintances.

That might be because she was always working and work was serious business.

Finding immediate welcome here was sweet.

The rest of the dinner was filled with typical family conversation. How the day had been. What they were going to do about a herd in some pasture. How the repairs were going at the fishing lodge next door. When Matt was going to hold the next planning meeting for the town's big spring festival.

"Now then, for this special occasion, I made Clay's favorite dessert in honor of all the hard work he's put in, keeping this renovation going and finishing up the development of his big subdivision in Colorado Springs." Prue held up a ceramic pie keeper with a flourish. Then she frowned. "Applause, please."

Travis bumped her shoulder as he laughed.

"I hope that's for display purposes," Clay said. "We're going to need more than one coconut cream pie to feed this crowd and send some home with me." Then he picked up his fork as if he was ready to dig in.

Prue rolled her eyes. "Of course I made more than one. You know I like to show off my pie keeper. It's one of Sadie's, from her first line of kitchenware." Then she removed the top of the keeper. Keena could see toasted coconut and was immediately intrigued. "Walt, start serving, please and I'll get the others." She handed him a stack of plates.

"Sadie Hearst, the Colorado Cookie Queen. Heard of her?" Walt peered down the table at Keena.

"I have. I loved her Christmas specials when I was a kid. She always had my favorite celebrities in the kitchen with her," Keena said.

"She was my aunt," Jordan said. "Great-aunt, actually, but she helped raise me and my sisters. When she died, she left the lodge next door to us, along with enough memorabilia for several museums."

Ten different questions immediately popped into Keena's brain about the Hearst sisters, the museum and plans for the lodge, but Keena knew she had a habit of overwhelming people with conversation that could transition to interrogation. That was how she made the correct medical diagnosis, but it wasn't great at the dinner table. Instead of launching into her first question, Keena took her first bite of co-coconut cream pie.

"Oh, my, where has this pie been all my life," Keena murmured. "Maybe I'll learn how to make it while I'm taking a break from emergency medicine."

"Tell us about that, Keena," Prue said brightly.

When Travis shifted in his seat, she wondered if he was preparing to divert the conversation away from her. As if he understood her discomfort at being center stage. For some reason, her usual jitters were quiet here.

Direct communication was her favorite kind. But what could she say that they would understand?

"Long shifts. Sometimes it's straightforward. Pretty standard admissions. Chest pain. Broken bones. Home accidents. Things that are serious but routine." She shook her head. "Then there are the nights when every decision is life or death. Those are the toughest, obviously. Can the bleeding be stopped. Can the person get to surgery in time." She cleared her throat. "You never know what will walk through the door."

Now the jitters rolled in, so she focused on breathing through it. "Sorry. That might have been more information than you wanted. It's hard work but also rewarding." Kenna had learned the polite answer early in her career. Often when people asked about her job, they only wanted the short, sweet answer, not the truth. The size of her next bite precluded any more talking for a while.

Travis ran his hand across her back. It was the same kind of touch Clay and Jordan shared, she noticed.

As everyone finished their pie, Prue asked, "Everything ready for the caseworker's return, Trav?"

The tension that swept through Travis's body was easy to feel as Keena's arm brushed his.

He put down his fork and tangled his hands together in his lap. "Believe so. This place is light-years different from what she saw on the first tour. The rooms are ready to go, thanks to Grant and his bunk bed design."

Keena noted how the pink spread across Grant's cheeks before he frowned at his plate. "Just built what I wanted when I had to share a room with Mr. Neat."

"It's a nice setup, lots of privacy, which even Mr. Neat would have loved to have had." Clay sipped his wine. "Still won't help if one of the boys never learns how to use a laundry hamper."

Keena ate the last of her pie as she watched Grant scowl at Clay. This back-and-forth reminded her of family dinners at her dad's house, but it felt less awkward to sit back and watch these brothers bicker.

Maybe that was because it was okay to feel like an outsider here, which made sense being at the Armstrong table. But there was also the sensation that the family was opening its ranks to draw her in. That was new.

"The caseworker is scheduled to finish the home study by the end of next week." Travis ran his fingers over his nape before clutching his hands together again. "I've done CPR, first aid, classes about working with children with special needs." He shrugged. "If we aren't ready now, I don't know that I ever will be."

Silence settled over the table. Without understanding the background or what the problem might be, Keena knew this was important to Travis, to all of them, but she could tell that he felt the pressure. She'd noticed his change from "we" to "I." In their first meeting, she'd discovered he was a man of few words. Being put on the spot probably made it harder to find the right ones.

She tried her trick with making physical contact again and reached under the table to squeeze his hand tightly. Something shifted on his face and his shoulders relaxed.

Then he turned to her. "We're trying to get the ranch set up as a foster home for boys. We were all fostered and then adopted by Prue and Walt when we were teenagers."

Keena glanced around the table to find everyone staring. Now she was on the spot.

"Wow, that is…amazing." Keena squeezed his hand again. The only thing she knew about the foster care system was how heart-breaking it was to see caseworkers called in to care for children in her emergency department, the ones who had no one else to protect them. It was easy to imagine Travis and his family being a safe space for those kids. "That you found the family you needed and that you're all going to do the same thing for more kids, it's… Impressive. There's one question I still have. Who's oldest and who's youngest?"

When Grant groaned loudly, Prue scowled at him. "Matt's my baby, but they're all close in age, Keena." She patted Matt's cheek. "And Wes is the 'oldest.'" Prue made air quotes with her fingers. "He arrived first, but they're all one of a kind, let me tell you."

"Like an irregular shirt, one of a kind," Jordan drawled. Everyone laughed but Keena watched the way Clay's arm slid over Jordan's back to squeeze her close. So casually. It was sweet.

To shrug off the melancholy that flared at seeing such a simple sign of their connection, Keena shook her head. "I need a couple of hours to draw my family tree to make sure I know exactly how many brothers and sisters I have because my parents have each been married three times, so the branches get confusing. I think I'm the oldest, but I'm not certain anymore."

When everyone laughed as she'd intended, Keena ran her thumb across the back of Travis's hand. "But a good family is a blessing, so I try to focus on that instead of the number of Christmas gift cards I send out in the mail every year."

"That is some wisdom right there, Keena. Thank you for contributing to this scatter-shot dinner conversation," Prue said as she pointed at Keena. "Consider yourself welcome at my table here or in town whenever you like. I've got the cutest little apartment not too far from the clinic and I can tell I need to know more about you."

When Travis turned to glance her way, she batted her eyelashes innocently and sipped her glass of wine.

The way all the men at the table shook their heads at Travis would have made Keena laugh if she didn't know she was the reason for the commiseration.

"Thank you, Prue. Three months in Prospect should be enough time to enjoy a meal or two, I'm guessing." Keena wanted to make it very clear that she was temporary. "I don't get a lot of home cooking working the night shift in Denver."

Prue nodded. "I will do my best to rectify that, you sweetheart." Then she raised her glass. "And you never know, time in Prospect moves differently than it does in other places. Three months might turn out to be a whole lot more before it's all over."

It was impossible to miss that she'd met an expert strategist in Prue Armstrong. She'd taken Keena's warning and lobbed it back in a friendly but firm return.

Was Prue right? Could Prospect turn out to be more than a momentary rest?

Into the charged silence that fell while Keena tried to find an answer, Travis said, "Mom, do you have time to help me pick out bedding tomorrow? Be nice to have some personality in the rooms, show we're ready for a foster right now."

She immediately said, "I do not." Keena was busy scraping the last of the coconut cream off her plate when Prue added, "Sorry, hon. Patrick, Rose and I have plans in the store tomorrow, and then Sunday I have to go to Denver." She sighed. "Rose insists she needs me to go with her to the radio station to pick up her Broncos tickets. She knew I wouldn't be able to claim the store as my excuse to get out of going. Little did she know I talked Patrick into coming along." Prue's broad grin convinced Keena that she was pretty proud of herself for doing it, too.

"We know Patrick and Rose share a love of football. Fingers crossed that some time together fans that tiny flame. We're going to do a trial run of a Friday night Sip and Paint at Handmade before the holidays gear up. Jordan and Keena will both be there, I'm sure."

Keena realized she was nodding before she was perfectly clear about what she was agreeing to. Sip and Paint? Were they painting walls or canvases? Either way, she didn't have much experience.

"Patrick is my father. Rose runs Bell House," Jordan said quietly to Keena before adding loudly, "I can't do it, either. Sorry, Travis. I'm too busy tomorrow." Then she took a bite of pie.

When she didn't offer anything else, Clay laughed as if he knew exactly what was going on before saying in a stilted, formal voice, "Oh, if only there was someone else who could help my dear brother create welcoming bedrooms for our new family members."

Keena finally realized everyone at the table was staring at her. She put her spoon down and coughed. "What? I'm sorry. I was in too deep with my pie."

Prue's lips were twitching as she said, "Dear, would you be able to help Travis with his shopping tomorrow? He could also show you around Prospect and you can pick up anything you might have left at home by accident."

"Um," Keena said as she looped hair behind her ear, "okay? I'm not sure I'm an interior designer, but I could help?" That uncertain tone would have sent everyone in the hospital into a panic, but here, the Armstrongs accepted it easily.

"Let me show you the rooms," Travis said. His tone was resigned but she didn't think he was unhappy with the way everything had turned out. He motioned her ahead of him toward the hallway.

They had almost made it all the way to freedom when Prue called, "Oh, Keena? One quick question for you."

Keena glanced over her shoulder.

"How do you feel about horses?" Prue asked sweetly.

Keena frowned, confused. It was clear that she was missing the part of the conversation taking place among the rolled eyes of those around the table.

"I don't really know anything about them. I grew up in the suburbs of Des Moines. We had dogs. I like dogs?" Keena turned to Travis for guidance but he shrugged.

Prue pursed her lips as she considered that. "It's not the end of the world, I guess. I've adjusted my views on the necessity of loving horses lately."

At the end of the table, Jordan straightened in her chair. "There are good people everywhere who'd rather drive than ride, Prue."

"Well, while you're in Prospect," Grant drawled, "it's an opportunity to add that skill to your résumé, Doc. If you'd like to go for a ride, I'll be happy to teach you. I've been working with a couple of horses that have the perfect personality for new and inexperienced riders."

"My son is a rodeo star, Keena." Prue tapped his shoulder as Grant squirmed under her proud stare. "You couldn't ask for a better teacher."

Keena wasn't convinced she needed riding lessons, but she took the phone he offered and entered her phone number quickly before sending herself a text. "I'll think about it. That's kind, Grant. Thank you."

Grant grinned as he dropped his phone into his shirt pocket.

"Let's go." Travis frowned at his brother. Keena noticed the rest of the table was busy scooting crumbs around on their plates.

Keena waved and then followed as Travis towed her away.

"Hey, are you mad?" Keena asked as she dragged her feet to slow his march.

Travis shook his head as he stepped inside a spacious room and flipped on the light switch. "Not at you."

"Whoa, these are more than bunk beds." She stood on her tiptoes to stare through the rails at the bed. "This is more like a tiny, tiny home. You know, how everything has multiple functions."

Instead of a ladder, each bed had a shallow staircase that also held books. A floor-to-ceiling wardrobe formed one side of the bed, complete with doors that locked. The other end was a cube with a built-in desk. Under the bed, they'd put in a bench and a place for a small TV. Curtains could be closed for privacy.

"I saw a news story about these bunk bed pods, spaces commuters could rent in the big cities where the rent is out of control. The spots were basically a bed and a TV, a rack for some clothes." Travis paused. "No way would I want to live like that, but for these kids…" He shrugged. "Grant and I agreed we would have thought it was perfect."

Keena trailed behind him as he showed off both rooms and the bathroom they'd installed between, impressed at everything the Armstrongs had done. She'd lost track of all the things she wanted to ask about the renovation and the foster process and the ranch itself.

If she agreed to help him shop, no way would those questions remain contained. "If we go shopping, you know I'm going to be asking about…all this." He deserved fair warning.

Travis propped one hand on the doorframe. "If you'll tell me how you can read my mind, how you know when the nerves are tying up my words, I'll consider replying to these questions."

She narrowed her eyes at him.

He waited.

"I guess we'll see how this shopping trip goes, won't we?" she murmured.

When she moved ahead of him on her way back to the kitchen, he said, "I guess *we'll see*."

Keena hoped Travis had missed the stutter in her step when his words registered. Something about his voice, the gravelly low tone, landed and stole her breath.

His family was painfully polite as Keena said goodbye and thanked his mother for dinner. Everyone was silent as Travis walked Keena to her car.

"I'll pick you up? Homestead Market opens at ten." Travis crossed his arms over his chest.

"It's a date." Keena instantly realized what she'd said, but no easy way out came to mind, so she moved on. "Your family is lovely. I'll see you tomorrow."

Keena didn't look back as she drove home. It had been a great opportunity to meet her neighbors. She'd help Travis and then she'd keep her distance. She'd come to Prospect, sure, but she would return to Denver and the career she loved better than ever. Disappointing Travis and his mother might be inevitable, but she could take care to make it as painless as could be. Maintaining enough distance between herself and the quiet cowboy to ensure that would be her goal.

CHAPTER FOUR

AFTER A LONG, sleepless night, Keena was relieved to watch the sunrise through the crack in the curtains over her unfamiliar bed. She'd learned some important lessons when her usual ability to sleep whenever and wherever failed.

First, she was not made for country life. She'd grown up in the suburbs and her apartment in Denver had plenty of comfortable white noise at all hours of the day and night. Traffic created a *shoosh* that she could pretend was the ocean. Her neighbors on all sides had conversations and televisions and radios to fill in any silence. She was never truly alone. Here? It was only Keena, her own breathing and whatever wildlife might be lurking in the dark outside.

Without sleep, her imagination filled that darkness easily.

No matter how often she'd told herself

nothing was roaming around this tiny, comfortable house, the fact that she couldn't peer out the crack in the curtain and see a well-lit sidewalk to satisfy those doubts meant she was never convinced, either.

Here, the moon was bright, but that was the only light available.

Second, having her fears confirmed by yipping coyotes that sounded too close for comfort had pumped more adrenaline through her body than watching an ambulance screech to a halt outside the hospital.

Instead of investigating the noise, Keena had yanked the quilt over her head and pretended she couldn't hear them.

Altogether, it had been a long night.

"You'll get used to it. No one sleeps well the first night in a new place." Keena pictured her mother's pragmatic frown as she tossed back the quilt, slid her feet into warm slippers, and headed for the tiny bathroom. The floors creaked with each step. Those moans and groans didn't bother her in the daylight. But at night, she'd had to settle her racing heart back down every time something in the house settled.

After brushing her teeth and tidying up

the messy bun that had unraveled as she tossed and turned, Keena decided her first order of business that morning would be unpacking the clothes she'd brought with her. If she was going to help Travis Armstrong decorate the room for his foster kids today, she was going to need something presentable for her introduction to her new neighbors in town. The mismatched sweatpants and T-shirt she'd slept in would not make a great first impression.

Keena studied the ancient drip coffeemaker and pulled some fragments of how-to from her memory to brew an incredibly dark, strong pot of coffee before moving into the living room to study her belongings. Sharita Cooper's house was warm, and all the basics were there, but Keena hadn't found a single radio in her hunt the previous night. That would have to change.

Spending too much time with only her thoughts for company would be a problem.

"Start a list, then." Keena pulled up the notes app on her phone and put down a wireless speaker that she could connect to her phone, and a single-cup coffeemaker. After she took a few sips of the brew she'd managed in the existing appliance, she removed that from the list. It was strong and dark and perfect as it was.

After dragging the largest suitcase into the bedroom, Keena unpacked everything quickly into the large wardrobe that stood next to the window. "A house with no closets may take some getting used to." Keena ran her hand down the smooth surface of the beautiful cedar wardrobe and thought it might be the simplest adjustment of them all. A shower, an exciting hunt for a hair dryer which ended at her growing list of things to purchase, and a bright red sweater to go with comfortable jeans made everything better.

Keena flicked the curtains wide open and studied the broad yard that stretched out in front of the window.

Sun rose over the ring of mountains that formed the backdrop in the distance.

Wide-open pasture dotted with a few cows stretched out between the window and those mountains. Whatever creatures she'd been imagining the night before were absent after sunrise. Would that be a comfort the next time she tried to sleep?

"Howdy, neighbors." Was she talking to

herself more often in Prospect? It seemed so. Keena tried to loosen her neck and shoulder muscles as she walked into the kitchen. Breakfast would help. "The fresh air might not be good for your nerves after all."

She pulled out the loaf of bread and the butter from the refrigerator to make toast. The toaster was adorably retro, but she had the feeling that it was not a reproduction, but an actual appliance that had been in use in this house since the style was new. It might also be a fire hazard at this point, but the toaster worked.

A little trial and error was all it took to get the charred edges she preferred on her toast. Slathering the slices with butter had her mouth watering. Then she noticed the long line of cookbooks that filled a shelf next to the sink. A tiny window was framed above the sink. The view from this side of the house covered the stump where she'd met Travis the day before.

The handsome, awkward lumberjack that she was somehow shopping with that day.

Keena hummed loudly, grateful to have the opportunity to purchase something that would allow her to have someone else singing soon, since her voice was nothing to brag about. She studied the titles on the cookbooks.

The thought that it might be a nice move to take treats into Dr. Singh's practice on Monday popped up. She'd never done that before. Since it didn't sound like Prospect had much in the way of a handy donut shop to swing by before work, maybe she should try her hand at making something? There was an entire library of cookbooks to choose from, most of them by the Colorado Cookie Queen.

"*Gimme Some Sugar* sounds like a likely place to start," she murmured before she finished off her first slice of toast and pulled the cookbook down from the shelf.

Keena immediately recognized Sadie Hearst's smiling face on the cover. *Fifty easy-as-pie recipes to share* was the tagline under the title. Sadie in her smart white cowboy hat was holding a decorative plate with a selection of cookies. "Ooh, this is what I need."

She refreshed her coffee and took her toast to the kitchen table as she thumbed through the recipes, studying the bright photos that accompanied each. Sadie was scattered throughout the book, along with "Sadie's Yarns," notes from the Colorado Cookie Queen herself about the best occasions for each recipe.

"Is there one for 'hi, I'm your temporary coworker and kinda sorta boss but I know almost nothing about what you do here and I want to be your friend-slash-neighbor so take this cookie as a sign of my respect' occasion?" Keena flipped to the beginning of the book to study the table of contents. When the last bite of toast was gone, she ran a finger down each line until she landed on "First-Place First Impressions."

Keena was surprised that in a collection of "So-Easy-It's-Cheating Christmas Cookie Exchange" suggestions, "Better Last-Minute-than-Never Potluck" winners, "Sorry, I Lost Your Lawn Mower" apologies, and other funny and sweet notes, there was one that fit what she was looking for.

Sadie was posed in a kitchen, wearing a red-and-white gingham apron. There was a little girl turned away in the photo, so that her face was hidden. "The first day of school can rattle even the bravest cowpokes, am I right? Send them off with two dozen of these and be ready to hear about six new best friends. Just don't send your good container, hon. Better than even chance you'll never see that again."

Keena pursed her lips as she considered that. Her last first day of school had been more than a decade ago but the nerves fluttering in her stomach as she considered finding her way around Dr. Singh's clinic were familiar. "That's not very Steady Murphy of you, Doctor."

Keena read the short list of ingredients for "Chock-full Cowboy Cookies" and checked her refrigerator before adding to her list of items to pick up in town. Then she scanned the recipes to see if there was a "thank you for inviting a stranger to dinner" suggestion because the Midwesterner in her felt the urge to return the kindness the Armstrongs had shown her. Her mother would have some good ideas on what to deliver as a thank-you gift, but she would also have so many questions.

Keena had always had a plan for her career. Her parents had been big supporters of that plan.

They didn't understand this need for a detour when everything was going the way she wanted it to in Denver, not even when she mentioned that she'd be helping out an old friend.

If the Armstrongs were big on helping neighbors, Keena knew her Midwestern parents would be the same. Neighbors helped neighbors, friends helped friends, but her mother had made it clear that Keena putting her own career on hold to help was a mistake and doing too much by her mother's measurement.

Keena hadn't explained the toll Emergency had taken on her lately.

If the staff at the hospital viewed her as unflappable, her parents had a whole lifetime of moments to rest that judgment on. They'd trained this self-sufficiency and keen focus into her in the first place, whether they'd intended to or not. Years of split custody and new stepparents and ex-stepparents and different formations around the family table meant that Keena had learned early on to take care of herself.

The anxiety that came along with it had required that she also learn to cope by herself. It didn't matter what her parents thought they knew about her and what she could handle or what she deserved. She was in charge of her decisions, as always.

Keena was going to make Prospect work, Dr. Singh would have the help he needed, and by the time she went back home, the whole town would know that she was a good doctor. They would miss her when they left.

And if she managed to make these amazing cookies, they would believe she'd been baking her whole life.

She'd added walnuts to her list of groceries when a grating scrape loud enough to be the roof sliding right off the house scared her out of her chair.

It was followed by another loud rip, the sound fabric makes when it's torn in a rush.

Was it coming from outside?

Keena rushed to the kitchen window, but she didn't see anything out of the ordinary. Nothing was amiss on the road or the small yard in front of the house, so she ran into the bedroom and shrieked in surprise.

Keena clamped one hand over her heart as she stared at the cow who was staring right back at her.

Through the window. Only the pane of glass separated them.

Grass was dangling out of the cow's steadily chewing mouth. With an audible gulp, the grass disappeared. So did the cow's head. Then there was another loud tear before the cow returned to face Keena, more grass being digested slowly.

"Was that you?" Keena demanded before she shook her head. Did she expect the cow to answer?

If the cow answered, she was getting in her car and driving back to Denver immediately. Forget her clothes. Forget Dr. Singh and forget Prospect.

When the cow blinked, seemingly unperturbed at the turn of events, Keena realized only one of them was acting unusual at this point.

Steady Murphy was not so steady this morning.

Then the cow showed how little she cared about the situation by meandering past the window.

Toward the road.

A vision of Bessie wandering out onto the asphalt and pondering life while straddling the double yellow line as a packed school bus hurtled around a curve and headed right for her popped into Keena's head.

"Why do you always have to go right for the worst-case scenario?" Keena asked, annoyed at her brain and the cow and country life in general. Racing through the small house took no time, and Bessie didn't know there was a finish line so she'd stopped to rip up more landscaping near the corner of the house. The slam of the door caught the cow's attention, and Keena realized she was half a second from actually chasing the cow out into traffic.

Not that there was another car on the two-lane road at this time, but there might be.

"Don't run, beautiful," Keena said in her best patient-soothing voice. "We're friends here. I don't care anything about those flowers that have probably been there for a century. The homeowner? Huh! It will be our little secret." As she spoke softly, Keena moved closer, ignoring the frosty crunch of dying grass under her slippers.

When Bessie glanced over at her, Keena hoped she was considering returning the way she'd come and shifted to cut off the route to the road. If the cow couldn't go forward, she would go back, right?

Bessie didn't do either.

She also didn't return to her breakfast.

Instead, she and Keena were locked in a staring contest while Keena inched even closer.

The sound of a car on the road behind her confirmed Keena's fears. "Do you hear that? You could have been the world's largest roadkill this morning. No one wants that. Go back through whatever hole you walked through, and we'll forget about the damages, okay? Come on, Bessie. Doesn't that sound like a plan?"

"Are you bargaining with livestock?" Travis asked. Keena craned her head over her shoulder to see that he had parked his truck between Bessie and the road. He shut the door. Bessie huffed out a breath at the noise. "And that is Chuck. Not Bessie."

Keena turned back. "Is that why you've been ignoring my courteous request? Because you're a bull and not a cow?"

Travis's chuckle assured her he was approaching them. Surely he would take charge of this situation. "Better watch out. If Chuck holds a grudge, you might be in danger. He's a steer, not a bull."

Chuck was wary, obviously, but he'd stopped destroying the flower bed.

"What's the difference?" Keena asked.

When Travis didn't immediately answer, she hazarded taking her eyes off Chuck to see that Travis was biting his lip. He said, "Castration?"

Keena blinked and willed the color she could feel racing up her body to flood her cheeks to just…not. She was a doctor. Embarrassment was unacceptable. "Sorry, Chuck."

"We're all very sorry, Chuck." Travis's laughter drifted behind him as he stepped around the steer to open a wide gate in the fence. Chuck considered it before returning to his buffet.

"Move over to close the gap up by the house, Keena," Travis said, "and if he decides to come your direction, get out of the way."

Keena froze, midstep.

"I don't think he will," Travis added.

Did she know Travis Armstrong well enough to follow his instructions here?

Since he was the only one of them with any hope of getting Chuck on the right side of the fence, Keena moved into place and held her arms out to make herself bigger.

Travis tilted his head to the side as he considered her stance before nodding. "All right. Head on home, Chuck." He moved cautiously toward the steer and clapped his hands. Chuck ripped one last bite out of the flower bed and moseyed toward the open gate. Travis continued the loud claps while Chuck took his own sweet time, but once he was in the field, Travis pulled the gate shut again.

Relieved, Keena dropped her arms. "Thank you."

"Good news, Chuck is contained." Travis stopped in front of her. "Bad news, he's going to show up again when you least expect it. He's an escape artist."

Keena exhaled, listening to the sounds of the morning, as she tapped her fingers against her thighs. She concentrated on the texture of the denim and counted her breaths. When her heart rate returned to normal, she realized Travis was watching her mindfulness routine. "Sorry. Old habit."

He shook his head. "No apology necessary."

"No time to panic when you're working in

the hospital, right?" Keena brushed her hair over her shoulder, relieved Chuck had chosen a breakfast time after she'd had a chance to shower and fix her appearance. Travis would not have been impressed by her bedhead or sweatpants.

Not that it mattered whether Travis was impressed.

Obviously.

"Intellectually, I know there was no reason for that fight-or-flight reaction here, but my body never got the memo."

Making excuses for an over-the-top reaction to a placid steer named Chuck was not how she wanted her encounter with Travis to go today, but life had other plans apparently.

"Stress reactions. I get it. Decades in the army showed me all kinds of ways to deal with that. Your way is probably the best. Everything else leads to trouble or heartache at some point." He crossed his arms over his chest.

Did he suffer from post-traumatic stress or was he thinking of a friend? Someone he knew? Keena knew the doctor in her was fighting to rise to the surface but she had learned that not everyone welcomed an on-the-spot diagnosis.

"Nice footwear. Are you wearing those into town?" Travis's lips curled in amusement as he pointed at her feet.

Keena glanced down at her slippers. They were shaped like hamburgers, complete with drooping lettuce and bright red tomatoes under a sesame seed bun. "I was chasing a cow around the yard with hamburgers on my feet."

Travis's grin was contagious, so Keena giggled as they stared at each other. She'd never seen someone so open; the amusement filling his eyes and lighting up his face were unforgettable. Thanks to that moment, she now recognized his eyes were blue.

Since blue eyes were her weakness, that was a game changer.

"You're lucky to have survived this, Keena." Travis chuckled and covered his heart with his hand. "I don't believe I've laughed this hard in… I can't even remember."

"Good. I'm glad my fright and overwhelming embarrassment has some silver lining," Keena drawled and coughed as giggles threatened again. "Are you ready to go into Prospect? I believe I will change my footwear in case we encounter any other cattle today."

"Ready when you are, but we can take a look at the fence before we go, see if we can find Chuck's point of entry." Travis stepped up on the porch and followed her to the screen door. She opened it and stepped inside, while he hovered in the doorway. Was he afraid to come in?

"Did you want some coffee before we go? It's so strong you'll be able to hear colors but I'm not sure that's a downside."

He shook his head. "No, I don't drink coffee. Don't need the caffeine jitters most days."

Keena didn't spin around with her prescription pad in hand, but his comment filtered into her brain as she changed into boots. Whether or not it was PTSD, Travis was on guard for the physical components of stress.

Keena grabbed her phone from the table and her puffy jacket. "Now that I've recovered from the shock of meeting Chuck this morning, I wonder if he was one of the critters I imagined walking around the yard last night. You'd think the coyotes would have every creature smaller than Chuck cuddled up safe and sound somewhere to avoid being dinner."

"Most of the critters around are more of the cute, mostly harmless type, and the coyotes always sound like they're standing under the window, but they could be miles away." Travis trotted across the yard to dig around in the bed of the truck before he pulled out a roll of wire and…a hammer. That she recognized. What was the other pointy tool? Her reminder to herself that no one liked interrogations floated through her brain. She could ask some other time.

Instead, she said, "I don't know anything about repairing fences."

He shrugged. "I'll say 'hold this' and then you'll hold it. I know enough for both of us."

Since he was the fence expert, Keena trailed behind Travis as he walked the edge of the yard lined by barbed wire fence. When he stopped, Keena nearly ran into his shoulder. She'd been so focused on watching where she was stepping that she missed the cue.

Travis slipped a heavy glove on. "Likely spot."

Keena studied the easy give of the barbed wire. Along most of the rest of the fence, it was stretched tightly. This section waved a bit in the breeze. "How do you know this is the spot? Because it's loose?"

He nodded. "Loose and…" He pointed at the wire. When she looked closer, she could see strands of hair stuck on the fence. "It's a sign Chuck got a little bit of hair trimmed when he went through."

She wrinkled her nose. "Doesn't it hurt? Why would a cow do that more than once?"

Travis cleared his throat. "Steers aren't known for being smart, Doc. It's a real problem that anyone who works with livestock has encountered. They are stubborn. They are almost always hungry." He shrugged. "They defy explanation sometimes, except to say they were on one side of the fence when they wanted to be on the other, so they do whatever it takes to go through it, even if it might hurt."

Keena took the hammer he held out and inched closer to watch him snip wire off the roll in his hand. Then she held the roll, too.

Travis stepped up to the sagging middle line of barbed wire and wrapped the small piece he'd cut off around it. Then he wrapped the unnamed tool around the new wire and twisted it. There was no strain showing on his face, but the way his shoulders and arms bulged was…impressive. If she hadn't watched him chop wood already, she might have been caught by surprise.

But she hadn't yet forgotten the way those muscles had worked. She was grateful to see this show, too.

When he'd twisted as far as he could, he handed her the twister-thing to dig in his pocket for a small bar thing. She had to lean in to see what he did, but he continued wrapping the loose ends of the new wire until the sharp points were tight against the fence.

Travis stepped back and tapped the wire. Instead of sagging loosely, it twanged. That was more like what she expected of the wire, so Keena was impressed again.

"Nice." She carefully poked the wire and watched it slide up and down the metal post. "But you aren't done, right?"

He shook his head, took the wire roll and the scary tool out of her hands. She watched him snip a length of wire, wrap it around the metal post and under the barbed wire and do the wrapping thing again with the little bar thing.

This time when he stepped back, he said, "Now I'm done."

Keena handed him the hammer, disappointed that the project had taken so little time. She was happy to watch Travis do that at least one more time.

"Imagine doing that a few million times a year." Travis sighed. "All because of hard-headed animals like Chuck."

His smile was so sweet, it made her happy to see it in this instant.

"You never get tired of it?" she asked.

"Oh, I get tired of fences, for sure, but never of this place." He walked farther down the line. "When I was stationed overseas, it took forever to get back home and I noticed this kind of ache. I never knew there were levels of homesickness." He glanced at her over the shoulder. "Did you, Doc?"

She huffed out a laugh. "I'm not sure there's an official diagnosis for homesickness, but I understand your point. Maybe it's tied to how much it feels like home in the first place. I haven't been home for the holidays in years, but I don't miss Iowa, you know?"

"What about your family?" Travis tipped his head to the side.

Keena studied his face as she drew up alongside him. Trying to talk to Travis was a challenge. He didn't say anything more than he had to.

Somehow that made her so much more interested in everything he shared.

"My parents…" Keena wondered if she was going to get into this. "Those families where there are multiple remarriages on both sides and you have half siblings and stepsiblings and you're the oldest on this side and the black sheep if you only talk about this group of kids but the golden child if you're considering those only from your dad's side…" She sighed. "It's not easy figuring out who you really are while you're in the middle of all that. Getting away from it made things much clearer. I love them, but when I go home, everything gets cloudy again. Talking on the phone one-on-one is much easier."

She wasn't sure she wanted to see his reaction to that. It wasn't easy to confess that family wasn't "everything" to her. She'd heard so many people talk about the sacrifices they made to stay connected in this modern world. For Keena, it was better to get snapshots instead of a running narrative.

"I might not get how all those connections change things, but I definitely understand needing to get away to figure out who you are." Travis took the wire from her and snipped off another piece. He repeated the steps to tighten the top wire near the corner of the lot that met the Rocking A fence line. "Becoming an Armstrong was a real process for me."

Keena bit her lip. He was talking. She didn't want him to stop.

"I can honestly see the question marks in your eyes, but you aren't letting any of them fly," Travis said as he led the way back to his truck. "Why is that?"

Keena hurried to follow him across the yard. Travis's easy amble had picked up speed.

"I've been on good behavior because I know unleashing a blizzard of questions isn't the best way to make friends." Keena frowned because she hadn't intended to be that honest.

Travis grunted. "With us, might be exactly what I need."

Keena crossed her arms over her chest at the relief that spread through her. He was giving her permission to be herself with this. How considerate that would be.

"What are these tools called?" Keena pointed at the items in the truck bed.

He nodded. "Ah, an easy one. You've heard of a hammer?" His lips twitched as he watched her face. Keena scowled in response. "The others are fence pliers, really good for cutting wire and protecting your fingers when you need to pull or twist. And the little bar thing is called a wire-twisty thing. I'll need to do some research to get the scientific name for you. My dad taught us to repair fences with lots of pointing and waving when we offered him the wrong tool. Repeat that by process of elimination until we guessed the right tool."

"It worked for you. Someday you'll teach it to your own son the same way, huh?" Keena watched him as he processed that and knew the instant something inside him changed. His face relaxed.

"Thanks. I hadn't gotten to that, the fun part, of what I could share with any of the kids coming through here. I was stuck on the responsibility." He tugged his hat up and rolled his shoulders. "Talking to you is good, Doc. You might have cured some of what ails me."

Keena laughed. "Yeah? I am very good at my job."

The warm gleam in his expression as he smiled at her did something to Keena's heart, as if it lit up in response.

His lopsided smile was almost as attractive as his ready laughter.

As she slid into his truck, Keena was warning herself not to fall for blue eyes in a nice face. Her career was in Denver. Nothing was going to distract her from that.

When Travis pulled out onto the road, he asked, "What made you decide to face off against Chuck anyway? Eventually he would have returned home with no intervention. He always does."

Keena pursed her lips, wishing she'd known that Chuck was a homing cow. "I was afraid he'd cause an accident in the road." Was that silly?

Travis looked thoughtfully at her. She didn't want to know that she'd made a fool of herself for no reason, so she didn't ask.

"And what about holding your arms out like that?" he asked. "What did that do?"

"Make me seem bigger? More threatening?" Keena couldn't keep the question marks out of her answer.

"Hmm, I don't think that would have fooled him." Travis smiled slowly. "You've been reading up on how to escape bears, haven't you?"

Keena narrowed her eyes to try for her best steely glare before the chuckles spilled out. "Maybe I have." Then she gripped his arm. "Do not tell anyone about this encounter ever, do you hear me? The arms, the difference between steers and bulls, the hamburger slippers…all of that better be locked away or else."

She waited for him to ask, "Or else what, city girl?"

But instead, he met her stare. "I would never. This stays between you and me."

Then he winked and she felt it all the way down deep in her soul.

Keena had tried to prepare herself for all the challenges of small-town life and medicine, but keeping her distance from this blue-eyed cowboy was going to be the real test.

CHAPTER FIVE

BY THE TIME Travis followed Keena back to the truck in the Homestead Market's parking lot, he was worn out, had spent twice what he'd intended, and had learned a lot about his new neighbor.

She was curious. He'd lost track of the number of questions that he'd answered. In no particular order, he'd shared: they had included space for four boys, many foster kids needed a temporary spot until family could be located, Prospect had originally been called Sullivan's Post, saying the store was "doing land-office business" meant it was a busy Saturday at Homestead Market in Western-speak, his favorite color was blue, there was no color he hated, his only decorating rule was no camouflage anything, and he hadn't set a budget for this shopping trip. Her brain moved quickly and he was almost certain it moved in a straight line somehow, but what came out of her mouth often seemed routed through left field.

Since he preferred listening to talking, catching up had been a struggle in the beginning, but her pleasure over each new fact she learned was a nice reward. He'd pushed the shopping cart in her wake, always alert for sudden stops at this cute thing or that important item she'd left off her list.

They'd only had two serious disagreements. Discussions, really.

Keena had argued passionately that the kids who came to stay needed some fun stuff, in addition to the bedding, toiletries and school supplies already picked out. Her choices: big puffy house slippers in the shape of cowboy boots or high-top sneakers, and small wireless speakers shaped like soccer balls, basketballs and footballs.

He'd given in on the speakers. They were fairly inexpensive, and he would have thought something like that was cool when he was a kid. She'd given up on the slippers but the firm set of her chin made him think she wasn't finished with the conversation.

He'd had more fun walking every aisle of the home goods section of the store than he'd expected. He'd have time to wash the denim-colored comforters, white sheets and pillow-cases with red or green stripes depending on the set, and get the rooms set up before the social worker came. Keena's reasoning about her choices was sound; everything was com-fortable, washable and easy to personalize when they knew who would be staying with them.

"Livery stables rented horses? Is that right?" she asked as she hefted one of the bags they'd crammed into the shopping cart after check-ing out.

"Horses, wagons and stalls sometimes. The blacksmith worked out of this livery stable, too." Travis handed her the next bag and watched her meticulously arrange it in the back seat of his truck. That care would come in handy since he wasn't exactly sure their haul would fit inside the cab. "Pros-pect was a boomtown and the livery was big business. Travelers would need fresh horses or repairs to their rigs if they made it this far before heading off on the next stage of their journey."

"I can't believe the building has been stand-ing all this time. That's a testament to human ingenuity and the materials they chose, for sure." Keena waved a hand at Prospect's version of the big-box store housed in the large space behind the old building's facade. "This is amazing." She took her smaller bags of groceries and settled them in the tight space behind her seat. "I can't wait to see what other surprises this town has."

That was the second thing he'd learned about Keena: she was enthusiastic. Instead of hanging back on their shopping trip, she'd taken the lead and made her selections confidently.

What he'd remember most was how generous she was. When she wedged the corkboards that she'd chosen carefully to be her housewarming gift for each boy against the seat, he said, "You didn't have to buy anything for my new family but thank you for doing that and taking so much time with me today. For everything."

She paused and met his stare over the shopping cart. "Every kid needs a corkboard, Travis. They can hold calendars and important assignments and mementos. Very useful. And if I'm here when you meet your kids, I will also personally arrange a welcome message for each one on these boards."

"And if you aren't here?" Travis asked. At some point in the hour-plus he'd spent trailing behind Keena, he'd realized he was going to miss having her nearby. Had anyone ever made such an impact in such a short time? Maybe Prue and Walt, but he couldn't name anyone else.

"Once I go back to Denver, you'll have to do the best you can to carry on my legacy," Keena said and shook her finger. "I bought plenty of extra cards and things to keep you in business for a while." She picked up the small bag that was filled with greeting cards, streamers and balloons and whatever she thought might add a touch of celebration for each new boy.

He hadn't had the heart to explain to her that few of these kids would be ready for a party when they arrived. There wouldn't be anything to celebrate for some time.

"You're thinking hard now." Keena arranged the cards against the corkboard. "Probably because I have no idea what the situation will be when these kids get here." She waited for his nod before doing the same. "You're right. I was never a foster kid, so I can't relate, but I have spent time with kids who have been through trauma." She shifted the bags around to make sure they were packed correctly. "There is a point in the emergency room when something normal, something that shows care and concern and that life goes on, makes a difference for that kid. Am I wrong that it's the same for kids in foster care?"

Travis braced his foot on the cart as he considered that. "No. You are not wrong." He sighed. "I'll never forget when Prue took me fabric shopping the first time. She was making me a quilt of my own, something she did for every one of her boys. My colors. My pattern. Mine to keep no matter where I went next." He still had it, rolled up carefully and stored in the top of his closet. Years of use had left the seams weak, but he could never give it up.

She had made something for him. He didn't exactly understand what went into making that quilt, but he had seen the time Prue had invested in a gift for him. That made it valuable then and priceless now.

"What did you choose?" Keena asked as

she took the cart and walked it around into the cart corral.

"The pattern is a star, I can't remember the name, but the colors are bright blue and purple. She added in some black, and it might be the loudest quilt ever assembled but I love it." His grin matched hers as they stared at each other over the bed of the truck. "My biggest worry is that so many fosters don't even have suitcases. I didn't. If I was lucky, I had a heavy-duty trash bag to throw all my stuff in when it came time to go. Other times I had to make hard decisions on what to leave behind." Travis wanted her to realize this but he didn't want to reopen old wounds. "It can hurt when the 'normal' from one place doesn't make the cut when you have to move on. That's all I'm saying. The speakers will fit in tight spaces. Great idea."

Keena bit her bottom lip as she studied his face. "Okay, I understand." She held up both hands in surrender. "We did good work today."

"And," Travis said as he motioned over his shoulder, "we missed the lunch rush. If we head for the Ace High now, we may have

the run of the place. I'm buying." He wanted the opportunity to talk to Keena without an audience, although Faye would be there. She ran the place for her grandparents and tried to do it singlehandedly as waitress, hostess and sometimes cook. She would spread the word back to his mother, but Faye was always at the restaurant. There was no way to avoid that exposure. She'd been his first friend in Prospect, not counting his brothers, so Travis expected her to share just enough gossip to appease his mother and no more.

"We could walk and take a look at the buildings as we go." Keena covered her eyes with one hand as she tried to avoid the late-afternoon sun. "Let's do that."

Before he could agree, he heard, "Hey, Keena, wait up."

They both turned to see Jordan trotting through the parking lot. "I want to introduce you to my sister Sarah. She surprised us all by coming into town earlier than we thought."

He knew Wes would be over the moon when he found out Sarah was back.

Sarah brushed her hair back into her ponytail before holding her hand out. "If I'd known my sister was going to drag me through the grocery store on the way home instead of taking the direct route, I might have put on some makeup before we were introduced." Sarah glared at Jordan before smiling pleasantly at Keena. "I'm Sarah Hearst. I think we're going to be neighbors."

Keena shook her hand enthusiastically. It reminded him a bit of the way Dr. Singh greeted visitors. Was that something they taught in medical school?

"Yes, I'm looking forward to seeing this lodge." Keena pointed at the bags in the back seat. "I found a whole collection of Cookie Queen cookbooks in the kitchen, so I'm going to try my hand at one of the recipes as a way of making sure my new coworkers are predisposed to like me."

Sarah clasped her hands together. "Oh, nice, you've heard all about our history, I guess? That will leave lots of time for us to find out all about you."

Keena shrugged. "No famous relatives on my side."

"But I bet you have plenty of wild stories to tell about working in the emergency room." Jordan held up a hand as if to stop her protest. "Let's make plans for lunch after Handmade's first Sip and Paint night on Friday." She pointed to Sarah. "This one's the marketing genius, so the name for Dad's painting event is still being brainstormed."

Travis was interested to see Keena wrinkle her nose. "I have zero artistic talent."

Jordan snorted. "Hasn't stopped my dad from trying to teach me everything he knows. The only real requirement for this is whether you drink wine." She waited for Keena to nod. "And do you like gossip?"

Keena glanced at him before nodding sheepishly. He was learning Keena liked information of any kind.

"Who doesn't?" Sarah drawled. "Friday night, join us at the Mercantile. You'll love Prue."

"Oh, I do." Keena smiled at Travis before returning her focus to Sarah. "She makes a wonderful red sauce."

Sarah's mouth formed a perfect O, which Travis took to mean that Jordan hadn't had a chance to update her sister on the dinner with the Armstrongs.

"We're about to head over to lunch. Should we save you a spot?" he asked Jordan. "I'm interested to find out what happened to all the plans you had today that kept you from helping me with choosing stuff for the new bedrooms."

Jordan blinked her eyes oh-so innocently. "No, no, no lunch for us, Sarah's in a hurry to get back to the lodge and her boyfriend." Jordan said the last word in the same obnoxious younger-sister tone she always used to give her sister and Wes a hard time. Travis appreciated anyone who kept his "older" brother on his toes. "I wanted to get Sarah's expert opinion on some dishes I was thinking of picking up for a continental breakfast at the lodge."

"Do we have anyone staying at the lodge? No. Do we have a plan for this breakfast? Not really. Have I been driving for hours and hours and hours to get from California to Colorado? Yes," Sarah said with a hiss as Jordan took her hand to drag her into the store.

"Whose fault is that?" Jordan asked brightly. "And you'll want your special drinks to be in the lodge's refrigerator this afternoon. Guess where we have to go to get those?" Jordan turned to wave over her shoulder at them, her eye roll very familiar.

"Sisters are pretty much the same everywhere you go, I guess," Keena murmured. "Arguing as a way of showing love."

Travis was skeptical. "I wouldn't know if that's true, but would you believe there's a third one? She lives in New York. We haven't had the pleasure of meeting her yet. Patrick Hearst, their dad, is a real nice guy. Quiet."

Keena smiled at him. "Can you blame him?"

Travis grinned. "Let's tour, shall we?"

They walked and talked. Keena asked him about the wood boardwalk, what the buildings were framed in, how much money would have been stored in Prospect's bank during the boom, and why the hair salon and barbershop had split the floors of the old bathhouse the way they had.

Luckily, she never got tired of his variations on "I don't know."

"What I'm hearing is that I need to take this tour again with Clay," Keena said and pulled open the door to the Ace High.

"If you want to know about old construction, yes. If you're interested in the history of the town, see if you can get Rose Bell, who runs the Bell House Bed-and-Breakfast," Travis said and motioned over his shoulder at the blue Victorian that took pride of place in Prospect's downtown. "Her family has been here a long time. She might be able to answer questions, too."

As they sat down in a booth, Keena said, "Thank you for being patient with all my questions. I get the impression that I've forced you to talk more than usual today. Have you used up your quota of words for the rest of the year?"

Travis grunted. "Not yet, but I am going to sit in silence this afternoon."

When she laughed as he'd hoped she would, he relaxed. Teasing her was a gamble.

Keena reached across the table to squeeze his hand and he knew for certain the gamble had paid off. "I have had a lovely day. I can't imagine a better way to get used to the town."

He wanted to ask why that was so. What had made the difference? Was it knowing that she could find whatever she needed, even in a place as small as Prospect? Or the way her curiosity was fired up in a new place with all these questions to be answered? Or was it the people she'd met?

Why did he hope his company was somewhere in the answer?

Instead of asking any of his own questions, Travis waved at Faye so she'd know they were ready to order.

"Tell me what's good here," Keena said as she moved the ketchup bottle and saltshaker around. "I need to study the menu."

Before he could reply, Faye slid to a stop next to their table. "I see Trav hasn't explained how the Ace works." She slipped her pen behind her ear. "Two choices. You can have whatever you want as long as it's one or the other of those options. Today, we have meat loaf and pot roast for dinner. Lunch is long gone at this point. The fixin's include fluffy mashed potatoes, charred brussels sprouts, glazed carrots, and rolls or corn bread muffins." Faye pointed at Travis. "He's having meat loaf, hold the sprouts. No sprouts will ever touch his lips voluntarily." The way she shook her head sadly reminded Travis that he and Faye would never see eye to eye on some of her vegetable offerings.

Faye pulled out her pen and said, "Now what can I get you, Dr. Murphy?"

Travis snorted at the way Keena's mouth dropped open in surprise. "How did you know? Pot roast and I'll have his brussels sprouts, too. With coffee."

"Oh, honey," Faye said as she patted her shoulder, "first time in a small town?" Then she was gone before Keena could comment on that. Faye didn't need to waste time standing around, especially with a large family entering the restaurant.

Keena raised her eyebrows at him, the question in her eyes.

"Is that your way of asking…" Travis watched her hold both hands out as if she meant to encompass Faye, the menu, their table and how Faye knew who she was. "Well, you understand there's no menu now. This place is named after the saloon that used to be here, the Ace High, fanciest one in town. Faye is your neighbor on the other side, unlucky owner of Chuck, and…"

"We've been friends ever since Travis landed in Prospect." Faye plopped a glass of water in front of Travis before sliding the bread basket and Keena's cup of coffee across the table. "Sometimes more, if you include three weeks one summer where I convinced him to be my boyfriend." Faye put a hand over her mouth to cover her chuckle. "No one counts that, though."

Faye dropped her bombshell and then hustled back to the kitchen.

Keena raised her eyebrows again.

"Does that look mean you're not going to ask all your questions?" Travis sipped his water as he watched her stir the coffee in front of her.

"I mean, I wouldn't know where to start. Did you break Faye's heart? Did she break yours?" Keena asked as she inched closer as if she couldn't wait to hear more.

"No hearts were involved. Lips possibly, but no other body parts were included that summer." Travis relaxed in the seat and watched as the information filtered through Keena's brain. Her face was so expressive. He read amusement, interest, and then he could see the questions start to build.

Sort of how steam escapes before a volcano erupts.

Luckily, Faye deposited two plates on the table and Keena's mouth dropped open again.

Faye laughed. "That's the reaction I like to see."

"Keena already met your favorite steer this morning, Faye. I patched a couple of spots on the fence, but I warned her he couldn't be contained by any fence built by man." Travis met Keena's stare. Was she afraid he was going to tell more about that encounter? He never would. He'd learned how to keep confidences early on.

"I swear, that troublemaker. He don't know where the grass is really greener, which is where I put it out for him every morning about dawn." Faye slapped the table. "I'll ask Gramps to keep a closer eye on that section of fence, Keena."

Since Gramps was almost ninety, Travis tried to help as much as he could. "Should be good for a bit."

Faye squeezed his shoulder. Travis understood the thank-you that she couldn't put into words. "The Armstrongs make fine neighbors but stop by without an Armstrong and I'll give you all the juicy gossip you need, Dr. Murphy. And I'll see you at this painting thing the Hearsts are putting together. Not sure the restaurant will be left standing if I leave for a couple of hours on Friday night, but it's time to find out."

Keena didn't have a chance to respond because Faye was already trotting across the dining room to answer the ringing phone. "Does she run this whole place by herself?"

Travis glanced at Faye over his shoulder. "Tries to. If a painting class will convince her to take some help, it'll be a good thing. And if you ever need to know anything about anything that is happening in this town, Faye should have the information. Somehow, the time she spends here, the people who come and go, she always knows things first." She was also the kind of friend who knew when to spread the story and when to sit on it. For that, she was one of his favorite people in town. "Her grandparents have had the smaller operation on the other side of the house you're renting for as long as I can remember. They're older now, and Faye is doing her best to run the place and keep the whole town fed here."

"So you fix the fence when you can." Keena smiled slowly.

Travis felt the color rising in his nape.

Something about the sparkle in her eyes felt like approval.

Or admiration?

Whatever it was, he was more comfortable with rapid-fire questions that put him on the spot. The way she stared at him now made him wonder how much she could read on his face. He worked hard to contain everything, but this pressure of stepping up to lead the family in fostering a new generation, something that mattered to all of them and that he was most likely the least qualified to do, was causing weak spots in his defense. Was Keena going to be the one to slip through the gaps?

CHAPTER SIX

By MIDMORNING OF Keena's first day of shadowing Dr. Singh at Prospect Family Practice, she'd discovered how the rhythm of her work life had changed.

The most obvious difference was the daylight. She'd spent so much time working the night shifts in Emergency, that she'd forgotten how cheerful morning people could be. Dr. Singh's office manager, Reginald, was possibly the purest ray of early sunshine Keena had ever met. He managed to hold on to that positivity even in the face of near-overwhelming obstacles, which included a jammed copier and the long-suffering stares of both Kim, Dr. Singh's physician's assistant, and Emily, who took care of billing and appointments.

Reginald was unperturbed by this. He called them Thunder and Lightning to their faces as he poured their coffee mugs to the brim.

She and Dr. Singh were in the exam room with Sam Walker, midseventies, retired rural postal carrier who appeared as healthy as could be to Keena but who seemed to have a monthly standing meeting with Dr. Singh. They could hear Reginald singing and whistling while he worked.

"Sam, Dr. Murphy here has made a rookie mistake." Dr. Singh dropped the stethoscope he'd been using to listen to Sam's heart and lungs. "Reg can be annoyingly chipper on cloudy days. With sunshine and the cowboy cookies Keena brought in, we may need to sedate him for his own safety. If we don't, the rest of the office will be ready to commit mayhem."

Sam sipped from the coffee cup Dr. Singh had passed him as soon as they'd walked into the exam room. "They're good cookies, ma'am. I almost want to sing, too, but it ain't nearly as pleasant as all that joyful noise." He finished the last bite of the cookie he'd taken the second time Dr. Singh insisted he try them.

"I wanted to make friends. Food seemed a good start. I like food." Keena rested her elbow on the counter, curious as to what was going on here, but nonetheless happy to watch Dr. Singh work.

In the pause of conversation, they could hear someone singing show tunes.

"Is that *Oklahoma*?" Keena whispered. Movie musicals were one of her nerdy hobbies. Listening to Reginald sing made her wish she'd packed some of her favorites to bring along.

"That's usually a Friday song. When the good news that the weekend is coming sparks a joy that cannot be contained, you will hear about the surrey with the fringe on top so often that you will wish fringe had never been invented." Dr. Singh slid down into the chair beside Sam and picked up his own cup. "Did you check on volunteering at the library, Sam? The sign I saw for part-time help was gone the last time I went in."

Since Dr. Singh seemed to be prepared to make endless small talk and the list of appointments Emily had shown her was long, Keena wondered if she was supposed to take the lead in this exam, to get them on track.

Before she could start asking medical questions, someone rapped on the door. "We've got an emergency in Exam Two, doc. Most likely needs stitches."

Keena immediately set her cup down and found Kim and their new patient in the exam room next door. When someone was bleeding, no one waited for backup in the emergency room.

She listened to the young woman, whose name was Lucky Garcia it turned out, tell Kim about the accident she'd had the night before while she was working on a car that she was restoring. She'd been wrenching at a carburetor when the tool in her hand slipped, leaving a gash in her palm. Two little girls were hanging on either side of their mother while she tried to explain how silly she felt about the clumsy accident.

"Looks like stitches to me. What do you think, Dr. Murphy?" Kim asked but was marching toward the door, already on a mission to grab everything they'd need to sew up the wound on Lucky's hand, she guessed.

Keena pulled the rolling stool closer to Lucky. "Since you are still bleeding, Ms. Garcia, I think so. Bring me…"

The door closed behind Kim before Keena had finished her sentence. Annoyance bubbled up because if the nurse had waited one more minute to listen to her instructions, they might have saved time. Instead they'd waste it when she returned, and Keena would have to make corrections. When the tense silence in the room registered, Keena focused on the kids. "And who are these young ladies?"

"Meet Eliana and Selena." Lucky ran a hand over each little girl's head. "Most commonly known as the Garcia twins around town. They are always in motion, so they create a blur that makes it even more difficult to distinguish who is who."

Keena laughed. "Must be tough to keep up with them."

"You have no idea." Lucky sighed. "I couldn't leave them with Dante at the garage because he's shorthanded today and you do not want to see what these two can get up to without constant vigilance."

Kim returned with the tray. "I know 3-0 sutures are pretty standard, but Dr. Singh would go with smaller based on the wound, so I also brought 4-0." She passed Keena the tray and moved over to enter notes in Lucky's file. Keena mentally ran through the usual checklist: nylon sutures in the smaller size, which Keena also preferred, needle driver, tissue forceps...Kim had gathered everything.

Keena's worry eased. Dr. Singh had built a strong team. She had help when he left.

Just as Keena dabbed the antiseptic along the edges of the wound, Dr. Singh stuck his head in the open doorway. "Oh, thank goodness. I was afraid I was too late!"

Keena turned to face him, prepared to state that she had the situation in hand, but he was holding out two cookies and making "come hither" motions toward the girls. "I was afraid I would have to eat these treats myself."

"Oh, no, we wouldn't want that." Lucky's voice was dramatic. She was committed to the bit.

"We'll go eat these in my office. Join us when you get all this taken care of," Dr. Singh called as he led the twins out of the exam room.

Lucky immediately relaxed. "I've been pretending this didn't bother me all day long. It bothers me."

Keena added more antiseptic around the

wound. "This will feel better any minute now. You should have had this done last night. This must be pretty painful," Keena said calmly as she made the first stitch, hoping to get this started and finished before Lucky caught on to what was happening. Making conversation while she worked had always been a simple but effective way to distract a patient from the worst.

"I had it stopped last night, but this morning, I noticed I bled through my bandage almost as soon as I got to work." Lucky rolled her other hand into a fist. "And I tried to find a babysitter, but Dr. Singh is so good with the girls, I knew it would be fine."

Keena bit her lip as she made quick work of five more stitches and then pressed gauze to the wound to stop the bleeding. Would she have thought to also distract the little girls while she worked? Keena wasn't so sure.

"No hospital around. Even the after-hours medical office is almost an hour away." Lucky glanced down and smiled when she realized Keena had finished. "Hey. That's amazing."

"I wondered about after-hours emergencies. Dr. Singh mentioned he sometimes gets calls, but they're filtered through an answering service. Why didn't you try to get him?" Keena scooted back on the stool and moved the tray to the counter behind her. She would have been available to help with something like this, too.

"Dr. Singh deserves to be off of work when he can, you know?" Lucky pressed her fingers lightly to the stitches. "I thought it was under control until this morning."

Being the only doctor in town was going to take some getting used to. In her estimation, this should have been an emergency call, but Lucky had made a different decision.

"Think you'll like small-town life, Dr. Murphy?" Lucky asked as she waved at Keena's scrubs and white coat. Dr. Singh preferred a simple shirt, jeans and running shoes. "We don't often see Dr. Singh in his medical duds, but I imagine you're facing even bigger differences than the dress code."

Keena stood to wash her hands. "Scrubs are comfortable. I don't know why everyone doesn't wear them. And apparently, cookies are dangerous to morning people. They inspire show tunes and excessive high spirits which can annoy their coworkers. I've been on the night shift so long I didn't know that." She tilted her head. Reginald was singing something else now. "Is that 'Happy' or…"

Lucky nodded. "I think so. He loves positive vibes. If you're still around for Western Days in the spring, be sure to catch Reginald onstage. He does the most amazing song impersonations. You're standing there, looking right at a cowboy, as if he'd just jumped off a bucking bronco, dusted off his hat, and picked up a microphone, but what you're hearing sounds like Frank Sinatra or Billy Joel or David Bowie. His range is wild."

Keena rested a hip against the counter as she tried to imagine the middle-aged father who coached his son's flag football team performing "Uptown Girl." It was easier than she expected.

Lucky was grinning when Dr. Singh swung by to drop off the twin girls. "If you're like Jordan and Sarah Hearst, Doctor Keena, they were both worried that life in Prospect would be boring." She managed to hide a grimace as her little girls hit her at full speed. "But one thing you can count on around here is that this town comes up with its own entertainment."

Dr. Singh nodded proudly. "Oh, yes, Keena, you missed the Halloween contest in the park. I enter every year but my costume hasn't won yet. And when the snow starts to fall, Prospect is a beautiful place. My wife and I will be sorry to miss winter this year."

Reginald groaned from outside in the hallway. "Winter, schminter. Give me sunshine."

Keena thought she and Reginald could agree on that as well as the best playlist, but she hadn't had a chance to experience snowy mountains. Maybe she'd like it? Blizzards in Iowa had been zero fun.

"Guess I better get back to the garage." Lucky stood and took the wrapped cookies Dr. Singh held out. "First-rate medical care with cookies to go? No way you can get that in Denver."

Keena nodded at Kim who was hovering. "If you see any signs of infection, come back in and let me take a look. We'll remove the stitches next week."

Lucky and her little girls were a happy, noisy parade down the hall when Dr. Singh clapped her on the shoulder. "Good work, Keena. I hope you see how easy it is to settle into Prospect."

Keena made a few notes on Lucky's chart and asked Kim to schedule a follow-up phone call for the next day so she could make sure there was no further breakthrough bleeding before she returned to her coffee mug.

"Reg, do we have time for a break?" Dr. Singh asked.

"Yep, next appointment isn't for half an hour," Reginald said as he juggled the ringing phone, waving goodbye to the Garcias, and topping off Keena's coffee cup.

"Keena, let's go sit in my office. I want to show you my files." Dr. Singh motioned for her to follow him, but when they were both settled, he stretched his arms with a happy sigh. "It's nice not to run from one emergency to the next, isn't it? Time to catch your breath, regroup. It has a positive effect on my well-being, you know?"

Surprised at the conversation opener, Keena sipped her coffee to take a moment to consider her answer. "It's only day one, Dr. Singh, but I don't believe I'll have any trouble settling in." She smiled. "Can't get too comfortable, though. You know I need my running shoes when I go back to Denver. Very few coffee breaks and breathing

has to be worked in on an as-needed basis."
She bit into the cookie and mentally patted
herself on the back. Following the Cookie
Queen's recipe had been simple.

She'd enjoyed the process so much that
she'd ended up trying a second and a third
recipe, so now Keena had a whole collection
of cookies to deliver after work. The pharmacy inside the Homestead Market would
get a container, for sure.

She wasn't sure it was important to have
a good working relationship with the town's
pharmacist, but it couldn't hurt.

Not as much as eating two dozen cookies
all by herself, anyway.

"Do you think you can work on calling me
PJ before you go back to your regular life?"
he asked with his broad smile and twin-
kling eyes. When they'd first met, Keena
had trusted him instantly. That was a rare
reaction to have as a resident at the mercy
of whatever attending physician was on duty
that day, but Dr. Singh had been all about ed-
ucation and compassion. Some of the other
doctors who'd taught her had been as good
with teaching technical stuff, but none had

been as thoughtful or encouraging as Dr. Singh.

"I'll try. PJ." Keena wrinkled her nose. "Sounds funny to my ears."

"But to mine, exactly right." He held a finger up. "I've mentioned how grateful I am for you stepping in here. Prospect has become my home and I worried about leaving my new family without someone to care for them. I don't worry anymore."

Keena chewed her cookie and swallowed carefully. It would not do to choke when he'd said such a nice thing. "I needed the break. This is going to work out very well for both of us."

"How is the house?" Dr. Singh asked.

"Sleeping is not easy. Yet. The change in schedule and the absolute lack of any noise has taken some getting used to, but otherwise, the place is great." Keena was prudently avoiding any mention of Chuck or her rescue from the beast thanks to Travis Armstrong. That story would go with her to the grave.

"It was nice to have Lucky mention how we make our own entertainment here." Dr. Singh motioned at Reginald who had transitioned to whistling. Keena couldn't identify the tune. "While you are here, maybe you could give some thought to how it would be to live here. Permanently."

Keena crossed her legs and braced her elbows on the arms of the comfortable chair as she tried to understand his point. Prospect was a lovely town, but she had no plans to exchange it for the career she'd built in Denver.

"Why did you need a break?" he asked softly. When Dr. Singh got serious, his expression transitioning from friendly smile to patient understanding, it made everyone around him nervous. He was very good at his job. This expression was a sign that things had gotten real.

This was what he meant by treating the whole patient.

"You remember how I was in the early days." Keena pinched a pleat in her pants and forced herself to meet his stare squarely. Convincing them both that she was in control and recognized her own limitations was important here. "Working Emergency requires steady hands, right?" He nodded in agreement. "And I always had steady hands when I needed them."

"You did. No one was calmer in the face of the unknowns that arrived at our door." He pushed his glasses up. "But as I recall, it still took a toll on you. Running on zero sleep. Very little food that counts as nutrition. Constant adrenaline. It builds up. Was that the first time you and I discussed how important sleep was, even for medical residents?"

It had been. She'd had to learn how to turn off her brain when it was time to rest.

She nodded. "You kept dropping notes and cards with the same website written on it in my coat pocket." Eventually, she'd surrendered and visited the site, and learned so many of the mindfulness exercises that she depended on today to siphon off the anxiety.

"Because being present is important." Dr. Singh said the words she knew by heart. He'd said them often enough.

"I haven't forgotten any of that. I needed to learn it and I still use it." Keena forced her fingers to relax. Something about this conversation was making her more tense than she'd been on her first day at a new place of work. That hadn't happened in years, so she'd had the jitters.

"There came a time for me," Dr. Singh said slowly as he stared at her over his glasses, "where my coping skills were failing me. I added exercise and cut out caffeine, but I still reached the point where sleep was impossible to come by. The time adds up and creates these memories that are easy to file away during the shift but harder to store when you should be free to think of other things." He braced his hands over his chest, covering the word *Vail* in the center of his sweatshirt.

"Right. So we take a break, we regroup, and then we come back to work stronger." Keena smiled. "I don't know if a mission trip to Haiti is going to be much of a break for you, but you will be so happy to see your small town again, whether or not there's a lot of nightlife to keep you busy."

He pursed his lips. "But of course. I know what Prospect means to me, my career and my life. I don't want to sacrifice one for the other, you understand. Here, I can have everything, do whatever it is I dream of. My question for you is…"

Keena braced herself. This had been the whole point of the conversation, of course.

She trusted Dr. Singh. If he had been diagnosing her, would she be able to ignore his judgment?

"What if you enjoy your time here so much that it's even harder to absorb the demands of Emergency when you go back?" Dr. Singh reached across the desk to grip her hand. "Just because there is only one doctor in Prospect now doesn't mean that this is how it has to be."

Keena gripped his hand tightly. "What are you saying?"

"Life and careers and medicine and family are all about timing." Dr. Singh smiled. "What if this is the perfect time for a break and for you to consider if you'd like to be a partner with an old friend in a small-town family practice?"

Keena laughed. "PJ," she said carefully, her lips forming the letters awkwardly, "I've built something in Denver. I could have left and gone to bigger hospitals and cities, but it's my emergency department. How could I leave it?"

He shrugged. "You wouldn't be the first

to determine you've gone as high as you could go there."

"Then why would I…" *Leave it for a place like this?* Keena didn't finish the question because she didn't want to insult him, but it floated in the air between them.

She could do more, for sure. Leaving Denver to come to Prospect would mean doing less.

Wouldn't it?

He shrugged. "Let's say the situation this morning had been reversed." He clasped his hands together on the desk. "Lucky and her girls came in first and I started the sutures. What would you have done?"

Keena shifted in her seat. She knew where this was headed. "Offered to take over the sutures so you could…"

His sly smile confirmed she was falling into his trap. "Instead of offering to babysit for a few minutes to give mom a break…" He held up a finger. "Or volunteering to have my monthly sit-down with Sam, you would have done only what you think you're good at."

Keena wanted to argue because this was going to turn into Dr. Singh teaching her something but… "Right. That's right. I couldn't tell that there was anything wrong with Sam."

He shook his head. "Nothing but loneliness. He retired and lost his wife in the past couple of years. She had a heart attack, so his initial visits were out of concern over his health, but he's fine."

Keena rubbed her forehead. "I should have paid better attention in my psych rotation."

His huff of amusement reassured her. "No real psychology needed. Empathy, compassion, curiosity, those are way more important here. Sam and I talk about current events, drink coffee and after twenty or thirty minutes, we both feel better and go on about our days. Next month, that will be you. What are you going to do?"

What a scary question.

"I was thinking about how different the rhythms were between Denver and here this morning. I don't have any idea what's in store for me yet, do I?" Keena asked.

"You have accomplished everything you can in Denver, Keena. You know it. I know it. What if, instead of a bigger city with a bigger hospital with bigger trauma..." He waited for her to meet his eyes. "What if you need to try bigger medicine? To learn new ways to heal people that might require more than technique?"

Keena sipped her coffee. "You are so sneaky."

He laughed until he had to wipe tears from his eyes. "I really am. Almost everyone loves me too much to point that out, but you are not like everyone else." He exhaled. "I wanted a new challenge when I arrived in Prospect. I found it."

"But you were always so good with patients, PJ." The nickname was a bit less weird this time.

He grimaced. "I wasn't so different from you when I started. Excellent medical skills but the struggle to slow down and connect with people took time. That requires maturity and confidence that you know what you know, I believe. I made myself do it and look at me now." He held out his arms to encompass his office. "On top of the world."

In a tiny town in the Colorado Rockies when he could have been running metropolitan departments anywhere.

But with the time to follow his interests, his passions, and be with a wife, grand-daughters, a whole town who loved him.

"The good news is you don't have to figure it all out today, Keena." PJ stood and pointed at the door. "And you won't have to do it the way I did. This team? They're really, really good. Getting them here to Prospect wasn't easy, but it was worth the trouble."

Keena followed him out of his office to go check on the next patients. Reginald was singing. Kim was unboxing supplies and putting them in the ruthlessly organized supply cabinet PJ had discussed so proudly. Emily was loading paper back into the copy machine. Prospect Family Practice ran efficiently. All it needed was a doctor who could continue to treat patients well.

For the first time in a long time, her job had changed. This was a different kind of medicine, one built on relationships.

Keena had three months to find out if she was capable of being that kind of doctor. Dr. Singh had given her a shot at something new.

Whether she was ready or able to take on that challenge was up to her.

CHAPTER SEVEN

THE WAY ELLEN MONTOYA, the caseworker assigned to review Travis's application to foster children, surveyed the crowded kitchen table upon her arrival had him second-guessing his request for his whole family to be present for the final home study. Travis knew it was important to introduce Ellen to everyone, because they were his support system, but when all the Armstrongs were gathered in one place, it was too much. Jordan and Sarah Hearst were on the periphery, too, hovering near the refrigerator.

In case.

That's what Sarah had said. They had wanted to be nearby in case they were needed.

Travis hadn't had time to consider what sort of event might require nine adults in total, but regardless, they were prepared for it.

Ellen cleared her throat. "Well, thank you for the introductions. It is lovely to meet you all. I know Prue and Walt by reputation, of course. They served on the board of the foster support foundation. Every now and then, Bridget Williams mentions how much they have contributed over the years." She smiled at Travis. "And I hope you know that we take every home study seriously. This is our chance to make sure you've considered the impact adding a foster child, even temporarily, will have on your home and family.

"When we meet someone who has even loftier goals like yours, to take on the older kids who may have reached the end of our ability to help, it's critical to take enough time to make the right decision." She patted his hand and Travis had to focus hard not to grip hers too tightly. As scared as he was of failing, he wanted this. It was almost impossible to put into words how important this was, but he was getting so close. They had already come so far.

"Wes, Clay, Grant and Matt…" Ellen made sure to look at each man directly as she addressed him. "You understand the impact of what we're doing here, and the work you've all done to create a comfortable, spacious place is obvious. The difference between the house I first saw and today is impressive."

"It's easy to get stuck in the past. The old house was bogged down, but these boys are the future, Miss Montoya." Walt nodded. "Took a minute for us old-timers to catch up." There was a sharp knock under the table and he winced but carried on. Travis thought his mother had shifted in her seat. Was she giving his father nonverbal signals under the table? "We'll be here to support but this is Travis's show to run. Nobody will do better for these boys who need the Rocking A."

No one? Travis wasn't sure he agreed, but he appreciated the vote of confidence.

Ellen nodded. "Then it's time to finish up this interview with Travis. Alone. Thank you all for coming."

When they started to drift away, Travis fought the urge to beg someone, anyone to stay with him. If he couldn't find the words he wanted, he could always count on Wes to step in and smooth out the awkward spots. If Wes didn't do it quickly enough, Matt would flirt with the nearest lampshade to lighten any tension. Clay and Grant weren't as skilled at the tough conversations, but both would do something, do anything they could to help.

Jordan squeezed his shoulder as she passed by, breaking into the runaway train of his thoughts. That helped.

Ellen was right.

This was his thing.

He needed to prove himself ready to take this on without them.

When the last clump of boots cleared the kitchen and the front door slammed behind the crowd, Ellen inhaled and exhaled loudly. "You ever have so many people watching you that you're convinced something is wrong? Your shirt's on inside out or your hair is being weird all of a sudden?" She fanned a hand in front of her face. "Not sure how you manage that much attention all the time."

"Ever since I told them I started this application process, that's been every family dinner and conversation. Out of the blue, everyone's watching me and waiting for something." Travis slumped in his chair with relief at hearing someone else say what he'd been feeling for too long.

He'd never have expected it to be her, but

he would take any gift he could get right about now.

"And try walking into the house all by yourself at fourteen. Prue and Walt seemed the perfect parents, you know?" Travis scrubbed a hand over his forehead as he remembered how awkward he'd felt that day. "It was like my shoes were too small and I couldn't remember how to work my mouth correctly. For that matter, I still have the problem with my mouth."

She grinned. "But your feet fit your boots now?"

He nodded. "Yes, ma'am. Any trouble I have walking cannot be blamed on the fit of my shoes."

She laughed at his weak joke, and Travis attempted to relax his shoulders.

"I can tell you're nervous about this, but I only want to be sure you're ready. This kitchen will serve up good meals and, around this dinner table, you will rebuild lives that have been shattered." She rested her elbow on the table and propped her chin on her hand. "I don't know everyone's story before becoming an Armstrong. What is yours like, Travis?"

The itch of the tag in his shirt made him

shift in his chair as he tried to come up with a good answer, one that was the truth without being too true. "I was one of those kids. Shattered. Runaway. Picked up by the police finally and bounced from one home to the next." For fighting. He wasn't going to say that, though. He'd had his reasons and they hadn't mattered a bit since Prue Armstrong had wrapped her arms around his bruised shoulders and welcomed him home. "When I got here, I had a hard time trusting that any of this was real. But it was. It is. Those people will help me take care of any kids who need a place."

The lump in his throat almost choked him, but Travis gulped in air.

"Prue was a big part of that, wasn't she?" Ellen asked. "It's too bad about their divorce."

"Yeah, there have been signs of..." How would he categorize this? "Re-acquaintance?" That was vague and modestly old-fashioned enough to fit his parents' relationship.

Even if his father had spent the night in town at his mother's apartment while they were all struggling to get the renovation of the ranch house finished. Neither one of them had much of anything to say about it to their sons.

Their sons appreciated the small bit of discretion.

Ellen made a note on her file, but he couldn't read it upside down. "They both made it clear that this is your thing. I wanted to talk to you about what it was like in this home with two parents, Travis. Kids are naturally drawn to some personalities, some styles. You understand? I bet the five of you boys each connected to Prue or Walt in different ways."

That much was true. He'd feared Walt was convinced he'd gotten a dud when Travis showed up. "I couldn't stay on a horse for the first three years I lived here. That put some strain on my ability to connect with Walt." Since his father had worked dawn to dusk, most of it in a saddle, Travis had missed out on some of the bonding the others had immediately. "I spent too much time with my nose in a book to be easily understood at first."

Ellen leaned back. "That must have been hard. The odd guy out, I guess?"

It had been.

There were still whispers of it, even though he knew his family loved him.

"Maybe. I believe it will also help me if I should run into a boy who doesn't quite fit the Rocking A at first glance." That was his hope. Foster care had a certain reputation. News stories covered the homes where bad things happened, but for every one of those, there were others like the Rocking A where lives were saved.

Travis had experienced one of those unhappy foster care stories first, so he knew exactly how wide the gap could be. If there was any way to build a bridge, he'd do it.

Ellen's lips curled. "You very well may be right. Have you considered how hard doing this will be on your own?"

Travis started to motion over his shoulder at the parade of people who had just left.

"I know. You have support." Ellen dipped her head down. "But Prue and Walt did this together. The fact is you don't have a partner, someone who's ready to make the hard decisions with you. Are you worried about that?"

Travis studied his hands on the table. There were a lot of answers here, but the only one he could trust was the truth. "Of course I am, but there's no guarantee I'll ever have that person in my life. I refuse to miss out on my purpose because I have a hard time asking a pretty woman out to dinner."

Ellen chuckled. "That is a fair answer, Travis Armstrong. Very fair."

She flipped through the certificates of completion for all the training he'd done. "I can't think of any other concerns I have. I expect this to be an easy approval. I'll meet with the review board and I'll let you know as soon as I have the final decision. I expect it to be quick."

"Our house tour was pretty quick. Want to see the boys' rooms again before you go?" Travis asked as he stood, ready to walk some of the nerves off. "We're pretty proud of all the work we did."

She nodded and trailed behind him as he marched toward the addition. "So we've got the two rooms, four beds total. Pretty sweet setup. We all wished we'd had something like this."

Ellen followed him inside the first room. He'd made the beds with the comfy bedding Keena had picked out, set up the corkboards she'd insisted on, and placed one of the wireless speakers he'd bought under duress on each desk. It was impossible to miss how much warmer these rooms were, thanks to Keena's input.

He sort of regretted not having the silly slippers to put on each bed, but there was time to fix that.

"A Broncos football," Ellen said as she picked up the speaker. "Interesting touch. Are you a big football fan?" Curiosity made her eyes bright behind her glasses. Why did the answer to this feel significant?

Travis cleared his throat. "Uh, no, not really, but we wanted to have something everyday, you know...something useful and fun. For little kids, stuffed animals make sense, but for older kids...speakers that they can connect to a phone or tablet seemed a good choice."

"What if they don't have a phone or tablet?" Ellen asked but waved her hand before he could stumble through an answer. "Never mind. That's a problem for later, right?" Then she crossed her arms over her chest. "Who is we? Did you and Prue pick all this out?"

"We..." Travis wished he'd been more careful there, but this seemed like another significant answer. "Keena Murphy helped. She lives next door." He pointed over his shoulder as if that was in any way helpful.

Ellen opened her file. "Keena. Someone I haven't been introduced to yet."

Before he could explain that there was no reason for an introduction as she was only visiting and not involved in this plan any further than this single step, he heard the front door open. "Travis? Are you here? Your mom waved me inside as she and Walt were leaving."

Before Travis could determine how to answer Ellen or head off Keena's arrival, they heard her coming down the hallway. It sounded like she was rolling something in front of her. What could that be? When she stuck her head around the doorway, Keena's cheeks immediately flooded with color. "Oh, I'm so sorry. I didn't mean to interrupt. I'll leave this here and go. Travis, call me later, okay?"

He'd wanted a rescue, but he hadn't imagined it this way—Keena appearing like a gift out of nowhere. Instead of allowing her to slide the wheeled suitcase his direction and scurry away, Travis quickly wrapped his hand around her wrist. He noted how she reacted to his touch. Her pulse sped up to match the pale flush in her cheeks. She brushed a loose strand of hair back into her ponytail before tangling her fingers through his.

Ellen held out her hand. "I thought I'd met all of the Armstrongs, but you're a new face. I'm Ellen. I'm the caseworker who will be working with Travis through the learning curve as a foster parent. You are?"

Keena nodded and shook her hand. "I'm Keena. I live next door."

Since Ellen knew that part, Travis added, "Dr. Keena Murphy."

"The decorator." Ellen patted the denim comforter. "What type of medicine do you practice?" Her pen was poised to make more notes.

Keena shifted back and forth on her feet, clearly uncomfortable at being the focus here. Travis had never seen her in scrubs. They helped him understand a different side of Keena. "General medicine for now, but my background is in trauma, running the emergency department in Denver's only Level 1 trauma center."

Keena must have realized she was giving more information than required. Her mouth snapped shut.

Ellen was thoughtful as she studied the suitcase Keena had rolled in. "Are you moving in?"

Keena frowned and then seemed to notice the way Ellen pointed at the suitcase. The pink in her cheeks turned to red. "Uh, no, this is for...Travis."

Ellen raised her eyebrows. "Is he moving out?"

Keena cleared her throat. "No." She stepped back as if she'd like to make a quick exit but stopped instead. "When we were shopping to finish out these bedrooms, Travis explained that we couldn't buy too many personal items because the kids might have to leave them behind. Because they don't have a way to carry everything." She brushed the hair behind her ear again, and Travis took a chance on touching her back. The way she'd broken through his anxiety when he'd been forced to talk to his family about all this that night at dinner had stayed with him. A simple touch had reset his brain, made it easier to put his thoughts in order.

Ellen pursed her lips. "I saw the speaker. That's a nice touch, too." Her eyes darted to meet his, but he wasn't sure what that meant.

"I wanted to do funny slippers, too, but Travis talked me out of it." Keena shrugged and grimaced as she met his stare. "One thing you will learn about me, though, is that it's not that easy to get ideas out of my head once they're there, so…"

Travis watched her bend down to unzip the suitcase. Stuffed inside were a few pairs of the boot-shaped slippers and a duffel bag. "I couldn't decide if a suitcase or a duffel was better, so now you have both. Your foster kid won't have to use a trash bag when it's time to leave here. That didn't seem right to me."

Her face was bright red at this point.

And Travis was speechless. Touched. Amused. But also aware of their audience.

Ellen studied them both silently for entirely too long. "Well." She brushed off her hands. "I'll do some research, check the references you've listed, verify all the trainings are complete, and give you a call when

I have the final approval from the board." She motioned between the two of them. "I'll leave you to the rest of your evening."

Confused, Travis glanced at Keena. She was staring at his hand wrapped around hers, and he understood what Ellen thought she saw: a romance between her prospective single foster dad and the beautiful doctor next door.

Exactly what she'd been in the process of suggesting before Keena had rolled in.

Keena was half a second ahead of him and determined to set everything straight. "Oh, we didn't have…"

"We didn't have any special plans for tonight, Ellen. Just the usual." He pulled Keena to stand next to him without letting go of her hand. "There's no need to leave."

Ellen huffed out a breath. "Third wheel? No way. Besides, it's a long drive back home to be in the office bright and early tomorrow." She picked up her file and notebook and patted Keena's shoulder. "Lovely to meet you, Keena."

Travis locked his eyes with Keena's to keep her from trying to explain any further as they followed Ellen back outside to her car. The social worker was happily driving away when Keena unwrapped her fingers with a yank. "What did we do? Why didn't you set her straight?"

Travis propped his hands on his hips and stared up at the darkening night sky. "I believe we just passed my home study." The relief that settled over his shoulders was light, comfortable. For the first time in the months since he'd gotten his first negative report about the dissatisfactory, cramped, out-of-date conditions of the house, Travis was truly relieved.

And a little weak in the knees to be over that hurdle. Some of the happiness he'd been waiting for bloomed in his chest.

"By lying to your foster approver. Great start, Travis." Keena shook her head. "Your motives might have been pure, but you dragged me into lying to her, too. And I don't think lying to the people charged with keeping children safe in this world is anything to celebrate."

She huffed out a breath. "Adults who care for children should tell the truth."

The anger was easy to see in her posture. And she was absolutely right, except...

"I didn't tell her we were a couple." She'd assumed it.

"You also didn't tell the whole truth about us when it was right there. Half-truths to make your life simpler are beneath both of us." Keena's lips were a tight line. "That's disappointing."

After she'd slammed her car door and backed out of the yard, Travis crossed his arms over his chest and came to terms with how the night had gone.

His home study was complete.

All signs pointed to success there. The whole evening would have been satisfying, really, except for Keena's reaction. What she said was technically true. He had dragged her into the chaos.

But what he'd said was also technically true. He hadn't made any false claims to his social worker. If she was happier to believe he was in a relationship, what was the harm in letting the misunderstanding continue?

Even if his logic was sound, Travis knew he'd have a hard time forgetting what disappointment looked like on Keena's face.

CHAPTER EIGHT

ON FRIDAY AFTERNOON, Keena stood at the back of the group as Dr. Singh said good-bye to his staff. Comparing her own politely restrained last night in Denver to this emotional going-away celebration illustrated the differences in her and Dr. Singh's styles. This group hugged. They took pictures in pairs and then a big group photo. They had given him a small camera and orders to update them weekly on how he was doing. There were tears, both sad and happy.

It was a lot to absorb. Keena did so from the outer edge of the party while she tried to ignore the increasing anxiety building in the pit of her stomach.

How had she ever imagined anyone would accept her in place of Dr. Singh? Even Keena would rather have him in charge. No way was her rudimentary bedside manner up to earning this kind of affection.

"Keena, I'm leaving you in the best hands." Dr. Singh smiled at her warmly. "I know you'll do well here."

She smiled in agreement and hoped they were both right.

Keena wanted Dr. Singh to feel confident he was leaving his practice in good hands even if she had her own doubts. It was important to her that he trust her.

Reginald picked up Dr. Singh's bag. "Let's lock up. Doc has an early drive to the airport in the morning." The whole group moved together to turn off lights and double-check that all the computers were shut down. Keena slung her purse over her shoulder and took one last glance around Dr. Singh's office. For the next three months, it would be hers. Alone.

Just like every bit of responsibility for the health of the entire population of Prospect.

No pressure.

"You'll do well, Keena," Dr. Singh said from behind her. "I understand your concerns. Just remember that this kind of medicine is about understanding the patient more than the problem quite often and you'll do fine."

She nodded. He thought he was helping her,

but he was actually speaking her biggest fear aloud.

"If you have the opportunity, please send emails and photos." Keena trailed behind Dr. Singh and tried to shove the anxiety down. Following along behind him like a lost child begging for comfort was a bad look. Her mother would have tsked if she'd seen it. "We all want to know how the mission is going." If she wasn't good at this, it might also help her count down the days until he returned.

He surprised her by wrapping his arms around her in a hug. "You're going to be fine. Thank you for doing this. My staff? They're pros. Don't hesitate to rely on them and ask for help when you need it." He raised his eyebrows and waited for her to meet his stare. They both laughed because they knew asking for help could be the sticking point.

Then he waved, slid into the driver's seat and drove off without looking back.

Just like that, she was responsible. For all of it. Everything. The weight of the world settled on her shoulders.

And specifically the future of Prospect Family Practice. Reginald, Kim and Emily were all watching her carefully. The brilliant smiles had transitioned to polite expressions.

"Big plans for the evening?" Reginald asked after receiving pointed glances from Kim and Emily. He'd obviously been elected spokesperson for the group.

Keena knew it was time to fake a little confidence until she made it. "I was considering going to the Sip and Paint at the Mercantile?" Her answer had a hint of a question at the end that she hadn't intended but it made perfect sense. She'd been wavering all week about going. In some moments, she was completely committed to jumping into the Prospect social scene and making new friends, even though she knew being the outsider at first could be uncomfortable. Then she'd remember she had no artistic talent and lacked the ability to make small talk easily when she was nervous and decide it was better to have people think her unlikable than *know* it.

Also, this divide between her and Travis made her uneasy about stepping into the room with his mother who he'd already told her would go to war for her sons. She expected Prue to be polite, but if any of the warmth of her welcome was missing, Keena would regret that.

Kim clasped her hands together. "Faye mentioned the class when I was over at the Ace yesterday. Apparently this is a trial run, only open by invitation, before Prue rolls it out for everyone to sign up. Patrick Hearst is going to be teaching everyone simple projects. Sounds like so much fun!" Her tone suggested she would have jumped at the opportunity to go if anyone had thought to invite her.

And newcomer Keena was lucky enough to have an invitation somehow.

All because she'd crashed a dinner party at the Armstrongs'.

That had worked because she'd done it without overthinking it.

Knowing the Armstrongs had improved her connections in Prospect by leaps and bounds, but she hadn't known that going in.

It had also indirectly gotten her wrapped up in Travis's half-truth to the social worker.

She'd been thinking about that night and him all week. Keeping her distance was the smart thing to do, but she'd enjoyed every minute she'd spent with Travis. Her mind had wandered his direction way more often than she was okay with.

Was spending her Friday night with his mother and friends smart?

Keena realized it didn't matter. She was definitely going to need something to discuss with her coworkers on Monday morning. Sip and Paint filled that need perfectly.

Once the decision was made, Keena didn't waver. "I'll let you know all about it on Monday. Maybe there will be cookies, too." After the rest of the staff left, Keena decided to have dinner in town at the Ace High instead of going home before Sip and Paint started. Otherwise, the temptation to stay on the sofa at home might kick in.

Since the sun hadn't completely set, Keena left her car parked behind the Mercantile. She could stretch her legs on the way to the Ace. The Prospect Picture Show drew her attention. Windows along the front of the building showed a two-story lobby that made her think of black-and-white movie classics. Framed photos of movie star cowboys lined the walls, and the carpet was a deep, rich red. The marquee displayed movie times for *Stagecoach* that weekend.

Next to the theater was a small furniture store featuring handmade wooden items. Keena studied the exterior, interested in what kind of business had been there during the early days, but she could only make out a name, Legrand. Then she noticed a small plaque.

She read, "Legrand Millinery was once Prospect's most exclusive milliner. Pierre Legrand created fabulous hats and other accessories that only the most successful could afford. When townspeople discovered the artist Pierre was actually Arthur Lee from Chicago, they called the sheriff in. After public discourse and trial, Arthur Lee continued to run Legrand Millinery until his death in 1924."

Keena shook her head as she crossed the street, aiming for the Ace High. "Arthur was able to fake it until *he* made it in Prospect. Good for him." The town offered opportunity and a pinch of forgiveness for him. If she stumbled in Dr. Singh's practice, maybe Prospect would do the same for her.

This time, Keena was prepared for the innovative non-menu at the Ace. Settling back to enjoy her pork chop with apple cinnamon glaze, roasted new potatoes and cara-melized broccoli, Keena observed the crowd and chatted with Faye who zoomed by as she worked to feed the dinner crowd.

"Last call for pie," Faye said as she pulled off her apron. "We've got about thirty min-utes until Sip and Paint starts. Want to walk over together?" The way she pointed vaguely toward the Mercantile and shifted on her feet made Keena wonder if they were going to run all the way there. Then she re-alized she had the conditioning to keep up after nights in the hospital, so she agreed.

"Great, I'm going to go grab a bite and make sure the kitchen is all set. Pie?" She pointed at Keena, eyebrows raised.

"Better not. No room," Keena said but realized Faye had somehow read the an-swer in her eyes because she was already halfway to the kitchen. She smiled and slid out of the booth to go pay for her dinner. Another benefit to the simplified "this or that" menu meant no one needed bills to say what had been ordered. She simply told the host, who was also running the cash regis-ter, she'd chosen the pork chop, offered her credit card, and was ready to go as soon as Faye finished her meal. Instead of going back to her table, she paused in front of the community bulletin board. There were flyers about upcoming holiday shows at the various schools, a garage sale hosted by the Methodist church the first Saturday of every month, and three babysitters looking for more work.

The cozy, small-town charm of the place settled over Keena as she scanned the board. She liked it. She liked all of it. The warm feeling about her new surroundings returned. Her neighbors were watching old movies, attending their kids' events and hiring babysitters they'd known since they were born for the occasional night on the town. Prospect was the kind of place people always imagined or dreamt of but here was the real thing.

"Ready?" Faye asked as she slipped on her coat. "Let's go before someone stops me, wanting intel on someone or something."

Keena followed in her wake.

Outside, Faye's pace was quick but not "busy restaurant server" level, so it felt permissible to ask questions. "Does Prospect have a newspaper?" In her head, the front-page story would be about who took first place in the spelling bee.

"No, not anymore. It closed down…" Faye paused as she considered. "Five years ago? Lucky Garcia runs a community page on social media and she tries to highlight all the big news around town." She got out her phone to pull up the website and show Keena. "You need to follow her. When the weather improves, she sets up food truck nights at the garage."

Keena favorited the site on her own phone. "Are you encouraging me to eat somewhere else, Faye? What about the Ace?"

Faye sighed. "Honestly, one night a month? I'll take the break, thank you. When you're the only one in town, the demand turns to pressure and I feel that." She wrinkled her nose. "You may, too, now that you're the only doctor around."

When they walked inside Handmade for their trial Sip and Paint, Prue hustled them upstairs. "Finally! I'm so excited about this night I can hardly stand it!" She then swept past them in the large open room. "Keena, I saved you a seat right by me. Faye, you're down there with Lucky."

Someone had arranged small easels and canvases on a circular table. There were eight seats arranged in a semicircle, all facing a man seated on a stool at the front of the room.

"Dad, this is Keena. I think she's the only one here you haven't met tonight," Jordan called as she patted the seat next to her. Her sister Sarah waved from the other side. "This is Patrick. You have officially met all the Hearsts now."

"The ones in Prospect." Sarah bent forward. "There is another."

Jordan rolled her eyes. "The most Hearst of them all, our baby sister is still in New York but we're working on her to come visit."

Patrick waved at Keena. "If you need me to separate them at any time, you let me know, Keena. They're trouble separately, but when they're together..." He shook his head slowly. "Prue, did you want to get this event started or should I?"

"You can," Prue said magnanimously, but before he could speak, she added, "though I would like to welcome everyone to our trial run at this Sip and Paint night. Patrick and I are making plans to build out the paint section downstairs, however, we're going to need to plant the seeds and get some painters in this town to make it all worthwhile. He had some concerns about teaching short classes and beginners like this, so I'm expecting you all to make him comfortable tonight." Then she picked up the wine bottle and started to pour. "I'll get us all started with a drink, how's that?"

Everyone turned back to Patrick and he cleared his throat. The bemusement on his face matched Keena's internal reaction whenever she got swept up by Prue so she connected with him immediately.

"Tonight, we're going to do a simple landscape. Since I've been back in town, I've spent a lot of time studying Key Lake, so we're going to paint a Key Lake sunset. There are individual containers of paint in front of you and three different sizes of brush. I want to start with a hazy sky, so we'll use the number 8 brush and the darkest blue." He held up the brush and waited for everyone to do the same. He pointed at the completed painting that was hanging behind him. "Here's the inspiration, but each landscape will be different and that's how you know it's art. Pick up some paint on your brush and move it to the palette, then we're going to add a few drops of water like this." He demonstrated, stirring lightly. "Watering down acrylic paint lightens the saturation and gives you a kind of watercolor effect. That will work beautifully with this sunset."

Keena anxiously watched her neighbors before attempting her first stroke.

"Keena, drink your wine. That will help." Patrick smiled encouragingly at her. "Some of us get stuck because we're afraid. Wine smooths all that out."

The laughter around the table made Keena realize she had a tight knot of tension between her shoulders, so she followed his direction. When the first glass was low, Prue topped her off. Then Keena picked up her brush and followed Patrick's lead.

"Don't worry, Keena. You will never paint as badly as Sarah and I do and our father has yet to give up teaching us," Jordan murmured as they cleaned their brushes to work on the darker foreground.

As the evening went on, Keena relaxed and started to enjoy the chatter and laughter. Sarah and Jordan bickered. Prue tossed outrageous zingers when things got quiet. Rose Bell, who she hadn't met yet but ran the lovely historic bed-and-breakfast, didn't say much, but the intense stares she traded between her canvas and the teacher convinced Keena that she was going to be good at this. Faye and Lucky were laughing together on their side of the table.

"Nice, isn't it? Having a chance to be silly and forget all the rest for a minute?" Prue asked. "I don't think the wine is strictly necessary but when in doubt, I always say 'do,' you know?"

Keena had no trouble believing that. Prue struck her as someone who lived full speed ahead.

"How was the first week at the clinic?" Prue craned her neck to see Patrick's example better before picking up some red on her brush.

The group turned its attention to her and Keena understood Prue wasn't the only one curious about how she was fitting in. "Good. It was really good. I've always loved working with Dr. Singh, and the rest of his office is so professional. Almost every concern I have, they deal with it before I can voice it." She glanced at Lucky.

"Stitches are healing as expected, Dr. Murphy." Then she toasted Keena with her wineglass and Faye motioned for the rest of the table to pass the wine bottle her direction.

"Everyone, please, it's Keena. In the office, out of the office, Keena. I'd appreciate that." As she said it, it felt right. She didn't want there to be any distance between these ladies at the table and her. "And seriously, if you have an after-hours emergency, do not hesitate to call me. I don't want anyone to suffer needlessly because it's after five o'clock. I'll never be as popular as Dr. Singh." Keena paused and studied her wineglass. How many times had Prue filled it? That was too much honesty. "But I'm a very good doctor."

Prue squeezed her shoulder. "Well, now, we sure are glad to have you here for as long as possible." Then she leaned in close. "Travis told me the two of you got a little sideways, but he didn't give me any details."

Keena glanced around the table. Every other woman was suspiciously engrossed with her painting, but she had no doubt their ears were straining to make sure they didn't miss Keena's answer. "Oh, it's nothing serious, Prue."

She sniffed. "There are two things you should know about Travis."

"Better be careful. Nobody likes to have their secrets spread around town," Rose murmured.

Keena appreciated Rose's words of wisdom at the same time that she regretted that Rose had said them. Why did she desperately want to know whatever Prue had been about to share?

Prue settled back in her chair as she considered that. "She makes a solid point." Then she perked up. "If you were to ask questions, I might be able to answer them."

Rose frowned, but Prue patted Keena's hand. "Go ahead."

Confused, Keena glanced at Jordan, the only person she'd actually experienced the Armstrong dinner with. Sarah caught her eye. "You might as well, Keena. You're in the middle of—" she pointed around them vaguely "—all this now. Becoming an Armstrong leads you to some unexpected places."

But she wasn't an Armstrong. For that matter, neither were any of the other women at the table except Prue.

"What did Travis say?" Keena focused on the frame of trees around the edges of the canvas.

"I went out to the ranch to fill up the fridge with some leftovers I had this week, and Travis mentioned you two had opposing views. Has to do with the social worker's visit, I believe," Prue said.

Keena finished the trees and decided to add more light yellow in the sun's reflection on the lake. If that's all Travis said, Keena knew it was in her best interest to keep the details to herself.

But she was even sorrier for Rose's well-meant words of caution. It would be nice to get some clues about Travis without spilling what had set them at odds.

Keena wasn't ready to admit that her biggest concern was how disappointed she'd been that he let the social worker leave with the romantic misunderstanding in place. She'd started to build this ideal man in her head based on his patience and humor, the care he had for the kids he hadn't even met yet.

No way was she confessing any of that to his mother. There was not enough wine in the world to loosen her lips that much.

"Well, I hesitate to interrupt the conversation," Patrick said as he finished the slow stroll he'd made around the table, "but it looks like most of you have completed your paintings. All that's left is to let the paint dry and show off your work. One at a time, we're going to turn the easels to face the center of the table. I love this part. It's where you see how many different ways there are to see something. Sarah, let's start with you."

"He's going from worst to first, everybody," Jordan said as she scooted back in her chair. "You will see proof that artistic talent can skip entire generations in three, two…"

Sarah sighed. "She's right. I want to argue, but she's right." After carefully turning her easel, Sarah flopped down behind it. "It's like if an alien was describing the scene to his dog and the dog tried to paint it."

Laughter swept the table as Jordan clapped her hands. "I love it." Then she spun hers around. "I was going to say that mine was like if you'd painted the scene and left it out in the sun to melt, but Sarah's description fits mine, too."

Both Hearsts had the suggestion of a lake in the golds, but they were surrounded by… blobs. So many dark blobs.

Patrick sighed and turned to Keena. "Moving on. Keep my hopes up, Keena."

She bit her lip, nervous as she turned her own easel. "Is this better?"

"There's no way to be worse," Patrick said dryly as his daughters giggled and clinked their glasses. "It's nice. I love the way you've worked in the shadow on the lake to show space and perspective."

Relieved, Keena relaxed into her chair to finish her wine. Being anything better than terrible was winning in her book, especially since she couldn't land in last place behind Sarah or Jordan.

Prue spun her painting around proudly. "I embellished mine a bit."

Keena leaned forward to see that Prue had added a couple sitting in a boat, facing each other.

"Are they wearing ball caps?" Patrick asked slowly.

"Broncos caps. Both of them. Cute, right?"

Prue grinned. "I love adding romance to the scene."

Rose Bell grunted as she tugged down her own Broncos cap, her lips a firm line. "Faye, Lucky, you go next. I need to add some finishing touches."

Jordan moved closer. "My dad is single. Rose is single. They're both big Broncos fans. Prue is matchmaking."

"She's not subtle about it, either," Sarah chimed in. "Prue is always pulling these strings, making couples where she wants."

Prue whispered, "Not true. I don't run around making matches. Sarah and Jordan made their own matches, Keena. I only encouraged them. That's my gift."

Sarah and Jordan communicated silently in head tilts, eyebrow raises and shoulder rolls, before Sarah said, "That's fair."

Faye cleared her throat. "Can I have your attention?" She displayed her painting.

"Beautiful strokes showing the individual leaves, Faye. That's nice attention to detail," Patrick said. "I'd expect nothing less from you."

Faye immediately started gathering up her brushes and paints to clean up her station.

"We aren't quite finished, Faye," Patrick said softly. "Besides, you let me take care of all that tonight, okay?"

Keena wasn't sure Faye agreed with his comment, but she settled back in her chair.

"That leaves me," Lucky said as she waved a hand at her own.

Patrick pursed his lips. "The way you've worked with the colors tells me you're making this scene your own, Lucky. That's something that's hard to teach. I like it."

Keena would have put herself solidly in the middle of the crowd as far as painting ability went. She might not have untapped talent, but it was something she could practice and improve on if she wanted to.

That might be something to pursue while she was in Prospect and had the time.

"Rose," Patrick said, his lips twitching, "you're up."

She sniffed haughtily and turned her easel around. Of them all, Rose had most closely followed the inspiration. Her painting was good.

It also featured what appeared to be a woman in a wedding dress and a man in a cowboy hat faced off in front of the sunset.

"Lovely. Very romantic. Two people no one in this room recognizes getting married in front of the lake." Prue patted Rose on the back.

"It's you. And Walt. See the hat?" Rose said baldly. "I can add in more details if you need them, but you should get your eyes checked. The whole world can see you two headed for the altar again sooner or later."

She and Prue glared at each other.

Sarah and Jordan perched on the edges of their seats, waiting for whatever came next.

Eventually, Patrick spoke up. "I hope you ladies have arranged rides home tonight. We might need to limit the number of wine refills when we do this for the real world."

Prue nodded. "Good point. Rose and I'll just be walking a couple of blocks. I figure Faye is headed back to close down the Ace."

Faye nodded.

Sarah waved her phone. "I already texted Wes to come get us. We can give Keena a ride and drop her off."

Prue beamed at her. "Sarah, I knew I liked you from the minute I met you." She was bustling away to help clean up the paints and easels when Sarah moved Keena out of the way.

"That is not true. I got the coldest of shoulders from Prue Armstrong when I introduced myself the first time. Her attitude about the Hearsts returning to Prospect has greatly improved." Sarah shoved her hands in her pockets. "Want to tell us how it's really going? We can talk about this town, the Armstrongs, Travis and any number of things without spreading tales. We don't know too many secrets to tell at this point!"

Keena laughed. "Everything has been so easy. Travis and I…" What could she say? "I had this daydream of who he was, you know? The cowboy hero, the white hat who lived for doing the right thing or whatever, and he's just a person. He didn't exactly lie but I expected more. Which is absurd. He's a neighbor, a maybe-friend, nothing else. There's no reason to feel let down about a little ol' bitty lie that doesn't change the outcome of anything after all." Keena closed her eyes. "I've had too much wine."

Jordan slung her arm over Keena's shoulders. "Proceed with caution, my new friend." She and Sarah exchanged a speaking glance.

What was it saying? "Sarah was going to make a quick stop and get the lodge ready to sell. She's half a second from settling down here permanently to raise more Armstrongs."

"And Jordan never stayed a second past when things got hard...until Prospect and Clay Armstrong showed her what staying could mean, like love and family, and community," Sarah added. "There's something about the men from the Rocking A in particular that makes you believe in old-fashioned goodness. It's like it goes all the way to their bones." She shrugged. "And it makes it hard to walk away from them. If that's not what you want, it makes sense to keep some distance between you and Travis. Whatever you thought you'd found in Travis, it's there. Maybe he messed up, but that thing you were starting to believe in, they have it, every single one of them."

"And Prue," Jordan added under her voice. "She's just hard to resist."

They all laughed.

"What's the story with the wedding couple Rose added?" Keena asked while no one was paying any attention to them.

"You saw how Prue and Walt are. They should not be a divorced couple, but the same stubbornness that makes them loyal and dedicated to the town and their family also makes it impossible for either one to give in and let go their small grievances." Sarah covered her heart with her hand. "That's my judgment but if either of you tells Prue I said any of that, I will deny, deny, deny."

Jordan pointed out the window at a truck parked below. "Wes is downstairs. Keena, ride with us. You may be fine to drive, but everyone will feel better if we see you home."

The urge to argue was strong, but she'd seen so many late-night accidents caused by drivers who would have sworn they were okay to drive that Keena agreed. She went to thank Patrick and Prue for including her.

To her surprise, Prue wrapped her arms tightly around her for a hug. Keena hesitated before returning it. "Do not be a stranger, Keena. Travis will eventually figure out the right way to fix all this, I promise."

She wanted to explain that there was really nothing to fix.

No hard feelings, even.

They were just neighbors anyway.

Weren't they?

Instead, she asked, "What makes you believe Travis is the one who needs to make a change?" Prue barely knew her. By the laws of family loyalty, wouldn't that make her the bad guy in any argument with Prue's son?

Prue smoothed Keena's hair back. "Hmm, I suppose it's possible that *you* made a mistake, but I can't see Travis holding on to that. Of all my boys, he's the one who understood best how easy it was to do that when I messed up. His forgiveness for honest mistakes by the people he loves comes easy. I don't believe that has changed about him." Prue held a finger over her lips as if she was sharing secrets. "Don't tell Rose I let that slip. Travis has a real soft heart under all that muscle. That also means his own mess-ups bother him until he makes them right. He'll do it again this time. I think you're already on the inside, pretty close to that soft heart."

When she realized Rose was watching them closely, Prue mimed turning the key to lock her lips and moved away. None of the questions Keena needed to ask were right for the occasion, so she locked them away, too.

Keena clattered down the stairs behind the Hearsts and out onto the wooden sidewalk, but she stopped as she realized Travis and Wes were both resting against the bumper of the truck in front of the door.

"Hey," he said softly. "I heard you might need a taxi ride home."

Keena glanced at Jordan. She had the offer to ride with them, but Travis's hopeful expression was impossible to refuse. "Are you going my way, driver?" Prue's secret was fresh on her mind and she wouldn't mind the chance to clear the air between them.

His slow grin landed in her abdomen, butterflies flitting and flapping wings.

Then he stepped around to the passenger side of the truck parked next to Wes's and opened the door. After she slid in, he shut it. Keena held Jordan's stare as Travis backed out of the parking spot. Whatever happened next, Jordan seemed to believe it was going to be big. Her warning about how the Armstrongs had changed everything was flashing across her face in the woman's wicked grin.

Maybe it was the wine.

Or it could have been the way she'd thought

about Travis every day since she'd seen him last, even if she was irritated with him.

But Keena knew letting Travis drive her home was the right choice. She wanted to know what came next.

CHAPTER NINE

BEFORE TRAVIS HAD followed Wes into town Friday night, he'd been at loose ends.

Late that afternoon, Travis, Grant and Wes had finished moving the cattle, grazing up in Larkspur Pass through the summer, into one of the lower pastures closer to the house.

They'd gotten a late start because Ellen Montoya had called to deliver her good news while they'd been working in the barn. Travis's application to foster had been approved. As soon as they matched a child who needed a place like the Rocking A, she'd give him a call. Telling his brothers that had been a relief. One weight rolled off his shoulders as another, a heavier one, settled in.

Now he'd have to provide a safe space for a kid he hadn't even met yet. He'd have to be a father, one good enough that no one worried about the missing mother in the equation. He'd spent some time remembering how much Prue had smoothed the way for him in the early days. Ellen Montoya's concern about him doing this alone had landed on top of all his other questions.

So much pressure.

The happiness he had expected to experience once everything was arranged had been elusive so far.

Travis had also confessed to the caseworker that he'd allowed her to leave with the wrong impression of his relationship with the beautiful doctor next door. Ellen had reassured him that his relationship or lack thereof had had zero impact on the decision to grant him fostering duties.

So he'd put that disappointed look on Keena's face for no good reason.

And then Ellen had advised him he might want to explore why he'd seized the chance to suggest there was more in the first place. Her chuckle as she'd hung up was what stuck in his brain, though.

He couldn't get that out of his head.

"This winter, we sure are gonna be glad we scraped together enough for the down payment on Sadie's undeveloped land in front of the Majestic," Grant had reminded the three of them in the barn. The sun had sunk below the ridge of the mountains. Now that the days were short, night came quickly. "You remember that year that the first snow fell before we got the herd moved?"

They all remembered. It had been a long December that year, waiting for the snow and ice to melt, so they could get the herd closer to the barn. Feeding and watering had been a struggle.

"It was a good lesson," Wes had immediately said. "When Dad asks why I'm bringing them in so early now, all I have to do is remind him of Matt's frostbitten toes and the way Mama threatened to move him into the barn permanently, and he stops singing that tune."

Travis had removed Sonny's saddle before filling his water and feed buckets. He'd had no clue his brothers were getting ready to corner him in the barn for a discussion about his emotions. He might have headed for Mexico, if so.

Instead, when he finally noticed Grant had propped one arm against the stall and was wearing that annoying half smile of his that always warned of trouble, Travis had yanked his hat off and prayed for patience.

"Am I going to need a whistle to referee this…whatever is coming." Wes's horse, Arrow, bumped Grant's shoulder as Wes led him into the stall next to Sonny, but Grant and Arrow spoke the same language, so neither one was upset by the contact.

Their mother liked to say that Grant was part horse himself.

When she wasn't around, Travis enjoyed identifying exactly which part of the horse Grant was.

"I've been good. For so long." Grant held out both hands, pleading. "I have bent over backwards, brother, to ignore your black cloud ever since I came home."

Travis straightened and stepped closer to Grant. He was partially right. They hadn't had a knockdown argument since he'd come home, but Travis's good behavior and long patrols of the fence line had more to do with that than any small amount of holding back on Grant's part.

Wes braced his hand in the center of Travis's chest. "I realize you might have something to say about exactly how 'good' Grant has been. We all do." Wes raised a brow at Grant. "But if there's a bruise on either one of your faces, I'll be the one to hear about it from Mama. I've got plans tonight and no time to paper over your shenanigans, so let's rip a couple of bandages here and now."

Travis was braced to be the first to do the ripping, but Wes turned to face Grant. "You go first. What's your deal?"

Grant's eyes grew round as his mouth dropped open. "What do you mean? I've been on my best behavior ever since I got back." Travis couldn't see Wes's face, but Grant could. There must have been something there to convince him to readjust his answer. "Listen, I…" He tipped his cowboy hat up. The frustration they sensed seething under the surface was right there, close to boiling over. "I retired. I came home. I pitched in on this renovation thing. I'm all good now."

"Retired?" Travis repeated. If he'd had to place bets on when Grant would leave the rodeo circuit, where he'd been a star, it would have been decades in the future.

Probably after some broken something kept him out of the saddle and not a second before. His whole life, Grant had been the star, the one who could do anything from the back of a horse. Clay and Wes and Matt were smart. They'd gone to college, finished their professional degrees.

And then there was Travis.

"Yeah, retired. What you do at the end of your career, so you can finally take it easy," Grant had said slowly, enunciating every word. "Like you did, Travis. Ending up here with Mom and Dad suited you just fine though, didn't it."

Wes grimaced, still with his arm out, a hard bar across Travis's chest.

Travis heard the insult in Grant's tone, if not the words, but Wes replied first. "Is this taking it easy? Ranching isn't what anyone dreams of for their golden years, is it?" Wes asked, disbelief clearly resonating in his voice. "Remind me you said that in February when every bit of water on this place is frozen solid and at least one calf comes early."

Grant rolled his eyes. "We don't do anything like other people, do we? Instead of picking up basket making and staring at the walls, we build houses and sleep in bunk beds. Why do we do that?"

At this question, both of his brothers focused on Travis. They'd done it for him.

"And I've said thank you." Travis propped his hands on his hips. "Why is this back to me now?"

Wes grunted. "Honestly, both of you are real burrs under my saddle."

Grant inhaled and exhaled slowly. "I get that, big brother. By now, you should be better at handling us misfits."

Growing up, he and Grant had been poles apart in terms of their personalities, and yet they'd also been closer than any of the other three. They'd done this quite often: switched sides in the middle of an argument to keep Wes and Clay on their toes.

Why? Hard to say for sure, but it was fun.

"You ever wonder what would have happened if Prue and Walt hadn't adopted all five of us?" Grant sat on one of the hay bales across the aisle. "Wes would have a lot less gray hair, I'm guessing."

Wes sighed as he took one of the other bales. "We'll never know."

Travis huffed out a breath, amused at Wes's long-suffering face.

"You've been stewing all week long. I expected some of this…" Wes gestured toward Travis "…this cloud to clear up once we met the renovation deadline. Nothing's holding you back now. Surely you know that. It's a matter of time, could be days even, until we have kids in the house. So what's your deal?"

Travis scratched his chin as he considered how to answer the question. None of the Armstrong men were overly open with their emotions, and he'd done his best to keep his own under tight wraps.

"Come on. We've shown you our support." Grant propped his legs up on the hay bale, Wes beside him. "I'm one hundred percent serious. This is a safe space."

Wes scowled at him. "You almost had it, but you had to keep pushing."

Grant covered his chest with both hands. "We all play our roles. You're the good one. Clay is the smart one. Travis is the heroic one. Matt is the cute one. I'm the problem." His smirk was the expression Travis expected to see, but he wasn't sure Grant thought it was as amusing as he was trying to pretend.

Wes shoved his boots off the hay bale.

"Problem? Maybe, but only because you work so hard at it." He pleaded, "Travis, go. Talk. Now."

"The heroic one." Travis paced in a slow circle in the open air of the barn. He could see the house, the neat yard with all their trucks lined up in front.

Grant made the continue motion with his hand.

"I'm guessing Travis doesn't agree with your list of our roles, Grant. I know I don't," Wes said.

Wes and Grant let the silence stretch whisper-thin, and finally, Travis said, "When we were kids, we talked a little bit about where we came from." He propped his shoulder against the barn door, staring out into the yard. "Wes and Clay both had pretty good homes, not their real family, but people who cared for them before things changed and they had to move to Prospect. Grant and Matt had never been in foster care before, so they had no idea what to expect."

"You never talked any more than you had to for the first five years of your life here on the ranch," Grant said. "Unless I made you."

Wes rolled his eyes. "True. Didn't have to talk much with you around."

When their smiles faded, Wes asked, "So tell us now. Was it bad?"

Travis nodded. "Sad news story at five, six and ten o'clock bad." Was he going to tell the truth? What was the point? He was so far away from that now that it might as well have happened to someone else. "Criminal tendencies. Juvenile detention. 'This is your last shot, kid.' That bad."

Grant sat up and braced his elbows on his knees. "Okay, so were you worried that would pop up on a background check or something?"

Wes shrugged. "The army's moral character enlistment standards would have flagged any criminal history on a background check, and I can't believe you've had any run-ins since then, so that can't be it."

"Prue and Walt refused to let me waste my last chance," Travis said, "but the things I did to survive… I just hoped either the good one, the smart one, or the cute one would decide they wanted to be a foster dad and let me fade into the background. Everyone would be happier, and the kids would be better off."

Grant frowned. "I'm going to ignore the fact that I didn't make the list of potential foster dads and say I understand."

"The worry makes me do things like let the social worker believe someone like Dr. Murphy would be stepping up to co-parent in the near future." Travis scrubbed his hand over his face. No matter how many times he replayed it, he couldn't get the image of Keena's disappointed gaze out of his head. "I'm afraid I'm not enough."

Travis wasn't sure they heard him. He hadn't wanted to say the words aloud, but it was a relief to finally let them loose.

He expected Wes to give him a pep talk. He took his role as "oldest" seriously and could usually be counted on to coach as needed, whether that was delivering the truth or a helping hand. Instead, Grant said, "Yeah." Rather than poking and prodding, Grant was completely serious.

As if he knew what that felt like.

"If you think you're alone in that, you aren't," Wes said softly. "I wish I had the solution, but it's not pretending. With us or the social worker. Or Keena." His emphasis on her first name signaled Wes was aware that the thing with Keena was more than incidental to his current mood.

"Fix what you can fix, Trav." Grant frowned, his gaze locked on the floor between his boots. "Everything else will have to work itself out in due time."

Wes raised his eyebrow at Travis. "It's solid advice. And from the problem," Wes murmured, "I didn't expect that."

"When it's right to hold him down and force answers about whatever happened to spur this retirement," Travis drawled, "please include me."

Wes laughed. "May take all of us to get it done."

Grant let out a fake laugh, slapped his hands on his thighs and stood. "On that note, I believe it's quittin' time."

"Hot date?" Travis asked as Grant left the barn.

"Something like that," Grant muttered before he slid inside his truck.

"Think we should be worried?" Travis asked Wes as Grant drove away.

Wes slung his arm over Travis's shoulder. "About Grant? Yes. But we have bigger issues at hand."

Travis hummed in agreement because that much was true. He hadn't seen Keena in days and he missed her. Finding a way to apologize and close this gap between them had him preoccupied.

"Our first crisis tonight is that it's your turn to cook dinner." Wes was laughing as he trotted up the steps to the ranch house.

Wes might not like it, but Travis only had one good go-to meal: hamburgers and hand-cut fries. So the decision was easy. Wes must have been satisfied because they were quiet as they ate and cleaned up the kitchen. Then they sat in front of the TV. Travis was bored with whatever movie Wes had chosen to watch but unmotivated to find any better way to occupy his time. And the replay of their serious conversation played on a loop in his head.

If Grant were here, this would have been prime time to start an argument purely for entertainment, at least on Grant's part.

Instead, Travis had stared straight ahead while his "older" brother cut concerned glances at him when he thought he wasn't paying attention.

Travis was ready for a distraction when

Wes had snatched up his phone and exhaled loudly. "Finally!"

"Finally, what?" Travis asked as he dodged the ragged throw pillow Wes tossed at his head.

"Finally Sip and Paint is over and I can find better company." Wes pointed at him. "All you've done all night is grumble under your breath like an old bear with a sore paw. I understand worrying. I do. This is more than that." He shook his head as he tugged on his boots.

Travis grunted but it was hard to argue the point.

"Thinking about something Ellen Montoya said," Travis mumbled.

"Nah, you're thinking about Keena Murphy. I know that look." Wes snagged his key off the long line of hooks by the door. "I've seen that hangdog look in the mirror more than once."

"Both things could be true, Wes." Uncomfortable that Wes had landed so near the real problem, Travis had said, "I guess Sarah's over at the lodge."

When Wes had paused with his hand on the door, Travis had been reaching for the remote. There was probably nothing better on, but it was something to do.

"Actually, she and Jordan had quite a bit of wine, so they're calling for a ride home," Wes said.

Travis nodded and watched the channels flicker by as he pressed buttons.

"Keena's with them." Wes had crossed his arms over his chest. "I could drop her at her home or…"

Travis had rolled up off the couch before he realized how quickly he was succumbing to Wes's plotting. "Your truck will be too crowded. I'll be happy to pick up Keena instead."

"I figured you wouldn't mind awfully much," Wes said dryly as he led the way out the door.

Travis had followed Wes and stood beside him outside the Mercantile to wait for everyone to come down.

It was one thing to understand how he'd come to be standing outside the Mercantile like he was picking up his prom date. But it was a whole different thing to realize he had no solid plan or clue about how to start the conversation after Keena was buckled in beside him and they were halfway back to the ranch.

Before he could find the right words to break the ice, Keena said, "Thank you." She faced him. "For picking me up. I appreciate it."

"Happy to help a neighbor." The awkward shoulder shrug was what convinced Travis he needed some kind of training session on how to adult correctly in public. He was a mess. "And I've been trying to find a way to talk to you this week."

She hadn't responded to that by the time he pulled into the front yard at Sharita's place. When he parked the truck, Travis inhaled slowly. "I'm sorry."

Keena sighed. "You don't really have anything to apologize for, Travis. I shouldn't have dropped in that way, and this thing with being a foster… What do I know about it? Nothing."

He stretched his arm out along the back of the seat. "I told Ellen today there wasn't anything between us, and she said it had nothing to do with getting approval anyway, so…it was a weird thing I did in the moment. That definitely deserves an apology."

Travis thought Keena was smiling but the cab was dark there in the front yard.

"You got the okay? Congratulations, that's wonderful." Keena squeezed his arm, and the glow of happiness he'd expected ever since he'd hung up the phone that afternoon finally spread through him.

Had he just needed to share the news with someone?

Travis replayed the reactions he'd gotten from Wes, Grant and his parents and realized he'd been waiting on her response. He'd wanted to talk to Keena about it.

Ellen Montoya's chuckle echoed in his head.

"I wish there was more light in the front yard." Keena snorted. "What am I saying? I wish there was any light in this yard at all."

"The front porch light isn't good enough?" Travis asked, determined to keep the conversation alive even if they had to talk outdoor lighting.

"For the three feet it lights up?" Keena wagged her head side to side. "Chuck avoids that circle, yes, but I'm afraid I'll step on something small and furry on my way to safety."

Travis relaxed in his seat. She was easing back into their normal pattern. If she hadn't forgiven him yet, she would. On his second unexamined impulse of the night, Travis got out and hurried around to the passenger side to open her door. Then he held out his arms.

"What? You're going to carry me?" Keena asked, giggles rolling out of her mouth even as he did his best to gallantly scoop her up. Gallantry lost to reality and Keena ended up braced over his shoulder instead. Carrying her the twelve or fifteen feet up to the porch would have been easier if she hadn't gripped one of his ears for safety while she laughed until she lost her breath.

"That's one way to avoid meeting the things that go bump in the night." Keena held her sides as she gasped for breath and fiddled with the house key. "Are you on call anytime I need safe passage through the dark yard?"

"Anytime you need anything. I'll answer." Travis wanted to keep their night alive. "If you'll let me, I'll show you how I learned to love the night here in the middle of nowhere. Took some adjustment when I first arrived at the Rocking A. Most of the foster homes

I moved through were in places where it's never really dark, thanks to streetlights and people all around."

Keena narrowed her eyes. "Will I have to go back out into the dark? Or can you teach me from this three-foot circle?" She motioned to the edges of the porch light.

"Either way, I'll be with you. You can trust me." Travis wished he'd planned this better. Or at all. He was going with the flow at this point. He was not that kind of guy.

"What do I need? A flashlight? A bat or something clublike for defense?" Keena asked.

"Quilts." Travis ran a hand over his nape and waited for Keena's reaction.

First, she studied his face. Then she shrugged and went inside the house. When she came out with a stack of quilts and two pillows, Travis didn't even hesitate to carry her back across the yard, laughing as she clung to his shoulder.

"We aren't going to get any points for style, but we're getting better at that." Keena fumbled with the latch on the tailgate and tossed the quilts down when it finally opened.

"At least my ear is still attached. I was

afraid you were going to take it as a souvenir the first time." Travis set her gently down on the tailgate. "Your feet aren't touching the scary dark ground, are they?"

Keena shook her head. "No, but I'm pretty sure raccoons can jump. Or is that squirrels?"

Probably both, but he wasn't going to say that.

Travis spread out one quilt for them to sit on, gave Keena another for their legs, and wrapped the third one around their shoulders. "Are you warm enough?"

"Warm enough for what?" she asked suspiciously.

Travis chuckled. "Good question. Okay, when I first arrived on the Rocking A, Wes and Clay were here. Grant came in a week or two after I did, and the space was so much smaller. I'd spent a lot of time…on my own." On the streets. Running away or hiding when he needed things to cool off before he went back home. "So to be surrounded by all these people and the noise… it was too much. Before, I would have hit the streets. They weren't scary, right? I knew them, day or night. Here, I couldn't see what was coming."

Keena studied his face. Since he'd spent time with her, he knew there were questions bubbling beneath the surface. Tonight, she held on to them.

"Yeah. I understand that." She rested her head against his shoulder. "Although I can't imagine being scared of anything when I have an amateur lumberjack at my side."

"Not even jumping possums or whatever?" Travis asked as he lifted her legs out of the danger zone to drape them over his lap. The way her giggles floated away in the night was sweet and satisfying. He took a second to commit them to memory.

"Straining to see the threat in the darkness made me miss so much." Travis watched her face. "What can you see?"

Keena tilted her head back. "So many stars. I wish I knew more about the constellations. A brilliant slice of the moon. The warm glow of the lights in the house. The outline of the mountains rising up. There are a lot of shades of dark out here, I guess."

"And what do you hear?" Travis asked as she relaxed next to him.

"Rustles that may or may not be steers intent on revenge," Keena said with a smile in her voice, "but they aren't nearby. If it makes sense, I can hear the silence. I can hear your breaths."

Travis was certain she could also hear the way his breath caught when she said that, but he didn't have any control over that.

"Once you taught yourself how to see in the dark, where did you escape to?" Keena asked.

"Took a while to find my spot, but eventually, I made a place in the hayloft. I could swing my legs out through the opening and see…forever." Travis hoped it didn't occur to Keena to imagine what kinds of creatures he might have spotted. That could undo everything she'd embraced there with him in the dark.

"This reminds me of my end-of-shift routine at the hospital," she said quietly.

Travis wanted to know more, but on the other hand he didn't want to break the spell between them. He waited to see if she would volunteer more.

"Working Emergency is a little like what you were saying about trying to see the threat before the attack happens. Your brain never stops running scenarios, you know?

Always assessing the patients needing help and figuring out which ones should be at the top of the critical list and which ones could wait and how long they could wait, not to mention what was coming in with the next ambulance, whether you had the right staff, equipment, knowledge, experience available for this case or that one." She exhaled softly. "It could be hard to see what was really happening because you were thinking of what the next crisis might be. I had all these mindfulness techniques. You've seen them. The counting down, centering myself, because my brain would run away and take everything I needed with it."

Travis stared at the top of her head, still resting against his shoulder, and realized the two of them understood each other in a way he would have never been able to put into words before meeting Keena.

"When you left the house that night, that look of disappointment on your face…" Travis concentrated on the night sky. "That's the kind of expression I am so scared of finding on my family's faces if I fail at this fostering thing. Seeing it on your face was like a punch to the gut."

Keena eased back. "I'm sorry. I do that. I build this outline of people in my head, one they can never live up to, and then..." She sighed. "My mother always said my unrealistic expectations would only lead to disappointment, usually when I was already disappointed because she or my father had missed something important in my life or broken a promise due to...whatever. It's too much pressure, so I usually stand on the outside. It's easier to be an observer than be involved, you know? I can get hurt if I'm involved. Being an observer builds in some safe distance from others. Being shuffled from one parent to the other, and the houses and siblings and schedules... I learned to do that to protect myself, I guess, but there's something about you and the way you...get me, that I fell into these old patterns. You and I, we're...different."

Relieved to hear her say some of what he'd been thinking, Travis tangled his fingers through hers. "We are different. I agree. Not sure exactly how we ended up here, but I feel that difference, too. Disappointing you felt wrong. I don't want to do that again."

Keena raised her head and looked at him.

"Were you going to ask me what I can feel, next?"

Travis chuckled. "Why am I afraid of that answer?"

"Oh? Maybe you should be." Keena's teasing voice was too cute for his heart. He was in serious trouble. "My nose is very cold, but the rest of me is comfortable. Relaxed in the deep, dark night because I'm safe with you." Keena wiggled closer. "I also feel that kissing you would make me happy, secure."

When she pressed her lips against his, Travis closed his eyes. The relief and pleasure and over-the-top joy he felt with her in his arms, sitting in the darkness, on the tailgate of his truck on a cold November night didn't make a lot of practical sense. Their first kiss was shy and sweet. Keena smiled at him. "I'm usually right, Travis."

He was amused and thrilled at how his nonplan plan had turned out, when Keena pressed her hand to his cheek to kiss him again. This time, they were more confident, as if this was the kiss they were each made for.

"Do you feel better about the darkness, Keena?" Travis asked, hopeful.

"Yes," Keena said, "but I'm still going to

need you to carry me up to the porch before you leave. I don't want to press my luck the first night out with the woodland creatures."

They were both giggling as he swung her over his shoulder.

CHAPTER TEN

AT THE ACE HIGH on Sunday, Keena happily slid across the seat to let Sarah into the booth and nodded acknowledgment to Jordan who slid in across from her. Keena was pleased to have the chance to talk to the Hearst sisters again. When she'd considered taking over the clinic for Dr. Singh temporarily, she'd worried how she would make acquaintances in a new town.

Keena hadn't counted on Sarah and Jordan.

"I hope this late lunch isn't too much of an inconvenience, Keena," Sarah said as she handed over one of the glasses of tea Faye deposited as she buzzed by. "We were hoping that we would miss the lunch crowd and have a chance to snag Faye for a minute. Jordan has been cooking up a plan." Sarah bent forward to say in a stage whisper, "And when Jordie has a plan, she drags everyone along with her."

"You say that like it's a bad thing, Sarah." Jordan was waiting for Faye to venture closer. Just as Faye did, Jordan whipped out a hand, wrapped it around Faye's wrist, and reeled her into the booth seat next to her. Then she crowed, "Look at that! I caught a Faye!"

Faye's deadpan stare at Keena surprised a giggle from her.

"About twenty percent of the time, I can catch her. I've been practicing." Jordan clapped her hands gleefully.

"I needed a break. You could have just asked me to sit down." Faye waved over her shoulder at the young woman behind the host stand. "But if you want food, someone is going to have to bring it to you. See how that works?"

Jordan pursed her lips. "A flaw in my strategy." Then she stretched across the table to say in her own stage whisper, "That is also one of Jordie's things. I never quite nail the plan the first time around."

When the young woman from the host stand delivered their late lunch, beautiful golden-brown fried chicken with coleslaw, green beans and baked macaroni and cheese, Faye said, "Now, what's the topic?"

Sarah held out a hand before Jordan could launch into whatever it was she was so excited to share. "First, family business. Jordan knows, but Travis met his first foster last night. His name is Damon. He's fourteen and he needed an emergency placement because of something that happened with his current foster family."

Keena put her fork down. She didn't want to miss any of this.

"The social worker called around eight o'clock or so last night to see if Travis could help. Apparently, she's hoping the issue can be worked out with Damon's first family." Sarah shrugged. "We haven't met Damon yet, but Travis wants to introduce us all, maybe tonight but maybe not, depending on how it's going."

"Any idea what kind of emergency it could be?" Faye asked as she glanced around the table.

"Wes said Travis was very quiet last night and even this morning," Sarah said softly.

When everyone turned to look at her, Keena wasn't sure what she was expected to say. "I know he's worried about being a good foster parent, but I think he's prepared."

For anything. Travis was the kind of steady that convinced Keena he could weather any storm and come out the other side stronger. "If this is only a short stay, Travis can build some confidence, and if it's longer, we all know how great the Rocking A and the Armstrongs will be for Damon."

She picked up her fork, mainly to have something to do with her hands.

Because everyone was still watching her.

"Did the two of you iron out whatever it was that Prue was buzzing about at the Sip and Paint?" Faye asked. She made a "so sue me" face as Sarah glared at her. "What? That's what you wanted to know. You were trying to send her psychic waves. I've discovered that actual words are a lot more effective." She took one of the rolls from the basket and slathered it with butter. "If Keena doesn't want to answer, she doesn't have to. Okay, so usually my manners are better than that." Then she muttered, "Sometimes."

Keena put her fork back down. Now she had a decision to make. She could gloss over the details, keep the ladies at arm's length and remain a pleasant acquaintance. That was her usual choice.

Or she could risk telling a bit more than the bare minimum, trust the women that far and see what happened next.

"Travis and I had a disagreement on allowing the caseworker to believe we were a couple. I think…" She sipped her tea as she fumbled for a way to sum up years of learning how important the truth was to her. "I'm like Faye. I want people to say what they mean. I don't expect most people to stick to the whole truth, but Travis had changed my mind about him, so when he let a trivial lie go, I…fell back to what I knew. I pulled back because that's safer. It hurt to be disappointed, but we've talked it over. I understand him better. I get it. We're friends."

Keena could feel the color filling her cheeks as she carefully avoided thinking about kissing him under the stars.

"Uh-huh," Faye drawled. "Friends. I believe that."

Sarah was obviously the peacemaker in the group because she immediately said, "Oh, good, I'm glad you worked it out. He didn't need to be weighed down by that, too, not now."

Keena nodded. She absolutely agreed.

She took a bite of the macaroni and cheese on her plate and decided the others might have to carry the conversation without her for a bit. Her lunch needed more attention.

"Let's come back to the newest budding romance in Prospect," Jordan said and raised her hand. "I want to talk about my plan."

Sarah nodded. "The floor is yours."

"Good." Jordan bounced in her seat. "You haven't been to our lodge yet, Keena, but we're going to fix that soon. The place was empty for years, but we've been cleaning it up."

"Mainly Jordan has been cleaning. She never stops," Sarah murmured and smiled brightly at her sister. "She's very dedicated. A hard worker."

Jordan cleared her throat. "Anyway, we have this restaurant that's attached. I'm not cooking. Sarah shouldn't, either. And so it's kind of just…there, for now."

Sarah jumped in. "Though, Michael and I have been kicking around an idea for it, in maybe early spring before the Western Days festival. Our cousin Michael is the new head of Sadie's Cookie Queen Corporation. Jordan and I were certain he would be a soulless number cruncher, but he has shown a streak of Hearst daring. He liked my museum suggestion, even agreed to bankroll it here in Prospect in exchange for a little help from me." Sarah clapped gleefully. "Wouldn't a cooking show, maybe a short competition of some kind, be fantastic? They could tape it at the lodge. The Cookie Queen Corporation would be the sponsor and have a TV crew here. We could offer to partner with one of the food channels or maybe stream it on our website or something." Sarah clapped some more. "We'll figure out the details later, but…"

Jordan had narrowed her eyes into a mean glare.

Faye laughed and pointed at Keena. "Sarah will also be roping us all into the plan. That is the Hearst way. From what I remember, their great-aunt Sadie was better at it than even these two, but what you are seeing is the cart before the horse. Whatever Jordan wants us to do for her will come before the TV show. Hearsts have a real eye for long-term strategy, but they also like the spotlight."

Keena smothered a grin as both sisters directed their scowls at Faye. Eventually, Jordan shrugged. "I mean, she's not wrong about any of that. Before Sarah's big, grand idea, I was thinking…" Jordan tapped her chest. "What if we host a community Thanksgiving potluck at the Majestic? You've seen the sheer number of Armstrongs crammed into the ranch house kitchen for a simple family dinner. If you add Sarah and my dad and Rose Bell and you, who will all be included in that number for a big holiday celebration, anyway, it's going to be elbow to elbow in there. A bigger, grander space is needed."

Sarah touched Keena's shoulder. "This is not to put any expectations on you to join us, of course. If you have other plans, like going home for the holidays, we won't kidnap you and force-feed you turkey, I promise. I won't let Jordan out of my sight, so you can make a safe getaway."

Keena couldn't contain the giggles at that. "Thank you for the invitation. Going home to Iowa is more stress than celebration for me, so I normally volunteer to work the holidays at the hospital so others can be with their families. I'd love to be included in your Thanksgiving crowd. Let me know what I can bring."

Jordan cleared her throat. "Okay, so let us return to the plan. We'll open up the lodge's restaurant kitchen. We'll provide the turkey, and everyone can bring their family's favorite holiday side dish. Since the Ace is closed for the day, we'll invite anyone who'd like to share a community Thanksgiving potluck out at the Majestic."

Keena nodded. "That's generous."

Faye pursed her lips. "Why do I feel there might be a catch here?"

"Because you know Jordan at this point," Sarah said under her breath.

"No catch!" Jordan batted her eyes innocently. "But, if anyone wants to come early or stay after to help us with refinishing the floors or painting or, depending on the weather, clearing flower beds or...what have you," she said airily, "we would be very thankful for that, too."

Keena waited for Faye's reaction. In the big Thanksgiving scheme of things, she didn't have much at stake. It sounded sort of genius to her.

"I'm in. I always enjoy a day away from the restaurant. Yes, please. My grandparents have been dying to see the Majestic since it reopened. I'll set Gram up in the kitchen to oversee the operation, arranging the dishes and directing all the volunteers with setup and cleanup. Making one dish instead of an entire meal? I love it. Hey, if we work this right, I might even fit in a nap somewhere." Faye grinned. "That's a winning plan, my friends."

"I like it, too." Keena rested against the seat, pleased with her lunch and the way the conversation was flowing. Driving into town, she'd been nervous. At Sip and Paint, she'd enjoyed herself, but Prue Armstrong was such a strong personality that she'd kept the event moving in the right direction. There was no space for awkward silence when Prue was nearby.

Here, the discussion might have lagged, but she was convinced that the Hearsts were born with something special, personalities or characters that made it easy to connect to them. Sadie had made it from this small town in the Rockies to become a famous TV chef, after all.

"Since I am next door, if I can also help get the restaurant ready beforehand, I'll be happy to roll up my sleeves and…" Keena wasn't sure where she was going with that. She knew nothing about what might need to be done to open up a restaurant. "Mop or something."

Sarah groaned as if defeated.

Jordan's smile should have made Keena nervous.

"Thank you, Keena. I know we can find something for you to do before the big day rolls around," she said sweetly.

Faye groaned in commiseration. "If I've picked up all the news, I need to go check on Gram in the kitchen. She wanted to scrap the week's menu the last time I talked to her, and we don't have time or money for that kind of artistic temperament."

"Her grandmother is the cook?" Keena asked.

"Never met her," Jordan said, "but I get the impression she's more like the 'executive chef' in that she tells people to jump and they ask how high. Runs the kitchen with a firm hand, but it's impossible to argue with success. They have this amazing apple pie that comes from one of Sadie's special recipes and it's worth all kinds of personality quirks and weird goings-on."

The three of them were all full and happy

when they stepped back out on the sidewalk. Jordan hugged Keena before she knew what was happening. "Lunch was great. Can't wait to show you around the Majestic."

Keena returned the hug and then gave Sarah one. "Thank you for inviting me today and for Thanksgiving. Maybe next weekend I can come over and you can put me to work."

"Oh, dear," Sarah murmured as Jordan lit up.

They were bickering when they got into the car and drove away. Keena knew the smile on her face might seem silly, but she'd had a blast.

The weekend had flown by. She'd spent it doing so many things she enjoyed, it was a new sensation. Resting. Painting. Hanging out with friends. Getting ready to go back to work on Monday after not spending time putting her apartment back together or preparing for the next crisis in the ER.

If Dr. Singh could see her smile, he might believe she was inching closer to accepting the offer he'd made out of the blue. Keena wasn't sure if she was or not, but it was difficult to argue with this bubble of contentment.

Prospect's pace left her plenty of time to

relax and even explore new hobbies. Adjusting to that was easier than she'd anticipated.

A quick trip through Homestead Market to pick up the groceries on her list and several cute plastic containers that could be used as gifts if this baking thing overwhelmed her, and she was back in her cozy rental house.

One of the biggest problems she'd discovered with her rental was the lack of internet access. Like most people, she spent entirely too much time online shopping for this, researching that, and generally wasting time. Here, Keena would have loved to pull up music and bake, but until she got the okay from Sharita through Wes to add service, she had to rely on the songs she'd stored on her phone...over and over. Sharita's aged collection of DVDs ended around 2012, so whatever was there was "classic."

Luckily, Sharita had an extensive collection of Colorado Cookie Queen shows on DVD to work through, thus the never-ending grocery list.

But Keena had an occasion to plan for and apple pie was on her mind. If it was good enough to smooth over personality quirks,

Keena needed the recipe. She hit Play on one of Sadie's earliest Christmas specials and settled on the couch with a stack of cook-books.

Sadie was cooking with celebrities. It was a cookie exchange–themed show, so she tried a new recipe with each guest. When Sadie and one of Keena's earliest and hardest crushes stepped onto the TV stage amid wild applause to make "Cute as a Button Butter Cookies," she sipped her cup of coffee and tried not to cringe. Was it embarrassing to remember the way she and her next-door neighbor had choreographed dances to his Top 40 hits? A little bit, but it helped that there was no way anyone in Prospect, Col-orado, would be able to find any footage of preteen Keena dancing to lyrics she most definitely had not understood at the time.

Watching Sadie now, it was so easy to see her warmth in Sarah's and Jordan's person-alities. Even Patrick had displayed the kind-ness Sadie showed when Keena's heartthrob tried to drop a hard glob of cold butter in the dry ingredients bowl. Sadie explained why that was a bad move, made a funny joke that had the whole audience laughing along, and then resumed her easy demonstration of the best method to make treats for Santa or "your favorite neighbor down the street. Do not waste these on a rascal, you hear?" The twinkle in Sadie's eyes convinced Keena that even the rascals in Sadie's life enjoyed pretty good cookies.

After the holiday special ended, a new show started. Sadie returned but she'd moved out of the studio. "Well, now, I was hoping we'd meet again." Sadie's grin and tone suggested this was how she always started her intros. She held out a graceful hand. "Here I am, in my favorite kitchen, back of the Majestic Prospect Lodge before the lunch rush starts. Got my trusty apron and my favorite hat." Keena scooted forward, immediately curious about the kitchen she had just been discussing with Sarah and Jordan. Sadie tapped the white cowboy hat before tipping it up. The sparkle of joy was easy to see in her eyes. "I'm a thinking today is a good day to make some molasses cookies. You ever had a perfect, soft molasses cookie? My mama used to make these, and you could never hold on to a bad day or a rotten attitude when these were around. That's powerful, right there."

She leaned forward as if she was about to share something top secret. "If I tell you how to make these, you gotta promise to use 'em for good in this world. That's one thing we ain't ever got too much of, good in this world."

As she listed the ingredients she'd be using, Sadie dropped little tidbits about the best kind of molasses to use for different applications. Blackstrap was too intense for these cookies and light molasses too mild. Dark molasses was the "Goldilocks choice" here. Her enthusiasm was contagious, so Keena started a new grocery list.

Sadie mixed the wet ingredients and then the dry. She talked about refrigerating the dough and then pulled out a fully prepped bowl from the large stainless steel refrigerator behind her.

"We're going to roll out some balls, about yea big," Sadie said as she held one up to the camera, "and scatter 'em across the cookie sheets. Now, getting them the same size is more important than what size they are. Leave breathing room for these beauties to bake."

"Better make sure I put 'dark molasses,'" Keena muttered as she pulled out her phone. "None of that bitter blackstrap molasses for me." She hadn't meant to say it the way Sadie did, but that's how the words came out. Did it seem right at the beginning? No, but she could see how easy it was to slip into.

Just like she'd slipped right into the flow in Prospect.

A text from Travis flashed on the phone screen before she set it back down.

Are you up for a visit?

Keena read it three times before she convinced herself that she understood it correctly.

Of course, she typed and bit her lip as she tried to decide whether it needed an exclamation mark or not.

Before she could commit, she heard a car in the front yard and went to check who exactly had arrived.

Travis waved from the driver's seat. She'd forgotten that Sarah had mentioned he was taking his new foster around to show him the town and make introductions.

Then she realized she'd somehow made the list of important people who deserved an introduction and wished she had a mirror hanging beside the door. What was her hair doing?

Didn't matter. He was sliding out of the truck before she could decide whether she had time to address it or not.

A tall, thin boy got out of the passenger side and stopped halfway to the door. His hair was long, hiding his eyes, but the way he held his left arm made it clear that Travis was stopping to introduce his foster to the doctor instead of the neighbor next door.

Which was fine.

Keena was both, so she was getting an early intro, even if she knew this was practical more than personal.

And honestly, she was too personally involved already.

"Hi, I'm Keena," she said as she stopped on the bottom porch step. "Please come in."

The kid eased closer and took the hand she offered but he didn't move to climb the steps.

"Nice to meet you." The kid glanced at Travis and away. Keena wondered if Travis knew anything pertinent to his injury.

"This is Damon." Travis moved to touch the kid's shoulder but stopped when he shifted away. "He's going to be staying for a bit. Thought he'd like to know who was living next door."

"I'm glad you did. I was going to make cookies. Do you have time to sit and wait for them?" Keena asked as she stepped down in the yard, moving slowly to give Damon plenty of warning.

"We better not. We've got a big day planned tomorrow, headed into town to visit the school." Travis frowned as Keena gently took Damon's hand and pulled on his sleeve.

"Can I take a look at your arm?" she asked Damon softly. "Dr. Keena is my whole name, but I want you to stick with Keena."

Damon licked his lips but let her remove his jacket sleeve. Through the neck of the thin T-shirt he was wearing, she could see a bruise. "Looks like you took a fall. Is it only bruising or…" Keena waited. If he had other injuries, she wanted him to share them without worrying about possible trouble later.

"Yes. No broken bones. I was climbing a fence and misjudged the height. Landed hard on the ground, but that's all." Damon shyly met her stare.

Keena whistled. "Oh, no, did you learn anything from that?"

One corner of the boy's mouth curled up. "Stop climbing fences?"

Delighted, Keena pointed at him. "Good one. I like it better than mine. I was going to say use the gate instead because you could have broken more than your arm from that height, but you're even smarter than I am." She took a chance and offered him her fist. His hesitation confirmed for Keena that fist bumps were no longer cool, if they ever were, but Damon humored her and returned it anyway. That successful interaction boosted Keena's confidence.

"If it's okay, I'll wait in the truck." Damon was pulling on the jacket as he walked away. "I like your hamburger shoes."

Keena stared at her house slippers and wondered if she'd ever get the hang of having the proper footwear for Prospect.

Travis watched him before turning back to Keena. "His record for words spoken. I'm glad we stopped."

Keena squeezed his arm. "You doing okay?"

He nodded. "Yeah, I just…wish I was better at talking, too. I might have broken my own record today, for that matter, filling in silence."

"I'm sorry for turning into a doctor." She smiled brightly. "Try some ibuprofen, but make sure he eats first. We don't want his stomach upset, just in case."

"Kid needs to eat around the clock for a month as it is." Travis rubbed his hand over his lips; the concern was clear on his face.

"Have you called in your mother to address the problem?" Keena asked, determined to lighten some of his load.

"Yep, she's headed our way with biscuits on her mind. I've also warned every adult Armstrong connected to the Rocking A that the kid doesn't need to be climbing fences. Ever." He relaxed. "And you don't have to apologize for trying to help. I appreciate it."

Keena sighed. "I have this weird compulsion. I see a problem or something I don't understand and I immediately launch into discovery mode. Sometimes people want to…just be and not answer twenty questions. Also, a fist bump? I don't know what came over me."

Travis laughed. "No apologies for that either. I understand compulsions. I have at least one myself."

"What?" Keena asked, reminded of Travis's comments about caffeine. Was that a sensitivity or did he have another trait that compounded an introvert's need for quiet?

Then he slid his warm hand around the nape of her neck, under the fall of her hair, and brushed his thumb over her cheek.

"Oh," Keena whispered as he bent closer, moving slowly, giving her plenty of time to decide about this kiss.

Then his lips were on hers. This kiss was different from their teasing kisses in the dark. They knew more about each other, what could be between them. This kiss was about missing each other for a couple of days and being uncertain when they'd be together again and warmth and need.

There was also a teenage boy in the front yard watching this kiss.

"Gotta go." Travis risked an injury of his own by backing down the steps and across the yard, his eyes locked on her face.

Keena collapsed against the door when she made it back inside, shaken by how much she missed him already. Had she known Travis Armstrong long enough to feel like this whenever he drove away?

Whether she had or not, the feelings were there.

What would it be like to leave Prospect to go home where she belonged when Dr. Singh returned?

Keena rubbed the ache in her chest before standing solidly on her own two feet.

That was a problem for later.

Today, she was going to watch Sadie Hearst finish these molasses cookies and then she was going to find the perfect recipe for the too-skinny boy next door and the man determined to keep him safe.

CHAPTER ELEVEN

TRAVIS REALIZED HE was humming to himself as he mucked out Sonny's stall and wondered how long he'd been doing it. It had been a busy few days since he'd taken Damon for the sightseeing tour of Prospect, and so far, everything was going…fine.

They weren't about to win any awards for most exciting dinner conversation, but Damon had agreed to attend school. He'd been doing his homework, too. And he and Travis had been learning their way around each other as Travis had shown the kid how to care for a horse. They'd covered how to saddle Sonny, how much the horse ate and drank every day, the places he liked to be scratched and places that would provoke a whiffle of disgust.

The kid was a lot like he'd been when he'd landed at the Rocking A, a complete novice when it came to horses, but Damon had one characteristic Travis hadn't. The horses didn't scare him.

That was a good sign.

This afternoon, Grant had offered to give Damon actual riding lessons, so Travis had jumped on the chance to get some work done in the barn. He enjoyed watching Damon learn, because the kid took everything so seriously, a little wrinkle appearing between his eyebrows as he listened intently.

That made it easy to imagine working with him around the ranch.

Grant was the best rider out of all of them, and Travis wanted Damon to know the rest of his family, so he'd stepped back and got busy with the chores he'd left undone that week.

While humming apparently.

When he moved the wheelbarrow back to its normal spot along the wall, he realized it was later than he expected. Dinner should have been ready half an hour ago, but no one had raised an alarm. Darkness outside suggested Grant and Damon had gone in for food and left him there entertaining himself in the horse stalls.

If they were getting along that well, it was hard to be mad.

Annoyed? Sure, that was normal.

He switched off the overhead light and pulled closed the barn door as his phone rang.

When he saw Keena's name, his mood did a one-eighty.

"Hey, neighbor, how are you?" he asked. He winced at the over-the-top excited tone. Keena would think she'd gotten the wrong number. It wasn't like him.

In fact, this whole…lightness wasn't like him. It might take a minute, but he'd like to have the chance to get comfortable with it.

"I'm okay. Have you seen Damon lately?" she asked quickly.

Travis hurried toward the house. "No, why?"

"I was walking through the living room and saw something out the window, along the road. I think it was Damon. He was walking toward town. I didn't think walking along a dark road in the dark night with all the creatures of the darkness waiting to pounce was a good plan?" Her tone rose at the end as if she was trying to be calm about everything. "I'll grab my coat and check if you'll stay on the phone with me."

Travis gripped his phone tightly as he stuck his head inside the house. Grant was standing at the stove. "Dinner's almost ready if you want to get Damon."

Travis listened as Keena's front door opened and closed. "Damon's supposed to be with you."

Grant pointed with a spatula. "He said he had a spelling test to study for."

"Spelling?" Travis and Keena both asked.

"Do teenagers take spelling tests?" Keena posed the question, although it sounded like she already had the answer. Travis could hear her quick breathing, as if she was hurrying across the yard.

"I don't think so. I'm headed for my truck, but don't hang up." Travis slammed the door shut and trotted through the yard, while he dug his keys out of his pocket. "Five minutes or less, Keena. I'll be there."

"No worries. I can see him from here. He's fast, but I've worked the night shift for years. I can catch him." Keena was quiet but Travis could hear her footfalls as she hurried down the highway. "Damon, wait up! I'll walk with you. I love the moonlight."

No way would the kid believe that, even

if Travis appreciated her attempt to tell her own harmless lie to stop the kid from getting hurt.

Travis couldn't make out what Damon said, but Keena answered, "I can't let you walk all the way into town by yourself. I'll keep you company."

Damon's response was muffled. "Yeah, it's Travis on the other end. I was worried about you."

Travis could hear a bit of apology in her voice.

"Want to come back to my house and wait where it's warm?" Keena sighed. "Nope, we're going to keep walking. I have cookies. Want one?"

Travis couldn't tell if Damon had accepted the offer or not.

"I'm close now. You should see my headlights coming around the curve." Travis slowed down. Speeding around the curve would put them in more danger than walking along the shoulder at night, even though that was so dangerous it made his stomach clench to think about it. Two city slickers wandering country roads in the darkness... that was how horror movies started.

As soon as he saw the bright pink back of Keena's jacket, Travis exhaled. He passed them and then eased over on the narrow shoulder ahead of them. Damon stopped and turned back toward the ranch, as if he was trying to decide if it was better to strike off in that direction on foot.

Keena was clutching a plastic container to her stomach and appeared to be ready to run behind Damon, no matter which direction he went in.

"Nobody is taking off into the dark tonight." Travis took his time as he picked through the right words. "We're going to talk. We can do that at home or in the truck or on Keena's porch or right here in the middle of the road, but we're going to discuss how running away is not going to work for me. Or you."

Travis leaned against the truck and crossed his arms over his chest. "Keena is freezing, kid. Let's get this conversation over with."

"I could go back myself." She sniffed. "It's probably safe. I might have heard Bigfoot in the trees over there before we rounded the curve, but I bet he's gone now."

Damon groaned loudly. "I have to go home.

I don't want either of you out here. You both go back. I'll go on to town. Everyone will be happy."

Keena popped the top off the container and took a cookie out. "I'm not a parent, Damon, but even I can see the flaws in your plan. Were you going to hitchhike all the way back to Denver? Do you know how dangerous that is?" She offered him the container. "They're Cookie Queen Chocolate Chip and I've already eaten six. Please take one."

Travis wasn't surprised when Damon took the container she offered. He hadn't had dinner. At fourteen, Travis would have been ready to chew bark off the trees if he'd missed dinner.

"And when you did get to Denver, if you ever made it at all, then what?" Travis asked. What could convince the kid to take such a dangerous step? He'd just been humming happily to himself about how well things were going.

"I'll convince the Smiths to take me back. I'll promise to never get in trouble again and things will be the way they were." Damon shoved half of the cookie in his mouth.

Travis could see how that might be something to daydream about, and if the kid had been happy there, maybe that was the best answer. But there was a piece of the story missing. How had a fall from a fence resulted in an emergency placement if everything had been going so well with Damon's foster family?

Keena was obviously on the same track because she said, "Spill the rest of the story, please. If it was that easy, why didn't you promise not to get in any more trouble before you landed here?"

Damon shrugged. "I did."

"Why would it work this time, if it didn't work then?" Travis asked as he intercepted the container and took one cookie for himself.

"I'll convince them." Damon scuffed his sneaker on the road. "I'm not a country kid, Travis. That's all. I need to be in the city. Don't worry about me. I'll be okay." He shifted the backpack over his shoulder. "I have some money and food. I'm all set."

"You loved every minute we spent in the barn with Sonny. No way were you faking that, kid." Travis held his hand out. Eventually, Damon slid the backpack off his shoulder and passed it over.

Travis unzipped it. "Jeans, good. Two sweatshirts, good. What about underwear?"

Damon didn't answer.

"Not so good. And the food appears to be…" Travis felt the crumpled wrapper of the chip bags he'd been sending for lunch. "Chips. I respect the choice but it won't provide much energy." He felt a hard something at the bottom of the bag. "And one wireless speaker in the shape of a football."

Travis couldn't read Keena's eyes in the darkness, but the way she snapped to attention told him she was pretty proud of the purchase she'd forced him to make.

"You can have it back. I don't need it." Damon's voice was firm, but he was still young enough that it was easy to hear the disappointment, too. He'd give up the speaker because it was the right thing to do in his mind, but he didn't have to enjoy it.

"It's yours. You can take it with you when you go," Travis said, "but that's not going to happen tonight." When Damon moved to go around him, with or without the helpful items in his backpack, Travis held up his hand. "Because I'll make you a deal. To-morrow, in the bright sunshine, I'll drive you down to Denver. We'll meet with Ellen Montoya to talk about you not being a coun-try kid even though you have horse fever now and we'll see if she has a better match for you. You aren't a prisoner here, but I have to keep you safe, Damon. Hitchhiking is dangerous. And life on the streets…" Tra-vis cleared his throat. "Believe me, I know it's not safe. I don't want that for you." Then he offered the kid his hand to shake. "To-morrow, we'll go and we'll find a better so-lution."

The boy hesitated. He'd probably had more than one adult make him a promise only to break it as soon as it benefited them. Damon might understand how Keena had felt about Travis slipping into his lie about them with Ellen Montoya. They both de-served to be surrounded by people they could trust.

Travis was resolved to keep every prom-ise. That meant he had to be careful when making them.

Damon shook his hand and Travis relaxed. "We'll take Keena home and then go eat dinner. After that, I'll text Ellen that we need to talk with her tomorrow and the Smiths, too. How's that?"

"Okay." Damon took the backpack from Travis. "Thank you."

Travis opened the door for Keena. "Everyone in the truck." After Damon slid in the passenger side, Travis backed up around the curve and into Keena's front yard. "Need me to carry you across the grass?" He slid out and held her hand as she followed.

"Nah, I'm a big girl." Then she pressed the cookie container into his stomach. "Take these away from me or I'll eat the rest." She squeezed his hand. "You gonna be okay? I know this is a challenge." Her voice was low. He wasn't sure if Damon would be able to hear what they said to each other.

"I'm okay because of you. Thank you for calling. I would have lost my mind when I found his room empty. After I murder Grant for believing the kid was taking a spelling test, I'll feel better," Travis said.

Damon's muffled chuckle answered the question about what he could hear.

"Good night. Call me and tell me how everything turns out, okay?" Keena hurried across the grass to the safety of her porch and stepped inside.

"The doctor's really pretty," Damon said. He was crammed up against the passenger side door as if he'd rather be riding on the outside of the truck if he could figure out a way to do it.

"Yeah, she is." Travis wasn't sure how to open up the conversation that needed to take place.

"You'll have more time for flirting when I go back to Denver," Damon said.

Travis grunted. "You were going to be my secret weapon. Keena's a sucker for kids."

Damon didn't answer and Travis wondered what Keena would think about that particular half-truth. Or maybe it was the whole truth. He didn't know. They hadn't discussed kids, but she was good with Damon. He still would have sworn in a court of law it was right to make Damon think twice about leaving.

Back at the Rocking A, Travis said to Damon, "Head on inside and get some dinner. Then, if you have any homework other than an imaginary spelling test, get started on it."

Damon stopped in the middle of the yard. "You aren't coming in?"

"Not yet." Travis needed a few minutes to himself first.

Travis now faced the same problem he'd had when he'd first arrived at the Rocking A. There was nowhere to go to have the time that he needed to work through his feelings. The house had his dad, Damon and most of his brothers, so he headed for the barn. He skipped the light switch because that would be the only clue any of his family would need to track him down. He climbed the sturdy ladder up to the hayloft that extended along one long side of the barn.

He didn't worry much about the darkness there because this was his spot.

Had been for a long time.

The first thing he'd done when he returned home for good was make sure the ladder was strong, the flooring of the loft was solid, and the path to his favorite spot was clear. He'd plopped down on the quilt he kept up there for nights when he couldn't sleep and needed to stare out the opening at the stars. Now, he heard boots on the ladder.

He didn't have to check to see who had followed him.

When Walt dropped down next to him with a grunt, Travis sighed. "Everything's okay, Dad. I needed to get my head straight before I try to unravel this thing with Damon."

His father didn't answer for a minute. They both stared out into the night as if the answer was outside.

"How many times did you run away before we ironed out an accord?" Walt asked. "Four? Five? All I know for sure was you scared Prue Armstrong to tears that last time, and I was almost certain that was a feat beyond mortal men, much less skinny boys with chips on their shoulders."

Travis's lips twitched but he contained the smile. That would not please Walt, a smile at the reminder of the way Prue had panicked the night he never came home. That wasn't the amusing part. It was that Walt had always been the voice of reason for Travis and he was happy to have his father nearby for this.

Even if it was going to try his patience.

And Walt's for that matter.

"I wasn't running away, though. That's

the difference." Travis had needed space. That's all. He'd had no destination to hitch-hike to in mind, no place called "home" that he wanted to return to the way Damon did.

"Maybe you knew that then. Maybe you only learned later, but your mama and I were in the dark." Walt wrapped his arms around his legs. "Thing we learned real quick about you boys was that each one of you was a 5,000-piece puzzle. Every piece had weird edges and only trial and error put them to-gether."

Travis closed his eyes. "I'm not good with puzzles. We should have had this conversa-tion before I upended the ranch to bring in more pieces."

Travis rested his head against the rough wood and wondered how his father had got-ten him to admit his biggest fear that eas-ily. There was almost no hope that Walt had missed it, either.

"You think we were good with puzzles in the beginning?" Walt snorted. "Prue was good. She's always had this knack of un-derstanding all kinds of people, even young ones who'd rather hide away than argue or fight. Me? I had to turn every single new piece thisaway and thataway until something clicked. Nobody explained to me how much flying by the seat of your pants is required in parenthood, but I'm doing you the favor of warning you now."

"Could be too late," Travis said. "What if I've already messed up my first chance?"

Walt yanked his cowboy hat off and tossed it on the hay. "By getting these nice rooms ready and filling them with special things and curving your world to fit these kids you haven't met yet. How can you mess that up?"

Travis shrugged.

"Use your words, Travis," Walt grumbled. "Can't believe you've got me talking to you the way Prue does me, but in this case, we need to have some words between us. What are you afraid of here?"

Something about the darkness and the open space around them made it seem possible to say the scary things out loud and survive it, so Travis said, "I've never been a parent. I wasn't even a child for long, you know? Until I got here, I only had me and I did things to survive. You know I was half a step from jail the night the social worker left me here and raced away. What if I can't learn what I need to in order to figure out these puzzles?"

What if I fail at this one thing that I've wanted more than anything?

What if I'm too broken to do this?

That was what Travis held close to his chest. If he failed at this, who was he going to be?

"You remember the first time I put you on a horse?" Walt asked. "Thought you might cry, you were so scared."

Travis scowled. "You were supposed to forget that and never bring it up again."

Walt chuckled. "Can't forget it. I think it was my moment, like the one you're having now. I only knew what I knew, Travis. My daddy never taught me how to deal with emotions like fear except to pretend they aren't there. Pretend you don't have emotions, period. Took me a while to learn how bad a lesson that was. Five boys and a wife, all learning that lesson alongside me, too. Wouldn't recommend that. Sure am grateful that Prue made it clear that you boys would feel the way you felt and that would be the end of it. Your mama made you all who you are today." Walt clapped a hand on his shoulder. "That's my biggest worry about this new family we're all building. You need a Prue to balance you out. Not a wife, I don't guess, but someone who can work alongside you to sort all the pieces. Wes is good at that, but the rest of us are about as good at puzzles as you are."

His father's grim tone wasn't intended to be funny, but something about the way he said it amused Travis.

That eased some of his panic and made it easier to think.

"All right. Call Wes. That's what you're telling me?" Travis asked. "Not surprising. That's often the answer to any problem."

Walt shrugged. "This particular question? We can figure this one out. Put Wes in your back pocket for real emergencies."

Travis turned back to stare out at the night. "Tomorrow I'll take Damon to talk to his caseworker one-on-one. If it's better for him to leave us, that's what will happen. It's not some commentary on what I've done here." Eventually, he'd get that through his head and he'd move on.

"Or you can talk to the kid tonight, spread

all the puzzle pieces out, and get a better look at what needs to be assembled," Walt said as he stood. "That's the correct answer. You wait here."

Walt was gone before Travis could argue.

He'd needed a minute to get control of his own emotions before he worked through the problem with Damon. His father knew it, too.

Moments later, the overhead light switched on and Damon walked down the wide aisle in the barn. "Hey."

Travis held up his hand. "Hey yourself, I know you have strict orders not to climb fences. Are you able to climb ladders safely or…"

Damon shrugged. "Guess we won't know until I give it a shot."

Travis was relieved that the kid didn't seem afraid of him or the barn. "The first few weeks I was here at the Rocking A, I didn't step foot in the barn unless Walt was with me."

"Why?" Damon asked as he followed Travis over to the open door in the gable. He sat on the quilt when Travis pointed at it.

"Scared. I knew there were critters in here.

Mice. Worse. Horses were intimidating, and I had to hide all that because none of my brothers had the same reaction. Grant would have slept in a stall with his horse if he could have. Then there was me, jumping at shadows."

Travis sat in Walt's spot and braced his arm on his knee.

"I was pretty sure Walt would have dropped me off on any other family's doorstep because I was never going to fit in here at the Rocking A. Spent a lot of time sneaking out of the house, too. Eventually, he made me a deal. I could leave whenever I wanted. He knew I needed the space sometimes to breathe, but I had to come here. No one else would know this was my spot, but he could find me when it mattered." Travis pointed at Damon. "Don't you spill my secrets."

"I won't." Damon shook his head. "You can trust me."

Good. That's what he'd wanted to hear.

"Trust me with your secret, Damon. I'll keep it. I promise. I need to know why you've got to get back to Denver. Did you leave something behind? We'll go pick it up. Our agreement still stands. I'll take you to meet with your social worker and we'll find whatever works the best, but I only want what's good for you. That's my only goal. I'd rather have the whole story going in, so I know how to help."

"It's… For some reason, I think you might understand this. The Smiths have another foster kid, a little guy named Micah." Damon glanced at him. "I'm worried about leaving him there alone. He needs me."

Travis picked up hay and broke it into tiny pieces as he tried to formulate a tricky question.

"It's not the Smiths, if that's what you're about to ask me. They're…fine." Damon bent his knees, his lanky legs forming a shield. "But Micah's…sensitive. Gets bullied on the bus. My bus usually dropped me off before his did, so I've been waiting at his stop to walk him home. Last week, my bus was late and these kids had Micah cornered."

"So you jumped in to defend him. How many kids?" Travis asked. This was a familiar story. He'd fought a few of these fights growing up, too.

"I don't know, four or five. Micah got free and I was losing." Damon grimaced. "Turns out watching karate movies doesn't teach you much karate, so I took off running, hit the fence to climb, made it to the top but they grabbed my leg and yanked me down. When I landed with a crunch, they took off running. The shop owner carrying out the trash got a big shock when he found me gasping for breath, since the fall had knocked it out of me. He called the cops, and the ambulance, and...everything escalated."

"Why were you in trouble? Seems like the bullies should have been the ones in trouble with the police," Travis said, offended at unfair treatment in general and for Damon specifically.

"I get in trouble for fighting. A lot. I mean, I've been on my best behavior because Micah was scared to death we'd get split up if he complained about the bullies or whatever, and there's something about the kid that makes me want to look out for him." Damon shrugged. "He still believes in happy endings, families that belong together and all that."

If Travis knew anything, it was that Damon wanted to believe those things, too.

He and his brothers had held on to that until they'd made it to Prue and Walt.

Damon met his stare directly. "Do I think that could happen here? Maybe. You and the Armstrongs seem nice, but I can't leave Micah. He's like my brother now."

Now that Travis understood Damon had been determined to return for a "who" instead of a "what," everything made sense. But he wasn't clear on the right answer. Was he ready to add a second foster, one younger than he'd expected to take charge of? If not, how easy would it be to say goodbye to Damon? He'd been imagining the kid riding in the Western Days parade with his family.

Before Travis could test the waters to see if Damon was receptive to bringing Micah here, his phone rang. He pulled it out to stop the ringing and noticed Ellen Montoya's name on the display. "Hello? I was about to text you to request a meeting for tomorrow."

"Oh? What's going on?"

Travis was very aware that the subject of the conversation was watching him from across the quilt. "We want to discuss some concerns Damon has about his brother, Micah." He would have explained in more detail, but he hoped Ellen Montoya could

remember enough about the boys to understand what he meant.

"Funny you mention Micah," she said.
"The Smiths caught him sneaking out of his
bedroom window tonight with a backpack
filled with what he thought would be enough
clothes and food to make it to Prospect. The
kid's not even ten years old, Travis. Is it any
wonder the Smiths were alarmed?"

"But Micah is okay," he said before he
realized how that would sound to someone else. Damon scrambled across the hay
to land next to him, his ear pressed hard
against the phone in Travis's hand.

"He is. The Smiths made a promise they'd
talk to me about bringing Damon back here,
to rejoin their family," Ellen said, "so this is
me talking to you about it. I'll be honest. I've
got concerns. Damon's influence might not
be what Micah needs. This running away is
new behavior. I wonder how much of that
has to do with Damon."

Travis pulled the phone away from Damon's grasping hands. The kid was desperate to defend himself. That made sense. This
was important to him. "Did Micah tell the
Smiths or you about the bullying he's been

experiencing? That's part of what I heard from Damon tonight when I stopped him from running away."

"Oh, no, him, too? This is a mess." She sighed. "And no, I don't believe the Smiths have that information. No one has shared it with me."

"The boys were afraid that would be what split them up. Damon's been watching out for Micah." Travis didn't want to give too many details. Damon's trust was new. It was important to treat the information carefully that he'd shared.

"We're coming to the office tomorrow. Could the Smiths meet us there with Micah?" Travis asked. Should he volunteer to move Micah to Prospect? That would get him away from the bullies, both kids would stop running away from home, and all he had to do was…open up the door and tell him to jump in the truck.

It seemed simple but it was another huge step.

"Come down. I want to talk to both boys, for sure, but I can hear the unspoken words, Travis. Micah is younger than you're prepared for. He's also got some trauma in his background that made finding a couple like the Smiths important. He's extremely cautious of men. I wasn't sure Ian Smith would make the cut."

Travis realized this whole time, even with Damon, he'd been worried about his own re-action, what he would do right or wrong, but he was dealing with kids who had their own histories. Had he even considered that piece?

The question reminded him of his father's analogy of the jigsaw puzzle.

"Okay, Damon and I will get a good night's rest and travel down tomorrow. We'll meet and then we'll all make a decision together. There's no sense in getting too far along in our heads tonight." Travis held Damon's stare as he spoke, hoping the kid was catching on to what he was saying.

"Yes. That's what we'll do. I'll see you tomorrow around…eleven?" Ellen asked.

"Perfect. We'll be there." Travis ended the call and slipped his phone back in his pocket.

Damon was quiet, his hands balled tightly into fists in his lap.

His fears were written on his face, but Travis wasn't sure what the right words might be.

"Thank you for listening," Damon said softly. "Is it okay if I sit here a bit longer?"

Travis nodded and stood. That had to be his cue to leave. "Thank you for telling me. Don't know what will happen tomorrow, but I'll go ahead and make a promise that you can tell me anything and trust me to keep it. Tomorrow, next week, next year, or beyond."

Damon nodded. Travis wasn't certain the kid believed him. Some things had to be proven first, but if he got the chance, Travis would keep his promise.

When he went into the house, his father and brothers were seated around the kitchen table.

Before he could speak, Grant said, "Sorry. I know better. I was the kid who had a story for every occasion. Gonna have to step up my game."

Surprised and touched, Travis waved it off. "Not sure any of us are truly prepared for this. I thought I had all the questions and none of the answers. Turns out, I don't even know all the questions yet." He rubbed his forehead, exhausted but certain he'd never sleep. "Tomorrow we'll get together with the other foster parents and the foster brother he left behind and come up with a plan."

Walt shifted his stance. "Ah, he wanted to get back to family. Makes more sense. Looks like we'll either be losing a Damon or gaining a…"

"Micah. He's almost ten. Not comfortable with men." Travis watched them trade stares around the table, all obviously reaching the same conclusion he had. The Rocking A was nothing but men at this point, which didn't fit Micah at all.

"Damon's taking over the hayloft. It's his spot now, for however long he stays." Travis squeezed his father's shoulder.

"Where are you going to hide out?" Wes asked.

Travis wasn't surprised that everyone knew about his hideaway. Walt had probably told them the same night he'd told Travis it was his and warned them all to let him have his space. It was a sign of respect that they'd followed Walt's direction.

"We may have to share it now and then," Travis said.

"You want company tomorrow? I'll be happy to tag along," Grant offered.

"Or a lawyer? I can go, too." Wes shrugged. "We could be backup."

Relieved that he had them to talk to, Travis tilted his head back. "Might need you more when I get home if Damon goes back. I'd already fitted him for his own horse and tack for Western Days." When he thought of the people he wanted by his side to navigate this conversation with the social worker and the Smiths, Keena's face popped into his mind.

But that didn't make sense. This was his thing anyway. He'd be fine on his own.

Walt slipped an arm around his shoulder. "We'll be here no matter what."

TRAVIS HELD ON TO his father's promise all the way through to seating himself at the conference table in the cramped office space Ellen Montoya shared with the other social workers. He'd dressed in his best button-down. Damon was seated next to him, one leg tapping out a nervous rhythm, and a small, well-dressed couple walked in behind Ellen Montoya. As she made the introductions, Travis caught sight of Micah for the first time. He stood carefully between Ellen

Montoya and his foster mother until Damon
said, "You aren't gonna hug me? Rude."

Then the boy walked quickly around the
table, and threw his arms around Damon's
neck. The hug went longer than Damon expected because he patted Micah's back and
sent Travis a silent plea for help.

"Micah, why don't you sit there with
Damon, okay?" Ellen suggested. Instead of
moving to the next chair, Micah climbed
into Damon's seat, made him scooch over,
and crammed himself into the too-small
space. Then he turned suspicious eyes on
Travis.

Travis pretended not to feel the weight of
that stare while Ellen did a recap of the situation. The Smiths admitted they had no idea
what Micah was experiencing on the bus.

Ellen asked Damon questions about the
ranch, Travis and his family, and school.

All in all, Travis thought the Rocking A
came out pretty well in the telling.

Damon said, "Micah and I should try Prospect together. There's plenty of room. We'll
go to the same school so I can watch out for
him. Maybe until the end of the school year.

Then we can decide which home would be better for us. That's what I think."

Ellen's eyebrows shot up, but no one at the table argued with him, so the solution had merit. She asked, "Micah, what do you think about living in Prospect? Travis and his brothers run a ranch."

The way the kid looked immediately at his foster mother confirmed Travis's suspicion. The ranch wouldn't be the best place for him. Micah needed a mother.

Then Micah turned back to him. "Do you have dogs?"

His foster mother laughed. "He loves dogs. When they walk down the sidewalk in front of the house, he stops whatever he's doing to watch."

Did that mean they didn't have dogs themselves?

Because Travis would add a whole pack of dogs at the ranch if that sealed the deal. He wanted this to work out in a way he had never expected.

"I don't right now, but I have horses. What do you think about horses?" he asked.

Micah tilted his head back. "Do I like horses, Damon?"

Damon laughed. "Yeah, kid, horses are good."

Micah nodded as if that was enough confirmation for him. "I'd like to meet your horses. We should circle back around to dogs at some point."

Travis bit his lip to maintain his serious expression, but wondered who this kid was, given he was talking like a corporate manager in his midforties.

Ian Smith's brow was raised. "That's what I say every time he asks if we can get a dog. We'll circle back around when he's older."

All the adults in the room smiled and relaxed because Damon had offered them a workable solution. If they tried it and it failed, they'd come back to the table and try something else. Travis shook the Smiths' hands, relieved and so pleased to meet the couple who were as committed to these boys' happiness as he wanted all foster families to be.

Then he noticed the way Micah continued to watch him closely and wondered how long he'd have to convince the boy he could be trusted. Even if all the running away stopped, Travis had a hunch he hadn't cleared all the obstacles yet.

CHAPTER TWELVE

ON SATURDAY MORNING, Keena made a mental note that she had to schedule the phone company to provide her an internet connection as soon as possible. She'd been busy at the clinic all week, but she missed her distractions now that the weekend had rolled around again. Finding a hobby had reached the top of her to-do list.

"Or else I really will do it," she muttered as she dropped the hank of hair she'd been measuring for bangs. Whenever the urge to cut her own hair arose, Keena started to worry. That was the sign of a desperate woman. Since her choices were limited, it was an easy decision that what she needed that morning was a shopping trip. She hadn't had a good opportunity to explore Prue's craft store. If Patrick was there, he could give her some tips on an inexpensive way to explore painting. "Or even expensive if that will keep you from cutting your own hair." The first time she'd chosen impulsive bangs had been in high school. Keena still couldn't look at her yearbook pictures from her junior year.

Not long after, she parked in front of the craft store and gave herself a lecture about walking into new places and trying new things and how other people managed to do it all the time and so could she. Tourist traffic was light on the wooden sidewalks in town. This was the perfect opportunity to go into the store because she would have space to shop and ask for help. For someone who had endless questions, the concept of being a beginner and having to start at the *beginning* was stressful. Tapping her fingers in her usual rhythm slowed her heart rate and Keena realized she couldn't remember the last time she'd done that.

Had she worked all week at Prospect Family Practice without once fighting back the rush of anxiety that had become routine for every hospital shift?

KEENA WIPED HER palms on her jeans as she stepped into the building with space divided for Prue's craft shop and a hardware store.

She needed to ask Travis sometime about how this came about.

"You were going to cut your bangs to keep from thinking about Travis, Keena," she muttered to herself. "Don't make me give you another lecture." As much as she felt the flutter of nerves before walking into any new situation, she usually managed to stop talking to herself before she committed.

Keena straightened her shoulders and stepped into Handmade.

Walt Armstrong had propped his elbows on the checkout counter with the cash register while Prue was staring down into his eyes. The way they immediately moved away from each other convinced Keena she was interrupting something…important? Or…

Prue recovered first. "Keena! My favorite doctor. I was wondering if I was ever gonna get you back in my store."

Walt waited for Prue to finish before tipping his hat at Prue. "Let's continue this conversation. Over dinner. Your choice."

Prue pursed her lips. "I'll think about it, cowboy."

Keena turned to study stacks of quilt patterns for a design called the Rocky Meadow. Keena knew nothing about quilting but the blocks were different kinds of flowers with embroidery details.

"We've got a small model hanging above the stairs if you're interested in seeing that pattern worked up," Prue said as she walked past Keena. She held the door open for Walt and then offered him her cheek for a kiss. Keena knew he accepted the offer because of the loud, playful buss and the way Prue giggled and said, "Oh, you."

Keena moved across the store to the section labeled Paint and prayed for the color in her cheeks to recede quickly.

"Patrick's gone back to LA for a week or so to pack up his house and talk to a real estate agent, but I'll do my best to help if you're interested in picking up things to give painting a shot," Prue called as she pulled a chair out from the large worktable. "He put together a beginner kit if you think you might be that interested. Has acrylic paints, two small canvases, a collection of brushes... The basics to get you started. There's also a couple of books for beginners over there in the stand next to the easels." Prue crossed her arms and rested them on the table in front of her. "I expect he'll have more to choose from when he gets back."

Keena pulled out one of the books. "I never realized how much the hospital took out of me. Days off were about errands and getting reset for hospital shifts. Here? I've baked so many cookies I'm starting to dread the idea of eating cookies."

She glanced over her shoulder at Prue to make sure the other woman understood that she was making a joke.

"Dire situation you got yourself there." Prue shook her head sadly. "If only I knew of a house filled with men and two growing boys that might be able to assist with your situation."

Keena paged through the book. Even though it said beginner, she wasn't sure she had enough experience yet to attempt any of the projects. "Two boys?"

Prue nodded. "Yep, Travis took one down the mountain and brought two back. It happens that way sometimes, I guess."

Keena moved over to where Prue was sitting. She needed more details. "I asked Travis to let me know what happened. I guess he's happy with this solution? I know he was already attached to Damon, making plans for the future. Letting him go wouldn't have been easy."

Prue smiled. It wasn't exactly a "gotcha" grin but it was in that family. She was pleased Keena was asking questions about her son. "He is, but he will enjoy telling you about that. I was surprised he didn't ask you to meet with the social worker. I tell you, every single time we were introduced to a new boy who might be ours and heard parts of his story, it took me and Walt some time to absorb the details and carry all the emotion. Travis is strong, but I'm not convinced anyone can be strong enough to do all that alone."

Determined to ignore the message being shouted clearly between the lines there and stuff down the confusion about why Travis would choose her for support over his concerned parents or any of his brothers who had lived the experience from the other side, Keena waited impatiently for more hints. Was Prue not going to tell her what happened?

Then Prue pointed at Keena's purse. "You have your phone, don't you?"

Keena frowned. Of course she had her phone. She never left home without it, especially now that she was the only medical care available in town. When it started ringing, she watched Prue's grin grow wider. What was that called? She'd passed right through "Gotcha" to…gloating?

Keena plucked her phone from her bag. "Hey, Travis."

"Good morning. You answered fast. Were you expecting a call?" he asked.

"No, but your mother was. How she knew it was coming to my phone is still a mystery." She laughed reluctantly at the way Prue brushed off her shoulders as if she was just that good.

"Let me solve that one. I called to beg for her help. She said she was swamped at the store today and she couldn't get free, so I should try calling you." Travis's dry tone convinced Keena he was aware of what was happening here, too. "Are you in Handmade this morning?"

"Yeah, I thought it would save me from cutting my own hair." Keena smiled at the sharp inhale Prue made in reaction to hearing that.

Travis obviously didn't understand the threat. "So you're busy, too?"

Keena laughed. "I am so unbusy I'm about to make serious hair care mistakes. What can I help you with? I'm going over to the Majestic to see if Jordan and Sarah can put me to good use this afternoon, but I have time now if you need me."

Maybe "need me" wasn't exactly the correct choice of words, but she had no way to remove them from the conversation now. *Want me?* Was that any better? Not really.

"Your mother did mention you now have two boys to care for. I guess things worked out with Damon." Keena returned to the Paint section and studied the kit for beginners Patrick Hearst had put together. Did she have enough talent to justify spending the money on that? Not really, but at this point she had more money than she'd ever have talent, so there wasn't much stopping her. She stacked the book for beginners on top of the kit. Optimism had swept aside reason with Travis's call.

"Yeah, turns out the 'what' Damon was desperate enough to hitchhike for was a 'who' named Micah who has some trust issues when it comes to men. Nothing too intense, but he's more comfortable with women present. He's also desperate to ride a horse. I wanted my mother to come out and take Lady for a ride, but she's busy at Handmade."

Keena took a long survey of the completely empty store before landing on Prue's pleased expression as she cut fabric at the table.

"You know I don't know anything about horses, right?" Keena asked.

"I wasn't sure, but I suspected. That's okay. I'm going to ask Grant to come along, so he can help with a lesson at the same time. Micah will be more relaxed. That will make Damon happy. And it's a nice warm day in November, so we should all get outside. Not sure how many more warm sunny days there will be before winter arrives."

Keena waited for Travis to wind down his sales pitch and wondered if he was as aware of how easy their conversations were now compared to that day they'd met over the tree chopping.

"What do you say?" Travis asked.

"I'm in. Give me twenty minutes or so, and I'll meet you at the barn." He whooped with satisfaction, so Keena hung up.

"Just absolutely swamped here," Keena murmured as she carried her stack of purchases to the cash register.

Prue sniffed. "Well, now that you're here, this is turning into a good sales day."

Keena had to agree. Prue's sales had taken a big jump, thanks to her maybe-someday hobby.

"My boys accuse me of being a matchmaker, but I'd say they're all lucky. Coincidences like this one, you needing something to keep you out of haircut trouble and Trav looking for help, always work for the Armstrongs." She slipped a receipt into the cloth tote stamped with her store's name and slid it across to Keena. "Born under lucky stars every one of those boys."

Keena shook her head. "Can't argue with success."

"Well, they try. They got too much of their daddy in them not to just take the win." Prue leaned against the counter. "I do not like to interfere in my sons' business..." Prue paused to see if there was any reaction and Keena wondered if the well-meaning woman uttered that whopper of a tale often. "They're grown, after all, but I would like to give you some advice. I appreciate that you have this career that you've invested your life into. It's an important job and Denver is lucky to have you, I have no doubt. Heck, I guess the whole state might need your expertise in an emergency."

Keena gripped her new tote bag with both hands as she waited for the "but." If Prue was building a case for a match with Travis, there had to be more coming.

"And I hope you remember what's important when it comes time to make a decision about what you do next," Prue said with a smile.

Keena stood there until it was clear Prue had finished her thought, although there was nothing else behind it.

Confused, Keena asked, "Aren't you going to make the case about how well I can do that right here in Prospect? With Travis? At the Rocking A?" All signs pointed to that being the logical next part of the dialogue.

Prue shook her head. "Honestly, Travis and his boys will take care of that for me. I'm gonna look out for you."

Did she need someone on her side?

Why were there sides at all?

Prue's smile was softer, a little bittersweet. "I am warning you that love becomes something else when it's for a man and his children. I swear, men will test your patience at every turn, so often that a smart woman begins to question her own intelligence some days. It ain't easy to walk away, but when you got all these other tiny connections, the memories of when this boy ran away from home or that one broke three fingers playing like he was a bank robber in a ghost town he shoulda never been in the first place and you and your husband have to make a flying trip together to the emergency room or when a boy you loved has the opportunity to go back home to his parents and you have to settle for occasional updates to know he's okay for the rest of both your lives…" Prue sighed. "Those are ties that never come undone, and that cowboy you'd like to erase from your life comes back around and you can see in his face how well he loved those kids…and you've got yourself a real dilemma." She held up her hands. "So I'm on your side, no matter what."

Prue didn't meet her stare. Was the emotion in her honesty overwhelming her? Keena understood how that could happen, so she held up the tote. "Thank you for your suggestion and the advice, Prue."

"Oh, now, this whole visit was definitely my pleasure." Prue waved goodbye.

Keena mulled over Prue's words on the drive and realized that her caution made sense. What had Prue given up to build this family with Walt? Were the regrets what kept them apart? And if she left behind the career she'd made in Denver for a possible new life in Prospect, with Travis and his boys, what kind of regrets might she have?

It was too much for a Saturday morning, even if Keena appreciated Prue's concern.

All this heavy thinking because she refused to cut her own hair.

Keena could see Travis and Damon leaning against the fence, watching as Grant worked with a young boy in the paddock. Both had one foot propped on the lowest rail.

"Good morning," she said, "good to see you again, neighbors." She waited for Damon to face her before smiling brightly. "Beautiful day to learn to ride a horse, I'm guessing."

"There's already a forecast for snow flurries at the end of the week." Travis gave a friendly wave and Damon's face immediately brightened. Kids loving snow must be a universal thing. Even in Iowa, they'd celebrated the first few snows every season. By March, they were ready to be done. "Will it amount to much? No, but it's a signal that our time outdoors on the ranch is drawing short. Once the snow arrives in full, we'll be locked inside together, and playing hockey in your socks across the living room floor can only burn off so much energy."

That was an oddly specific example. How often had Travis and his brothers done that? Prue must have been very laid-back or on the edge of desperation to survive the winters to allow that.

What would it be like to be snowed in at the Rocking A? That was another big question to consider, but she was tired of those. She wanted activity.

Keena crossed her arms over her chest. "This is my waiting patiently pose."

Travis couldn't contain the grin. "What comes next? Or should I not ask?"

She narrowed her eyes. "You don't want to know."

He immediately surrendered. "Let's get

this lesson started." Travis waved Grant and his student closer to the fence. "Micah, this is Keena. She lives next door. I was thinking about taking her out for a horse ride. What do you think about that?"

An actual horse ride? Keena tried not to overreact. She'd intended to watch Micah and Damon have a lesson, not attempt climbing on a horse herself. Still, she'd been asked to help, so she shielded her eyes from the brilliant sun as she smiled up at Micah. "I don't know much about horses. Do you think it's a good idea?"

He nodded. "Only you might need some lessons before we go."

The kid was obviously smart, too.

"Good suggestion," Grant said as he moved toward the barn. "Let's go saddle up some horses. You can show Keena how it's done."

Grant and the boys headed off. Keena stepped closer to Travis. "You're going to saddle my horse for me, aren't you?"

He laughed and draped his arm over her shoulder. "Yes, ma'am. We've been trying to convince Grant that he ought to be offering riding lessons out here, but he's not falling for it. I'm hoping working with you might change his mind, but he's not off to the best start, picking the kids over the beautiful woman."

Keena raised her eyebrows. "Wow, you're different today. Must be having some of the weight off your mind?" The first time they'd met, he'd been awkward enough to be charming and set her own social anxiety at ease. Today he was flirting?

"Could be. I'm also glad to see you. I'm excited to show off the ranch." Travis paused midstep. "I'm happy." He frowned as if the word tasted funny in his mouth.

Keena laughed. "Don't celebrate too soon. This ride can still go awry. I'm whatever stage of rider comes before beginner." She bit her bottom lip as if she was admitting a horrible secret. "I don't want you to judge me harshly."

Travis took her hand in his and smoothed out the fist. "If you'll agree to give it a shot, I'll tell you a story so that you will understand why I would never judge your horse riding ability."

She huffed. "But only if I agree to go with you all over to the Majestic. What is that, twenty miles?"

He blinked. "More like three or four miles. This is not a weeklong trek. We'll saddle my mother's horse, Lady. She is the easiest ride we have. All you'll have to do is keep your feet in the stirrups and your…self in the saddle. Lady and I can do the rest."

"My…self in the saddle, you say?" Keena's lips twitched in amusement. "They have trail ride companies who take city slickers up on the mountains for rides like this. If they can do it, I can, too. Right?" Some reassurance would be nice.

Travis nodded. "There are kindergartners who manage to do more than stay in the saddle during the parade for Western Days. That was one of the things I got excited about with Damon and Micah. They're going to love it."

"Kindergartners?" She straightened her shoulders. "Surely I can keep up with them. You sold me with the comment about the snow. I've been in Prospect long enough to know that Sharita's house is comfortable, but the cabin fever will be intense when I'm shut up inside it for days at a time. I want to hear about playing hockey in the living room, too." Keena pointed at the jacket she was wearing. "How does Lady feel about hot pink?"

"She's pretty stylish. My mother wouldn't have it any other way. I bet she'll love that color for you," Travis answered, his lips curved in amusement.

Keena watched as Travis saddled up two horses, both beautiful and extremely large. He was going to ride Arrow, Wes's horse, while she was going to cling to the saddle of Lady, and theoretically, this was going to be a lovely afternoon excursion. Damon had been learning to saddle and ride Travis's horse, Sonny, and to Keena's inexperienced eye, he seemed comfortable as he waited for everyone else.

"Micah, you want to ride with Grant or me?" Travis asked as he paused in front of the smaller boy. "Your choice. Next time, we'll put you up on your own mount if you feel up to it."

Keena held Lady's reins and tried to send her horse friendly brain waves, while they waited for Micah to make his decision.

"Come on, squirt. You can ride with me, the rodeo star, or with that guy." Grant held his hands out as if he was displaying his charms better. "It shouldn't be this difficult.

Only one of us will never tell you to eat your vegetables or go to bed before you're ready."

Travis huffed out a breath when Micah pointed at Grant's horse, Bandit. Grant picked the boy up and dumped him like a sack of potatoes in the saddle, and Micah laughed with his whole body. Grant swung up behind him, tipped his hat at Keena with a roguish grin, and walked the horse out into the sunlight.

"I would have handled him like spun glass. Grant tosses him like a football," Travis muttered under his breath. "I should take a page out of his book."

"Are you familiar with the term 'fun uncle'?" Keena asked while she watched him check the saddles. "I have a step-brother, single, no kids, who likes to give out hundred-dollar bills to all the kids in the family every Christmas. He's not going to teach them right from wrong, necessarily, and they love him for it. I think we know which one of your brothers is the fun uncle."

Travis considered that. "They haven't even met Matt yet. These kids are going to have choices to make if there can only be one fun uncle."

Keena realized that the closer she got to

physically climbing onto the horse, the more her nerves fired up. The longer she stood there, watching him do things she didn't know how to do, inhaling unfamiliar odors of the barn, and picturing in her head how awkward she was going to look attempting this for the first time, the faster her heart pounded. Breathing became something she had to concentrate on. And the funny little comments Travis threw out now and then had stopped blocking the alarms in her head. Eventually, Keena leaned against one of the stalls and started working through the exercises that pushed away the panic.

She counted each inhale, held it for five beats, and exhaled slowly until her lungs were crying out for air. She tapped each finger against her thumb and did her best to clear her brain of any images depicting her embarrassing fall from a saddle.

"You okay?" Travis asked, his voice a low rumble next to her ear.

As if he'd been patiently waiting for her to grab control of her runaway brain.

"Sorry. I'd almost gotten used to not having this panic take over here in Prospect." She flexed her fingers. "Glad to know it's still with me, like a ratty old blanket I've been dragging behind me."

He bumped her shoulder this time. "You don't have to ride, you know. This is completely optional. No reason to put yourself through it if you don't want to. Micah seems to be overcoming his own fears quickly."

"I want to try this." She licked her lips. "If you'd asked me a month ago if I ever dreamed of going horseback riding, my answer would have been a dumbfounded no. But even as I know I'm going to be terrible at this and I, as a hard-and-fast rule, do not do things I am terrible at, I still followed you into this barn." She glanced over at Lady who was definitely judging her, even if Travis wasn't. "She's beautiful. I understand why your mother loves her so much."

"Yes, Lady's the daughter she never had until Sarah Hearst popped up next door."

Keena raised her eyebrows.

"Daughter-in-law? In my family, they're blood relatives. We haven't had one yet, but I'm certain of it." Travis shifted his hat back. "Why don't you head on inside? I'll unsaddle the horses and we'll go with four wheels instead of legs."

"Eight." Keena pointed as he tilted his head to consider that. "Eight legs. Two horses. If my math is correct, that's eight legs."

"Good to know you can still do multiplication, Doc." Travis stood slowly.

"Wait." Keena wrapped her hand around his arm. "I want to try, but this is definitely one of the stories that go with us to the grave. You don't tell anyone whatever Lady says to you behind my back when this is all over."

His slow grin eased some of the anxiety. "I swear. Nobody will hear about it from me." Then he grasped her hand. "I'm going to take you over to the mounting block. That will make the whole thing easier."

Keena's mouth was suddenly dry so she nodded her agreement. When they were back out in the sunshine and Lady was calmly waiting, Keena stepped up and slid lightly into the saddle. Travis murmured softly to Lady as he adjusted the length of the stirrups and made sure the saddle was secure. Keena couldn't understand what he was saying to the horse, but his tone had a positive effect on her nerves, too. She realized she was breathing better. The pounding of her heart in her ears had receded.

As long as Travis was close by, she knew everything would be okay.

She watched him put a foot in the stirrup and swing up in the saddle and immediately knew she would never be able to do that. Her horse riding life would depend on having a tall something to climb up and step off of.

Before she could ask a million questions about their plans at the Majestic and the setup or proximity of a nice step stool, Travis took the reins she'd been holding on to for dear life and forced her cramping fingers to loosen. Keena relaxed a fraction when she saw that Grant plus Micah, and Damon had already moved out into the pasture. She didn't have an audience for this first attempt at being on a horse.

"We're going in a slow circle here in the paddock to get a feel for Lady's gait and to make sure the saddle feels right," he said in a low voice. "I've got the reins. You concentrate on the saddle part."

"And staying upright in it," Keena muttered as she clutched the saddle horn so hard her fingers turned white.

Travis hummed an agreement and he kept up the steady stream of encouragement to the horses, an indistinct murmur that Keena could feel more than hear. Eventually her spine relaxed a fraction and she could settle into the rock of Lady's gait.

"Okay, what do you think?" Travis asked.

Keena forced her eyelids open. She hadn't even realized she'd squeezed them shut, but the whole experience improved with sunshine, open space, Lady's placid brown eyes blinking back at her, and Travis's amusement. "Part of the challenge of horseback riding is that you have to keep your eyes open. The horse can see, but she doesn't know where you want to go, so you have to give directions."

Keena let go of the saddle and shook her hands to send blood back into her fingertips as she smiled. "Fine. I'll try it your way. Let's see if we can go in a line. Lady's tired of walking in circles."

"Sure. First, tell Lady she's doing a good job. Run your hand down her neck, give her some scratches if she wants them."

Keena froze, midreach. "How will I know if she doesn't want them?"

"You will know. She'll shake her head or most likely give you a death stare. Lady might be mostly human at this point. She and my mother have been together for years." Travis pointed with his chin. "Try it and see."

Nervous, Keena did as he directed, running her hand down Lady's neck, surprised and charmed at how warm and soft the horse was. Lady tipped her head to the side in a broad clue on where to scratch, so Keena followed her and was rewarded when the horse huffed a happy breath.

How Keena could tell the difference between a happy horse and a mad horse at this point, she wasn't sure, but something in her gut told her she and Lady were building a connection.

"Okay, let's work with the reins. Hold these loosely but don't drop them. Lady will follow Sonny, so you aren't going to need to give her much prompting." Travis urged Sonny a few steps forward. "Squeeze lightly with your legs to tell her to move forward. Since you're both learning here, you can also say 'go.'" Travis held up a hand. "And for stop? You pull lightly on the reins. Never tug. Never yank. That will hurt the horse and my mother will kill us both without waiting for a trial or a judge to render us guilty. Light pressure and say 'Whoa, Lady.' That's all it will take. Try both."

Keena wanted to call it quits again, but Travis was watching her proudly.

Even Lady seemed to be urging her on, so she followed his instructions. Her shout of terror and elation, all tangled together, instantly died in her throat as the image of a startled Lady rearing and dumping her in the dirt flashed in her brain. Keena held her breath as Lady moved in the same lazy circle they'd been working on in the paddock and stopped immediately at Keena's signal.

"Why do I know in my heart it won't always be that easy?" Keena said under her breath.

"Could be because you've got the heart of a cowgirl and you know animals have their own minds," Travis answered. "Either way, I think you're ready to give the open pasture a try. Do you?"

Keena wasn't convinced she was ready, but his steady regard made her want to give it a shot. "Lady's ready, for sure. I'll hold on." When she realized her jaw was aching from gritting her teeth, Keena took a deep breath. "This is so much fun."

His low laugh improved her mood a fraction. "Give it a chance. Follow me."

More than anything, Keena wanted to do this well, and by the time they made it to the fence that separated the Rocking A from the Majestic Prospect Lodge property, she had managed to yank her stare from her white-knuckled grip on the loose reins to how the land rolled gently before rising sharply into the mountains.

"Travis, I understand your homesickness. This place is gorgeous." She could see in the distance how the shadows changed on the mountainside as clouds interrupted the sunshine and then moved away. The dying grass was dull now, but in the springtime, she could imagine a rich green. And the autumn colors would be so intense that a person might never forget them. When she realized that was a season she wouldn't see in Prospect, Keena felt a pinch of regret.

"Larkspur Pass." Travis nodded to the valley between the mountains. There was a faint trail worn that disappeared over the edge. Grant and Damon had reached the gate between the ranch and the lodge next door. "We moved the cattle we graze up there down closer for the winter. Once the snow comes, it's a tough ride." He shrugged. "If we get a chance, we'll go for another ride before that happens. You need to see how pretty it is then, too."

Keena nodded enthusiastically, grateful that her less-than-natural ability to ride Lady hadn't convinced him she never needed to slip into the saddle again.

After a few hundred trips, she might be able to do this without any trouble.

Keena followed Travis through the gate Grant had left open.

"We bought this part from the Hearsts, used to belong to Sadie." Travis and Sonny closed the gate behind them. "Normally, we'd leave this open, but I don't have the energy to chase down one rogue Chuck that would pick my first ride with a pretty lady to make a fool of me."

"Are you calling them all Chuck now? My Chuck isn't special?"

He pointed toward the lodge on the hill. It faded so well into the surroundings that she might not have seen it without hunting for it. "I like the name."

"I guess they aren't pets," Keena said as she followed behind him. Lady was quite content with their speed and distance so far. Keena couldn't imagine a better partner for her maiden ride.

"No, not pets, although Chuck the first has been over at Faye's for long enough to meet the pet criteria. Since her grandparents have slowed down, she's got her hands full with the restaurant and the farm. She doesn't have a lot of time for buying and selling livestock right now."

"She was telling me about the food truck nights that Lucky arranges like they're such a relief to her. But I wondered if she ever got a break. She ran out of the Ace High for the Sip and Paint like she expected the dinner crowd to stop her."

"She works too hard, but it's next to impossible to convince someone who loves what they're doing that they deserve time to do other things, too." Travis led the way up a faded trail. "Letting go of the small farm they have would be a big help, but it also might break her grandfather's heart, so she's stuck doing what she can."

Keena watched him sway easily in the saddle as she considered his words.

Maybe it should have been harder for her to walk away from the hospital, even for a temporary reprieve.

She'd understood immediately the way Faye spoke about the restaurant. She was proud of it, enjoyed what she was doing, and at the same time it was sucking every bit of life out of her. At that point, anyone would be desperate for a break.

Even a doctor who had built the emergency department she dreamed of and couldn't imagine herself anywhere else.

Those people, like Faye and Keena, who loved what they did but sacrificed so much to do it, might gamble on something new, just to have a chance to breathe again.

Keena wondered what Prue might say to that. In Handmade, she'd considered what Prue had given up to make the Armstrong family work. What if life on the Rocking A, where winter might mean so much snow that five growing boys played hockey in the living room when they weren't struggling to keep livestock fed and watered, had been her emergency department? Had this divorce been Prue's way to get breathing room, some space for herself?

If so, that made Prue's promise that she was watching out for Keena sweeter and so much easier to understand.

"I'd love to meet Faye's Gram. The food she sends out at the restaurant is amazing."

"She's...intense." Travis wrinkled his nose. "Has a firm opinion on everything related to the Ace and keeps Faye running. Prospect could easily support another restaurant which would lighten some of Faye's load. I'm hoping that when the lodge reopens, they'll follow up with redoing the restaurant, too. This place used to be for special occasions, the date-night destination for Prospect and other little towns around. When Sadie shut it, it was a big blow."

"Whoa, Lady," Keena said and did a mental high five for herself when Lady smoothly halted next to Sonny. They were in front of the lodge, a large open space that was...rustic. That was the kindest adjective Keena could come up with. A bridge from the parking lot crossed over a stream that flowed into the lake, and on the other side was the lodge. The lodge's siding was dull and graying, but it was clear someone had been doing improvements.

"Is that a new roof?" she asked.

He was surprised as he turned to her. "Good eye. It's a repaired roof. There was an episode with bats. In the attic. They had to be remediated immediately, so while the crew was working on that and the improvements needed to keep any bats from returning home, they got the roof fixed. Jordan and Sarah are pushing hard to get the place reopened in time for the spring Western Days weekend." Travis slid out of the saddle and looped Sonny's reins over a low branch there at the edge of the parking lot. A few hardy sprigs of grass survived in the sunshine around it. Travis did the same with Lady's reins. "After the first of the year, if you see my mother headed in your direction, turn and go the other way. Right now, the push for Western Days volunteers is low-key, but she will turn up the heat once the preparations get serious. She's determined to make this anniversary weekend bigger and better than ever." He moved to stand next to her. "How are the legs?"

Keena wrinkled her nose. "I forgot I had legs somewhere around the gate. I can't feel them."

He whistled. "You will." He offered her his hand. "Good news is, that gets better the more often you try this. The bad news is, they are going to remind you of this ride for days."

Keena sighed. "I figured. Lucky for me I know a good doctor who can tell me how to cope."

"Yeah?" Travis said as she slipped her hand in his and tried to swing her leg down. It was so much harder than it should have been. "What will the prescription be?" he asked.

"Water. Ibuprofen. Lots of both. That's a start on a lot of the things that I treat." Keena held on to the saddle tightly, afraid to trust her legs, until he touched her hips and guided her to the ground.

When both feet were planted, Travis said, "You let me know when I can let go." She nodded and took a step, relieved that her legs responded as requested. Maybe she would be sorry when she woke up tomorrow, but she wasn't going to make a fool out of herself now.

Not yet, anyway. Keena refused to worry about how she was going to make it back into the saddle when their visit was over.

Instead of warning him that he might need to get a strong team to help hoist her back into the saddle, Keena turned as the door to the lodge opened and Jordan stepped out. "Keena! Travis! I'm so glad you're here. Doc, you are so brave."

Keena blinked and looked to Travis for more information. "Jordan doesn't like horses."

Jordan shivered as if she'd felt someone walk across her grave. Keena laughed. "I'm not sure horses like me, but after today, I feel better about them."

Travis's smile felt like something only the two of them understood and shared.

And that was nice.

"Let me show you the lodge." Jordan clasped Keena's arm tightly and pulled it through hers, the woman a force of nature towing her along. Inside the lobby, Keena understood why Jordan was excited to show the place off. On the outside, the lodge showed some wear and tear, but inside, the beautiful wood floors were lit with golden sunshine streaming through large windows. There was a bright rag rug in yellow and orange and a few pieces of charming rustic furniture that seemed to fit the place perfectly.

"You've been doing some hard work here," Travis said. He propped his hands on his hips as he did a slow circle. "It's nice to see the painting hanging where it belongs."

He had to mean the large landscape positioned over the check-in desk that lined one long wall. It was of the mountains, snow covering the tops, and lots of lush evergreens. It was striking and seemed as if it had been made to hang there.

"My dad. He painted that for Sadie." Jordan smiled. "You see why he despairs any time Sarah and I pick up a paintbrush."

Keena laughed and followed as Jordan urged her down the hallway to show off more of the hard work they'd been doing. Most of the guest rooms were empty except for bed frames and mattresses, but they were spotless. She listened to the plan for a "soft launch" to give the sisters a little practical experience running a lodge, since none of them had ever done so. Jordan explained how Sadie had grown up here before her career and her family took her to LA.

It was a sweet tour of a place that was going to be fantastic someday, because the Hearst sisters were determined, and it was clear that they loved the Majestic and Sadie Hearst a lot.

Along the way, Keena was aware of two things.

At all times, she knew where Travis was. If he was trailing behind them or he'd stepped away to study something more closely, Keena was aware of it without watching it happen.

And there was the faintest scent of vanilla that wafted along with them.

"Have you already fired up the oven?" Keena asked as Jordan and Sarah led her back through the lobby to the restaurant. "Something smells good."

The glance the sisters exchanged immediately caught Keena's attention.

"Oh, yeah? What do you smell?" Jordan asked.

Travis sniffed the air. "Sweet. Are you baking cookies? A cake?"

Sarah's smile was kind as she hugged Keena's arm closer. "Vanilla. I can't smell it right now, but is that it?"

Keena nodded. She'd been baking enough cookies since she'd gotten to town that she knew Sarah had nailed it.

Jordan wrinkled her nose. "We have a small ghost story to tell you. Not a scary one. It's a friendly ghost and seems to be living in our kitchen."

"It pops up now and then, almost like Sadie would if she were here, so we aren't too bothered by it," Sarah added. "It doesn't surprise me a bit she'd want to welcome you to the Majestic herself."

Keena turned her head to catch Travis's eye. He shrugged as if to say he had no response. They were going to have to go along with the ghost story.

"Well, I've been watching all of Sadie's old shows since I got to town. I'm happy to have the chance to tell her I'm a big fan." Keena would examine later whether she believed in ghosts or not, but it was hard to deny that the smell of vanilla intensified after her statement and stuck with her while she was in the Majestic.

CHAPTER THIRTEEN

TRAVIS RESTED ONE shoulder against the door-frame as he watched Grant, Damon and Micah work as an efficient team to sand the floor of one of the lodge's guest rooms. Damon was guiding the floor sander while Micah vacuumed up dust along the sanded edge. Grant was hands-on, offering advice and correcting techniques when needed. His brother saw him and said, "Wouldn't have guessed learning how to use one of these things on the living room floor of the Rocking A would be put to use again so soon."

"Are you using the experience, or are they?" Travis drawled.

Grant pursed his lips. "I am a teacher. You told me that. I taught them how to saddle their horses and ride, giving you and your doctor some privacy. Now I am passing along another valuable skill here. Are you making good use of the time I've bought you is the real question. It's hard to court after the kids come along, dontcha know?"

Travis nodded. He could understand how that might be true. "I'm glad you put them in safety equipment." He pointed at Damon's and Micah's eye and ear protection.

Grant nodded. "Soon as we finish this room, I think we ought to call it a day. The horses have been tethered outside awhile. They've got water and sunshine, but Lady will be ready to get back to her comfy stall."

Travis had headed in this direction to suggest they start wrapping up. He hated to leave because it was clear everyone was bonding over their work. Damon and Micah exchanged a high five. The younger boy had pointed out something on the floor and Damon moved to hit it with the sander.

"I'll have to drag Keena down from the ladder. She's painting the restaurant wall that has all the windows." Travis wasn't going to add that she'd made such painstaking progress that it would take her three full days at the rate she was going.

"I bet she's a perfectionist, isn't she?" Grant asked. "I'll help Keena paint if you want to take the kids back to the ranch." His tone clearly said, "If I have to," and Travis knew that Grant was poking and prodding him to admit he wanted to spend more time with Keena.

"Or Wes and I could take the horses and you can bring my car over," Sarah said from behind them. "Jordan is pushing my buttons with all her orders. If I don't take a break, I will make a break…possibly all the way back to California."

Grant held his hands up. "Easy, Sarah. No need for more folks to start running away. Travis is such a gentleman that he will be happy to meet your terms. You and Wes take their horses home, and then we'll all invade the Rocking A kitchen to find something to feed these hungry boys. How does that sound?"

Sarah said, "Why do I get the feeling that you won't be the one doing the cooking?"

Grant pretended shock. "Now that you mention it, it's Wes's turn and he mentioned a pot of chili, I think." Then he blinked innocently.

"What do you want to do, Trav?" Wes asked as he joined the group. "We'll be happy to watch the boys, including this troublemaker, if you want to take Keena to town for dinner or…" He shrugged. "Yeah, that's about all I've got to offer. I'm not exactly known for my romantic sensibility."

Sarah squeezed the hand he'd extended to her. "If you'd find a place to hang up a porch swing around here, we'd have plenty of places for…romance."

Grant and Travis exchanged smirks while Wes cleared his throat. "We'll be riding off with the kids. You figure out your own romantic moves, brother."

Grant went to fetch Damon and Micah and when he explained it was dinnertime, both boys perked up. Travis realized he was going to have to pay more attention to when it was time to eat. They weren't ready to make demands yet, so he needed to watch these things closely.

"You guys okay to go back with Grant and Wes? Keena's in the middle of a project. When she finishes, I'll bring her over to the house."

Micah nodded. "Can we ride by the lake? I didn't get to see it."

Travis noticed he'd asked Grant instead of him. That wasn't a problem.

"It's cold and the sun's setting. Let's save that for our next ride, okay? We'll get back and let Uncle Wes feed us. Then I want to show you the wonders of my collection of video games." Grant's smile showed he knew he had both boys.

Damon watched Micah trot down the hallway behind Grant, Wes and Sarah. "I can stay behind with you. I like doing this. I like helping."

Travis took a chance and squeezed his shoulder. Instead of shifting away, Damon watched him curiously. Then he smiled and Travis felt it direct in the center of his chest. The emotion of that tentative smile, the first one, left a mark. He wasn't sure he'd ever recover.

"There's so much to be done here, we'll drive back over tomorrow. I know Jordan will be happy to have your help. How's that?" Travis asked, proud and excited at how the single afternoon had shifted things between these boys and his family.

"All right. It's a deal." Damon followed the group toward the lobby.

Travis called out, "Hey, Damon, will you watch out for Micah? Grant will keep him safe but he's a horrible influence." Damon's lopsided grin wasn't a big reaction but it was new and Travis felt stronger because of it.

Keena was still at the top of the ladder, still holding her tiny paintbrush because it was "better for cutting in" though it would take years to finish the job, and waving at Damon and Micah as they said their good-byes. Jordan hit them both with high fives and clapped when Damon told her he wanted to return to help with the sanding.

Sarah ushered Damon out the door ahead of her before Jordan could promote him to operations manager, while Travis wandered back over to Keena. She immediately glanced down at him. "Thank you for saving me. I wasn't sure I had it in me to climb back in the saddle for the ride home. I was trying to decide if walking all the way might be easier."

"Is that why you're channeling Michelangelo with the interior latex paint? You were avoiding the ride home for as long as possible?" Travis pointed to the lobby. "They probably have a bed here you can use if you want to stay the night."

"Nope, I want my comfy couch, thank

you." Keena handed him the tiny brush. "I took my assignment seriously. That's all. I finished cutting in. Tomorrow I'll work on the rest." Then she moved slowly down the ladder.

"Muscles stiffening up?" Jordan asked as she plopped the top back on the can of paint. "I wasn't sure you were even moving there for a minute. Were you actually waiting for the paint to dry between each brushstroke? Interesting technique."

Keena narrowed her eyes at Jordan. "Are you saying I'm a slow painter?" She cupped her hand to her ear. "Surely you aren't complaining about free labor." Travis loved watching her tease Jordan. It was as if they'd been friends forever or at least long enough to give each other a hard time now and then.

He liked how Jordan and Sarah and now Keena had become parts of Prospect and the Armstrong family.

Jordan held up a finger. "Excellent point. Free labor is my favorite kind of labor. I am so impressed with your attention to detail and appreciate you being here. How is that?"

Keena turned to him. "Reading between

the lines, I'm still getting that I'm not good at painting walls, either."

"Or you're entirely too good," he murmured and brushed a drop of paint off her forehead.

Her sweet smile matched the glow that lit in his chest as they stood there.

"Gross," Jordan groaned. "If it's not Wes and Sarah, it's you two." Her awful grimace suggested she was about to revolt.

"When is Clay coming home from Colorado Springs?" Travis asked.

"Sometime this week," she responded sadly. "Then I can make my own lovey-dovey faces."

"I have Sarah's keys. Want to go for a joy-ride through Prospect?" Travis jingled the key ring at her.

Jordan snorted. "Nah, my baby sister, Brooke, wrecked her car once when we were teenagers, and Sarah's revenge was cold. Brooke did all the laundry for five years after that."

"You okay here on your own?" The sun was setting quickly now that the days were short. Travis knew Clay had his concerns about Jordan staying at the lodge alone, but he'd heard enough of the debate to understand Jordan was confident in taking care of herself.

Also, there was a ghost on duty.

"Yes, I'm going to throw a frozen pizza in the oven and watch trash TV. Sarah hates all the reality dating shows. Want to join me?" Jordan's sly grin was proof she knew the answer was no even as she asked the question.

Keena sighed. "TV. That reminds me to call the phone company on Monday. I need to stream something besides the Colorado Cookie Queen. I do love internet cat videos."

They were all laughing as Travis and Keena left the lobby. He noticed she'd braced her hands on her low back as if the muscles there hurt.

"Regrets over the horse ride?" Travis asked as he stopped her.

She shook her head immediately. "None. I want to do it again…whenever my legs have forgiven me for this lesson." Her bright grin reassured him that she meant every word. "You aren't going to believe this, but I don't like to do things I'm not great at. Trying this…it was a huge step. I also expected to be good at painting walls. Imagine my surprise to hear that I am not."

Travis chuckled. "You might not know this, Doc, but you aren't alone. There are people all over the world who'd prefer to be good at everything right out of the gate."

Keena rolled her eyes. "That's not really what I meant."

Travis flexed his fingers. "I understand. I do. Is it okay if I rub the muscles in your shoulders? Might help." It would help.

She hesitated but eventually swept her hair over her shoulder. When he pressed his hands carefully on her shoulders, his thumbs working against knotted muscles, her head dropped forward and she moaned.

"I promised to tell you why I wouldn't judge you." Travis concentrated on the tender spots at the nape of her neck, glad she was turned away. Telling stories he wasn't particularly proud of was so much easier when he could do it without eyes on him. "After arriving at the Rocking A, I hid away because I was so terrible when it came to the horses. Just couldn't stand it with Wes and Clay being comfortable and Grant riding as if he'd been born in a saddle from day one. Then there was me. I hung on for dear life, and I had trouble sleeping at night because

I knew Walt was going to need our help the next day. It's hard to settle in when you're aware you don't fit."

Keena tilted her head to the side, a silent clue on where the pain was centered. He smiled as he shifted to work on the tension there.

"You figured it out, though. Now you have something else to teach your sons, and you'll be able to do it with the understanding that not everyone gets it the first or second time, but you don't give up."

He was silent as he considered her words. There was something about Keena that led her to exactly what he needed to hear when he needed to hear it the most. "I guess so. That's a nice way to look at being absolutely terrified of horses. So much so that sleeping in the scary darkness seemed like a good way to handle it."

Keena grasped his hand as she turned to face him. "It's the only way to look at it. Maybe you didn't fit in at first, but of all the Armstrong sons, you're the one doing the big work now, opening the ranch up to fosters again. You picked up on a character trait of

Walt and Prue that makes them rare in this world."

He studied her face. "I don't know how you do what you do. You must be an amazing doctor. Patients must come just to pour out their troubles."

Keena squeezed her eyes shut. "Funny you should mention that. I'm good with the technique, but I never trusted my bedside manner. Turns out, that will get you pretty far in the emergency room, where you patch together patients and then send them on to others who heal them, but in Prospect?" She sighed. "Dr. Singh leaves enormous shoes to fill, you know? He was always the only doctor I could talk to as a resident. You've seen it, too. That's been my worst worry, that I'll connect with patients as well as I ride a horse."

Her mouth dropped open, as if she was inviting him to laugh along with her.

He shook his head. It wasn't funny because it wasn't really a joke. He understood admitting his fears and pretending it wasn't all that serious to keep others from comforting him, or worse, reassuring him, which only made him feel less capable in the end.

"Thing is, as long as you can overcome the fear, you can practice and get better." He tilted his head back. "I'm strictly speaking about riding here, you know. I am not a doctor so…"

He waited for her to meet his stare. "Right. Only a cowboy, not a doctor…even if that advice sounds more like something Dr. Singh would say to encourage me." She smiled. "Thank you. I was worried how I'd do without him. I'll come back to you when I need pep talks."

He nodded. "I like this arrangement. For you, I've got encouragement."

"And I believe you're going to be an amazing foster parent, even without a make-believe girlfriend waiting in the wings to lend a hand." Keena blinked innocently up at him.

"I guess, although I would put you and me against all odds, no matter how hard the job was."

Her eyebrows shot up in surprise.

He knew the feeling. "I didn't mean to say that out loud."

And it was clear she didn't have a clear response. "I like you, Travis…"

"But not like that." He'd heard that more than once, so the sting didn't register anymore. "I get that."

"No, I like you like that, too." Keena laughed. "Any woman who watched the way you chopped wood, the muscles in your back and arms rippling like waves…" Her words trailed off. Travis waited.

"Where'd you go?" he asked when he was convinced she wanted to stay exactly where she was in her mind.

"You're very good-looking. You know that." She said it so matter-of-factly that Travis wanted to believe her. "A man who is reshaping his comfortable world to help kids who need a safe place. That's hero stuff, Travis. You should have a line of the best women waiting for a turn to be your real-life girlfriend. The fact that you don't see it makes you that much sweeter."

Grant had said something similar, calling him the hero in their lineup, but he hadn't spent much time considering it.

Keena's opinion shifted something inside of him.

She wasn't family.

Keena hadn't watched him grow and change and mature in Prospect, either.

With her, he was only a man.

A good man.

Keena Murphy had the power to take a look at the wounds he hid from almost everyone else and say the words he needed to begin the healing. How did he convince her to spend more time with him?

"I have a babysitter tonight. Didn't even know I was going to need one, but I'm glad the fun uncle showed up right on time." Travis ran his hands down Keena's arms. "Would you be interested in exploring Prospect's nightlife with me?"

She frowned. "Are we back to joyriding in Sarah's SUV? I don't enjoy doing my own laundry, much less someone else's."

"Maybe after. I was thinking first you might like to eat junk for dinner and watch whatever old Western is playing at the Prospect Picture Show." Travis shook his head when her eyes lit up. "Let me make something very clear before you say yes. If we go, we might be the only ones in the theater watching the movie. The rest of the audience will be watching us, and the story of

our outing will sweep through the town like
the wildfire that destroyed Sullivan's Post
the first time. It was fast, if you don't know
how that went."

Keena bit her lip as she weighed the pros
and cons. "I want to see the movie. Will you
kiss me during the show?"

His mouth dropped open and she shrugged.
"If we're to be the story going around on
Monday, we should at least make it good."

Travis opened the door to the SUV and
waited for Keena to slide in. He wasn't sure
why his whole life had suddenly turned into
a romantic comedy but he was excited to see
where it would lead next.

CHAPTER FOURTEEN

ON THURSDAY AFTERNOON, Keena was resting against the main counter at Prospect Family Practice, blearily staring at the computer screen in front of her.

She was entering notes about the fourteenth student from Prospect Middle School who had come down with the flu. None of the cases were critical, but it was a lot of miserably sick kids to see and absorb over the period of four days.

As always happened, adults were also trickling in with flu-like symptoms, and most of them handled it with a lot less grace than the students did. She and Kim had worked out a steady routine to diagnose each and prescribe antiviral medication if they were within the effective window.

Keena was glad that folks in Dr. Singh's office knew their jobs as well as they did. It was easy enough to figure out her part of the process. After work each evening, she'd been spending time with Sarah and Jordan as they focused on improving the lodge's restaurant, so she was busy. She liked busy. Her worries about how she'd spend her time in Prospect seemed silly now, but after a long week, she needed a boost of energy stat.

A water bottle suddenly blocked her view of the screen and it took Keena longer than she liked to realize what had happened.

After she opened the bottle and drained half the contents, she smiled at Reg. He was shaking his head in disapproval. "We can't have the doctor getting dehydrated or sick, Dr. M. You realize how much trouble we'd all be in then?"

She nodded her agreement.

"I get it. I used to do this every night, where I got so overwhelmed with work that little things like food and water got lost in the shuffle." Keena realized how much better she'd been feeling now that days like this were by far the exception instead of the rule. "Thank you for watching out for me."

Reginald sniffed to make sure she understood she was pressing her luck. He pointed at her. "Always will. The difference between those nights and these days? You're all we've got. This is definitely a situation where, if the airplane is losing cabin pressure, you put your own oxygen mask on first before assisting others." His stern expression convinced Keena that he was a successful flag football coach, too. Keena didn't want to disappoint Reginald.

Emily hung up the phone. "That was the school. The principal thinks we've made it through the worst. They didn't have any new absences today." She picked up her notepad where she'd checked off a note on her to-do list. "And the pharmacy supply of the meds is holding up. The pharmacist placed a special order after you asked me to let him know about the first case we had on Monday. That was good thinking, Dr. M."

Keena exhaled slowly. The praise meant more to her than it should have, but when she'd seen the first flu case walk in, she'd been afraid of how bad it could get in the close confines of the Prospect schools. During heavy years, her entire emergency waiting room would fill with people, some of whom had reached the critical stage before they forced themselves to get medical attention. Getting overwhelmed at the hospital was one thing. The resources they'd need to call in for assistance—more staff, more meds—were close at hand. Here? Reginald was correct. Looking out for herself and her team was the smartest thing she could do to take care of the rest of the town.

They all needed a boost at this point.

"I wish I had a cookie," Reginald muttered under his breath.

Keena nodded. "Yeah, I was thinking the same thing."

"I'll run over to the Ace for pie. We all need a slice," Kim said and hurried out the door before Keena could stop her.

When Kim walked back in with an entire pie held in victory over her head, Keena said, "I wasn't hinting that we needed pie!" And if she had been, she certainly would have walked over to pick it up and pay for it. She was the leader here, after all.

Sort of. In name only?

"Faye sent it over, no charge. She's been hearing all week long about the sick kids so she knew it was important to the health of this town that we get a sugar boost." Kim cut the pieces and handed them out while Reginald poured coffee. The first bite of apple pie hit like it should have been accompanied by an angelic choir. Keena's energy rose, her eyesight cleared up, and she was almost certain she could make it through the rest of the day.

Kim laughed. "Sometimes the doctor needs someone else writing the prescription."

Keena nodded. "I've been searching Sadie's cookbooks for this recipe. I didn't understand it was the same thing as finding hidden treasure. I need to take off the rest of the afternoon because I must find the gold."

Emily tipped her head to the side. "Nope. Not this afternoon, Dr. M. We've got a well-baby checkup and then two patients who need physicals for insurance purposes."

"Good thing you got this pie, then," Keena said with her mouth full.

They laughed at her garbled words and Keena realized everything about that moment was right. She had been successful running Dr. Singh's practice. His staff liked her enough to volunteer to go on emergency pie runs. And she still had plans for a life after work and on the weekend and in the future.

If Dr. Singh could see her now, he would be celebrating, no doubt. She should send him a message.

"I was thinking of sending Dr. Singh an email today," Reginald said causally. "Anybody have any updates they want to include? Tidbits of town news?"

He didn't glance at Keena but she was almost certain the words were aimed at her. Instead of answering, she sipped her coffee and waited.

Kim wrinkled her nose. "I'm sure he's missing the gossip, Reg. I heard the most interesting story."

Keena braced her elbow nonchalantly on the corner of the desk. She loved gossip but she wasn't sure she should let them know that, so pretending to be a bystander was the way to go.

"Oh," Reg said as he spun in his chair. "I wonder if it's the same story I heard. Did it happen at the Picture Show this weekend?"

Keena closed her eyes because now she understood what was coming next. Travis had warned her, but the flu epidemic in the schools had delayed the story's spread. It had taken a couple of extra days to make it around to Keena. Watching a movie at the Prospect Picture Show while she and Travis had split an enormous tub of popcorn and a family-size box of M&M's was more fun than she expected.

Kissing him in front of that audience made her feel young and silly in love.

That was something she'd never regret, even if she must face the consequences today.

The idea of falling for Travis Armstrong flitted around in her brain. If she tried to examine it too closely, it flew away but that didn't mean Keena could forget about it.

"There was a couple making out, right in the middle of the theater. All lips and hands, there in front of everyone." Kim held her hand over her heart as if the scandal was too much for her. "Can you even imagine?"

Keena sighed. "We… The couple wasn't making out. There were lips but no hands. It was a kiss. That's all."

Reg inched his glasses down. "Were *you* there, Dr. M?" His tone was so innocent, as if he would never imagine such a thing happening.

Keena cleared her throat. "I was."

"Who was the couple, Dr. M?" Emily

leaned forward as if she was desperate for the answer. Keena hadn't learned to read Emily as well as the other two. Had the admin really not heard the story yet?

"One of them had red hair. That's what I heard." Reginald's grin was slow and sly.

Emily straightened immediately, her eyes locked on Keena's casual updo.

"Who was she kissing?" Kim drawled.

Reginald shrugged and stared at Keena.

"Dr. Singh doesn't need to know about any redhead kissing any cowboy at the Picture Show. And that's all it was, a kiss." Keena stepped back from the desk with her best severe frown. It would have been more powerful if she could have kept her lips from twitching in amusement before she walked toward her office. "Let me know when the next patient gets here."

Whatever they said to each other didn't make it to Keena's ears, but the stage whispered "Travis Armstrong" was loud and clear. She covered her hot cheeks with both hands before she forced herself to get back to business. Keena checked her email first. Every now and then, she considered sending a message to Angie Washington to make sure that things were running smoothly in the ER, but she knew there was no way she could step back in to help if they weren't. Right now, her priority had to be Prospect.

The rest of the afternoon was quiet and easy, so Keena was relieved as they locked up the clinic. She considered driving home to make a healthy salad for dinner, nixed that almost immediately because this string of work days required something stronger, and headed over to the Ace to see what Faye was serving.

She'd taken the first bite of a warm corn bread muffin while she waited for her steak to cook just as Faye trotted out from the kitchen, her eyes locked on Keena. There was something about her expression that told Keena her friend's urgency wasn't to do with the usual dinner rush. "What's up?" she asked and put her muffin down. She realized she'd forgotten to turn her cell phone ringer back on after leaving the office. She had two missed calls from Grant Armstrong. "Is there an emergency?"

"Yes, Grant needs you to meet him at the ranch. There's been an accident. They're out searching for Damon right now, but they want you to be nearby, in case…" Faye left the sentence unfinished. Based on that, Keena understood the Armstrongs were afraid the outcome was going to be bad.

Keena stood and pointed at the table. "I'll pay up next time." Faye waved her off as she hit the door at a run. Keena dashed into the clinic and grabbed anything she could think of that might help with an accident at the ranch and then sprinted to her car. Traffic was light so she pressed the gas pedal hard on her way out of town. She wasn't sure how long the trip was taking, but it felt like forever because she knew Damon needed her now.

Grant was waiting for her at the barn, horses saddled. "We'll go slow, Doc, but this is the best route to reach Damon and Travis. You trust me?"

Keena nodded and accepted his help to get into the saddle. She handed him her bag, gripped the reins and said, "Let's go."

Keena had never wondered how smart horses were, but it was clear that Lady was aware this was an emergency. She followed Grant without urging and matched his speed without waiting for her clueless rider to give the commands. All Keena had to do was hold on and pray.

Grant handed her a flashlight as they neared the first ridge that led over toward Key Lake. She'd never seen the lake this close in person, but it was a dark shadow. The moody tone wasn't reassuring.

Then she saw Travis and Walt on their knees next to the edge of some kind of bank or drop-off. "Hurry, Grant." When she was close enough to spot Micah clinging to Travis's shoulder, she slid out of the saddle and caught herself against Lady. "Thank you, Lady." She was running before Grant could catch up and managed to brace herself in time to catch Micah as he launched himself at her. Tears were silently streaming down his cheeks, but he didn't say a word. Fearing the worst, Keena pressed Micah's head against her shoulder and inched closer to Travis.

From here, she could see over the edge. There were two large bright lights pointed down to an outcropping where Damon was lying on his back. At first she thought his eyes were closed. "Has he been conscious?"

Travis seemed to realize then that she was there and he grasped her hand. "He's awake, raises his hand or answers when we ask a question. I've been waiting for Grant to show up with you and the rope. I'll climb down and lift him out of there. Just needed more hands." He ruffled Micah's hair, the worry clear in the tension on Travis's face.

"Have you called in the emergency? Is an ambulance coming?" Keena asked as she took the bag Grant offered.

"Yeah," Travis replied. "Wes is waiting for the sheriff at the closest gate over at the lodge." He paced. Keena slipped her arm around his. "Dispatch said they'd request an air ambulance and would connect them with the sheriff when they were nearby." He held his hand out for the rope that Grant had. "Let's get Damon ready for when they arrive. No time to waste."

Keena tugged at him to get his attention. "Wait, Travis. If he was unconscious when you got here, he could have a head injury, a spine injury. We need to make sure it's safe to move him before we do anything else." She knew he wanted to argue, so she spoke first. "I can do that. I can go down and see if it's okay to pull him out or if we need to stabilize him first. That will help the EMTs when they get here." She held up her bag. "I'm ready. I have everything Damon might need and emergency blankets to make the waiting easier. Send me down, then we'll figure out the next step." They had to know Damon's condition before anything else happened.

"I don't want to lower you down there. It's too dangerous," Travis said.

"So make the climbing part as safe as you can. I need to be with Damon. Now." Her firm tone must have convinced him, since he took the rope Grant brought and tied one end over her puffy coat, wrapping and knotting, wrapping and knotting until Keena had no idea how she'd ever get herself free. She wasn't worried about falling. Travis would keep her safe.

That was the thought she kept repeating to herself as she inched down the side of the steep drop toward the lake. Travis had her. She was safe. All she had to do was be a doctor and that was what she did best.

When her feet touched down next to Damon, he said, "How did they talk you into this, Doc?"

The relief that swamped Keena at hearing his strong voice made her weak in the knees. Carefully, she sat next to him. "We arm wrestled and I won." His lips curved in a grin that got Keena's heart pounding again. She immediately unwrapped the emergency blankets she'd shoved in her bag and covered him. Damon's skin was pale and clammy and his pulse was racing, classic signs that shock was going to be their initial problem. "How is the head? Any pain?"

Damon licked his lips before speaking. "No, not really. I don't think so."

Keena lifted the blanket up and gently ran her hands over his arms and legs. "Tell me what hurts."

"Back. Pretty sure it's torn up from the slide." Damon closed his eyes. "Leg."

Keena paused. "Which leg?"

"Left. Can't feel my left foot, either." Damon blinked. "That's a bad sign, right?"

As she resumed her examination, Keena analyzed all the possibilities. "Could definitely be worse, young man. I hope you're prepared to be literally grounded for years and years. They won't even let you sit in a chair until you go to college… Too high. You might fall off." She smiled down at him, relieved that he was with her and she could speak to him like this.

He gripped her hand. Another good sign. "As long as this doesn't convince Travis to close up the Armstrong foster home I will be happy to stay off any elevated surfaces."

Keena realized he'd had enough time to imagine more than the worst-case scenario. Poor kid.

"Keena, talk to me." Travis was angling the light over them so she could see better. Micah was still clinging tightly to him.

"He's making jokes, Travis. That's a good sign. See how far away the air ambulance is, okay?" Keena yelled and then whispered, "Damon, can you wave at Micah? He's a little frightened."

Damon let go of her hand and held his own hand close to his face before wiggling his fingers. Keena couldn't tell if that had any positive effect on Micah, but it helped steady her. "We'd be better off waiting for the EMTs to lift you out of here. You gonna be okay with my company for a few more minutes?"

He nodded.

She took his hand in hers. "No way Travis

is going to change his mind about you. You better decide you like being a cowboy. He has big plans for both of you boys. I hear there's a parade. Matching outfits. That kind of thing."

"I like it here. Micah's getting better. Hope we can stay." Damon blinked rapidly. "Think I'm paralyzed or anything, Doc?"

These were the questions that had always stopped her in her tracks in the emergency room. Patients and their families desperately wanted to hear the best scenario, but as a medical professional, she knew how often the worst came true. She couldn't lie about this. "Honestly? I don't know if there's some kind of injury causing numbness or if it's shock or what, but we'll figure it out together. You and me and Travis and Micah and about a million Armstrongs for backup, okay?"

He nodded again.

She knew she had to come up with a diversion, but what?

She couldn't tell if her brain was playing tricks on her, but she wanted the faint noise she could hear to be the air ambulance. That would mean the sheriff was nearby and help was coming. "Have you ever ridden in a helicopter, Damon?"

The kid huffed out a breath. "Of course. On the way back and forth to the bank to deposit my lottery winnings."

Keena narrowed her eyes. "Sarcasm. In this case, I'll allow it." She smiled at him. "What color do you think the one you're about to ride in will be?"

Keena might not be able to lie to comfort the patient. She might not know exactly the right words for every situation. But she could ask questions. As soon as Damon answered this one, she'd fire another one at him. Keeping him alert and talking would be the best thing for both of them.

"I'm going with blue. What color do you think?" he asked.

Keena pursed her lips. "Blue would have been my pick, too, but it's no fun if we choose the same color, so how about...green? I'll go with green."

He shifted slightly. "What does the winner get?"

Keena whistled. "Oh, he wants to run a bet while we're waiting. Okay..." She brushed his dark hair off his forehead. The sound of the helicopter was becoming much clearer now. The struggle to get him back up to the top would take a lot out of everyone, but most especially Damon. "Loser bakes the winner her favorite cookie."

He rolled his eyes. "Or *his* favorite cookie."

She laughed. "Fair enough." This time when she tilted her head back to see what was happening, Travis and Micah were still there but they'd been joined by sheriff's deputies and one paramedic wearing a dark blue uniform.

"Good news, Damon. It looks like you are about to take a ride in a blue helicopter, my friend," Keena said, keeping an eye on the growing group above them. "We've got a fourteen-year-old male with possible spinal injury or compression, temporary loss of consciousness, and pain in his left leg which may indicate a break."

The paramedic nodded. "Are you able to assist with loading the patient up for extraction if we lower the board?"

Keena straightened her shoulders. This was a new part of trauma medicine that she hadn't experienced before but she knew she could handle it. "Lower the board and give me clear instructions. This boy is ready for his helicopter ride."

CHAPTER FIFTEEN

THE RESCUE CREW that gathered at the edge of the steep bank pulled Keena up right behind Damon. Travis's knees turned too weak to hold him up any longer. He settled on the ground next to Damon and gasped for air. His lungs burned as if he'd been holding his breath ever since he'd looked up from the tack he'd been mending in the barn to see Micah clinging to Sonny's back with no Damon behind him.

"I'm really sorry, Travis," Damon said softly. "What a mess."

Travis rubbed his eyes hard and realized they were leaking tears of relief. He couldn't remember ever being as scared as he had been staring down at this boy who needed help.

"I knew I shouldn't take Micah to see the lake, but he kept going on about snow coming and missing his chance for months and months and months." Damon closed his eyes. "It's a lake, you know. It would still be there, even if it did snow, but it should have been simple enough."

Travis realized he didn't have much time to fall apart. Micah was around there somewhere, and the kid hadn't been able to speak as they'd ridden out to find Damon. After watching all this, he might never speak again.

Damon tried another apology, and Travis put his hand on the kid's arm. "Listen, this was an accident. Taking off on your own wasn't smart, but you know that already. Everything else could have happened whether I was with you or not. Let that go. Help me reassure Micah and we can discuss what sort of boring chore you'd like to do for the rest of your natural life as a reminder that poor judgment has consequences, when we're all safe back home." He waited for the kid to nod before smiling at him. "We aren't done yet, but everything is going to be okay. You will be fine. We'll all be fine."

Travis took a chance that his knees would hold him and stood to peer over the crowd. He needed to check on Micah before the EMTs got Damon on the helicopter.

When he spotted Keena's bright red hair, he realized Micah was glued to her side. Keena pointed at Travis and asked Micah something. Her frown made Travis think that Micah's trauma still had a hold on him, but she pasted on a brave smile when they stopped next to Damon. "Look who I found." Micah immediately knelt beside Damon and pressed his face to Damon's chest.

Micah's sobs took every bit of tension inside Travis and twisted hard. Keena reached out to comfort him, but before she could say anything, Travis wrapped his arms around her and pulled her close. "I was so scared."

The weight of her hands on his back eased some of his trembling. "I knew I would be fine, Travis. This is what I was meant to do. Painting? No. Herding loose cows? Also no, but I am good in a crisis." She squeezed him tight. "You found him. You saved him. Now talk to Micah. You don't have much time before the EMTs will be ready to leave."

Travis knew she was right, but he didn't want to let go of her. Or Damon. Or Micah. He clutched her hand but squatted down to run the other one over Micah's back. "Hey, bud, we're all okay. Damon's going to ride in this cool helicopter while you have to go home and when you're ready, go to bed, because life is totally unfair. But he'll be home soon to tell you all about it."

Micah still didn't speak but he pressed himself tightly against Travis's chest, his arms gripping tightly. Travis rubbed a hand up and down the boy's back and nodded at the EMT who stepped up. "We're going to load Damon now. You'll be coming with us, correct? We need a family member."

Travis nodded and squeezed Micah. "You hear that? I get to ride along. I'll make sure Damon doesn't make any stories up about flying to Denver, okay?" When tears started streaming down Micah's cheeks again, Travis broke. Then the bigger pieces splintered until Walt came forward.

His father squeezed his shoulder and helped loosen Micah's grip. "Micah and I have a big job, taking care of all these horses while you're gone. We'll be countin' the hours until you get back."

Micah stepped back to take Walt's hand and some of Travis's panic receded. The boy who didn't trust men more than he had to trusted Travis's father. Walt met his stare. "I will call Prue, tell her everything. She'll stay at the ranch with us tonight. Wes and Sarah will be driving down to Denver to meet you in the hospital."

Travis inhaled a ragged breath, grateful they'd already come up with a solid plan. What would he have done without this family behind him? This was the kind of emergency he'd never planned for, one son headed to the hospital while the other was shattered at home.

But his parents were there for Micah. His brothers would step up to help him.

And then there was Keena who was pointing at Damon and saying something forcefully to the EMT.

"Ma'am, I can't give you permission to ride along. You aren't a family member, that's up to the family." The EMT held up his hands at whatever expression Keena flashed at him.

"His father is giving permission for me to accompany Damon to the hospital, although I am his personal physician and that should count for something." Then Keena raised her eyebrows at Travis in a clear "Tell them I can come along or else" look.

Travis nodded. "Yeah, she's coming with us." Then he wrapped his arm around her shoulders and the EMT crew lifted Damon into the helicopter. "I'll never be able to thank you for this. Ever."

She jerked back. "Thank me? No thanks needed. This is my job. This is my calling, Travis. Your purpose is to help these kids. I can heal them…" She tilted her head to the side. "Or I can find the right doctor if I can't."

He wasn't going to argue with her, not here and not over this, so Travis bent down to squeeze Micah tightly one more time and sent a silent thank-you to his father before he and Keena followed Damon into the helicopter. They were buckling themselves in when the EMT asked, "Closest hospital, right?"

Keena immediately bent forward. "The best hospital. Take us to Denver Medical Center."

Travis wasn't sure when the power had shifted but the EMT didn't turn and ask for confirmation or permission this time. The blades got louder and the weird sensation of the earth falling away caught all three of them by surprise. Damon was the only one who managed to speak. "Whoa. They need to warn me before they do that."

Keena smiled at him, then at Travis and reached for his hand. At this point, he was going purely by instinct. Grabbing her hand, following her lead, made perfect sense, and in no time, they were landing at the hospital. A team raced out to meet them, and Keena started shouting Damon's condition as they hurried inside. "Fourteen-year-old male, his pulse is still fast but steady, lost consciousness briefly but has been able to provide updates on his condition since. No blood or bruising to the head, but signs of abraded flesh on his back and left side. Pain in the left leg and some numbness in that extremity. We'll need to check for concussion and run the usual tests to see what may be causing an impingement in the nerves of his..."

Travis glanced away from Damon as Keena's words halted.

Another doctor had met them at the sliding doors to the ER. "And I am not in charge here so we will need to see what Dr. Shane orders to diagnose further treatment."

Keena put her hand to her forehead. "Sorry, Dr. Shane. Old habits die hard?"

The older man who was already listening to Damon's chest nodded. "That they do, Dr. Murphy. I'm happy to have the chance to shake your hand." He did so quickly before sending a nurse scrambling to make a call to find out how quickly they could get Damon in for scans. "The tales I have heard of the amazing Steady Murphy. Your night shift crew talks about you like you're a myth. It's a pleasure to meet a legend in the flesh. I believe this whole team is counting down the days until you return to take charge of Emergency again."

Keena's pink cheeks could be the result of the adrenaline rush from this rescue.

Or it could be embarrassment at being treated like the conquering hero by her successor.

Either way, Travis finally completely understood that Keena wasn't just a good doctor. She was a superhero to the people in this hospital. And she'd been hanging out in Prospect all this time without anyone knowing what she was capable of.

How would it make sense that someone who was capable of doing this, who could without hesitation climb down to Damon, keep him calm and evaluate his health, then hop in a helicopter for emergency transit, and impress the coolly confident doctor on call at the time…how would she leave this for small-town life?

Her insistence that she was only a temporary neighbor made perfect sense.

"I'll find a place to sit in the waiting room. Travis is going along with Damon for his tests." She said the words firmly as if there was a possibility the doctor would argue with her decision.

Dr. Shane held up his hands in surrender and said, "Travis, if you'll go with this nurse, we'll make sure Damon's not suffering from a concussion first, and then evaluate from there."

Travis stared at Keena until the doors between them closed and then he focused on Damon. He spent what felt like hours waiting while Damon was checked over, but eventually, they returned together to an open room in the emergency department. Keena was already there, and Travis was happy to see that Wes and Sarah had arrived. And Grant, too. Travis hadn't expected that, but it was a welcome surprise. When they all turned to face him, he said, "And now we wait."

Grant took up a spot next to the bed. "Well, this is not looking good for your career in the rodeo, kid. A little fall from a horse and sliding a hundred feet or so? Even the clowns would tease you about that."

Travis gripped Keena's shoulders before she launched in to defend Damon and waited for the kid to plead his own case. "I've decided not to waste my time with the rodeo. Going straight to Hollywood stunt man." Damon's voice was weak but steady.

"A man with a plan," Grant said and offered the boy a wide smile.

Sarah shook her head. "Boys are weird, but these two are okay, if you guys want to take a walk? Keena, you and Travis could find some coffee. It's been a long night." She pointed at the small window on the opposite wall. "Or night and morning." The pink sky of sunrise filled the window.

"Good idea." Keena took Travis's hand. "Let's go to the cafeteria for coffee." They were silent as they rode the elevator down to the cafeteria on the lobby level. Travis managed to keep it all together as they got through the cafeteria line and Keena greeted coworkers. He poured too much sugar and creamer into his cup and stirred it while the coffee turned pale.

They chose the closest table and sat down. Before either of them could say anything, he put his head in his hands and waited for the emotional fallout.

Keena came around the table, wrapped her arm around his shoulders and waited silently. When someone walked by, she said, "Hey, Frances, can you grab a cold bottle of water for me?"

She put one hand on his back and moved it in steady circles, and then said, "Thank you. Yeah, we'll be okay. Thanks." She unscrewed the lid and offered the water to him. "I forgot you don't drink coffee. I'm sorry. This will be better for you anyway."

Travis pressed the cold bottle to his forehead. "I'm okay. I was afraid I was losing it there for a minute."

Her hand never stopped rubbing and eventually he felt like himself again.

"You're a rock star, Dr. Murphy." He sipped the water before adding, "Or should I call you Steady Murphy. That is what Dr. Shane said, isn't it?"

Keena huffed out a breath. "If you knew how unsteady I was the last time I worked the night shift, you would understand how a nickname can weigh on a person. Every single night, I was holding on tightly to make it back to the locker room where I could fall apart in private. People depended on Steady Murphy. They told each other stories about her as if she was different." Keena clutched her cooling coffee cup with both hands. "I was so scared to let anyone down."

Travis was solemn as he studied her face. "I can't believe how lucky we've been to have you next door all these weeks without understanding who you are." Travis hadn't had a moment to dig down to the problem he was having with the revelation, either. It was a good thing that the best at anything was in town, right?

"It was the hamburger slippers, wasn't it? You have no faith in a woman who wears shoes like that, I bet." Keena wrinkled her nose as she teased him. "I was afraid I'd lose my edge in Prospect."

"But you haven't." What a relief she'd been nearby for Damon.

How many other emergencies was she missing while she'd stepped off the beaten path, Travis wondered.

"No," Keena agreed with a beautiful smile, "I haven't. I don't think I will, either, which I'm kind of glad to say out loud. It's a bit of a revelation, that this emergency response mode, this ability to think in the middle of a crisis, is really who I am. I love medicine and the rewards are so sweet when I can make a difference like I did tonight, or last night? You know what I mean."

Listening to her talk illuminated the unease he'd been feeling since they walked through the hospital doors. He'd been imagining a future with Keena next door to the Rocking A. His off-the-cuff decision to pretend she was his girlfriend in front of the social worker had been wishful thinking and he'd never recovered from that.

No matter how often she made sure to mention that she was only in Prospect for the short term, he'd been doing his best to change that in his own mind.

Seeing her here, though, there was no way

to avoid how far she was out of his and Prospect's league.

It was going to hurt when the inevitable happened and she returned to her calling here. But he was someone who understood fulfilling a purpose. Damon and Micah had confirmed his.

And this rescue had clearly proven Keena's.

He'd been doing his best to weave her into his plans for Damon and Micah and whoever came next. Keena made every bit of this up-and-down foster process feel better.

Depending on her was easy.

Loving her was even easier.

But that didn't change who she was or what she was meant to do and losing her would sting. When she clapped a hand to her forehead, he eased back.

"I better call Reginald to see what we do about the clinic until I'm there." She got out her phone. "I'm still struggling with being the only doctor on call and letting people know how to get ahold of me."

Travis listened to her one-sided conversation where Keena and Reginald decided to move all of her appointments for that day to the following Monday. They were closing the clinic early on Wednesday, and then all day on Thursday and Friday for the holiday, but they'd fit everyone in who had an appointment before then.

Travis wasn't sure how to return to their conversation, so he was happy to see Grant walk up. "I drove your truck down so you'd have it if you need to stay over." He offered Travis the keys and they watched Keena move over to another table to make conversation with someone in scrubs. "Your doctor has been amazing."

"I told her." Travis sipped his water and wondered if he had any gas left in the tank for another deep conversation at this point.

"I expected a lot more to come with that answer." Grant pulled a chair out and sat. "You okay? For a man who has to be deep in love at this point, you sure are playing it cool."

Travis nodded. "Just realizing how much I've been depending on Keena." He motioned around the cafeteria. "And here's this whole place that could be benefiting from her amazing-ness."

He rubbed his forehead, aware that he was on the verge of making no sense.

Grant said, "Uh-huh, but there are other

doctors here, too. They deserve a chance to show off their own talents. Prospect only has Keena. Let's keep her."

Travis grunted. "She's been clear all along that keeping her wasn't on the table. Seeing her in action here makes it crystal clear why."

Grant opened his mouth, so Travis braced himself for something annoying. Instead, his brother simply shook his head. "There's time to figure that out after Damon comes home, right?"

"Yeah." Travis would spend a lot of time thinking about it in the meantime, but Grant had a point.

"Let's go upstairs and check on Damon. Mom was in a panic when she found out all she'd missed, so she and Dad are planning to come later today." Grant rubbed his eyes. "Wes and Sarah are going to head back now to stay with Micah and I'll ride with them. We all needed to see that Damon was okay for ourselves."

Travis could understand that. Seeing everything in full color made some things so much clearer. For now, Keena was the only person available to help in an emergency in Prospect. He'd make sure she went back with

Grant. Then he'd figure out how to keep the distance he'd failed to maintain between them in the first place for the rest of her stay.

Keena was coming back to Denver.

A smart man would take care to remember that.

For himself and his kids.

CHAPTER SIXTEEN

KEENA REALIZED THAT something had changed when she returned to the table in the cafeteria and Travis was gone. On the way up to Damon's room, she replayed their conversation in her head, but the only thing that stuck with her was the fact that he'd called her a rock star.

At the time, she'd thought he was teasing. That was their thing, trading funny things back and forth. If Travis seemed out of it, he had good reason. They'd been up all night, most of it spent in the windy cold. Damon was going to be fine, Keena was certain, but they'd burned through tons of energy to get to this point. If she counted the busy days at the clinic and lack of food for hours and hours, it was a miracle she was still putting one foot in front of the other herself.

But the fact that Travis had left without telling her was a bad sign. Ever since she and

Travis met over the woodpile, they'd had this invisible link. Walking away from her like this seemed a deliberate move to cut that tie.

As she stepped off the elevator, she was having the usual internal debate, where one side convinced her to shut down, step back and accept the distance he was putting between them because it was the safest option here. She would be fine. Everything would be fine.

The other half? That half of Keena was angry.

Since she needed to think clearly, Keena stopped to stare out the window overlooking the hospital parking lot. Bright sunshine warmed her face as she inhaled slowly and then exhaled.

Was Travis putting space between them here? That might have worked if they'd never rescued Damon together, but it didn't work for Keena anymore.

The long night had shown her that she'd already tumbled too far into… What? Not love.

If she left Prospect, she would worry about Damon and Micah.

And whether Prue and Walt would ever figure things out.

Then there was the lodge and the Hearsts and this friendship that she didn't want to lose.

She might never find Sadie Hearst's treasure of an apple pie recipe and learn to make it or paint mediocre mountain landscapes.

Her panicked ride to help Damon might be the last time she ever climbed in a saddle if she returned to Denver to step back into her old life.

Keena closed her eyes to focus on the quiet conversation at the nurses' desk and Dr. Singh's smile flitted through her mind.

PJ would welcome her to Prospect Family Practice with that smile every day.

If Travis had decided he wanted distance from her, they were going to have to learn to share Prospect.

Because Keena couldn't leave.

And love was definitely part of that equation, but she wasn't convinced she had the final solution regarding Travis.

Even if the anger simmered below the surface, she knew Damon's hospital room was not the place for an honest airing of feelings, so she pasted on a calm smile and joined the group gathered around Damon. He was awake. At some point, Dr. Shane had come in to say there was no evidence of head trauma. Damon was cleared to eat and drink, and he was doing his best to do both at the same time while Travis juggled a fork and his glass of juice.

"Looks like we got some good news," Keena said softly as Damon swallowed whatever it was he was chewing. He gave her a thumbs-up and then pointed at a piece of bacon on the tray in front of him.

Travis hmphed. "Seems like if you can point, you can pick up the bacon yourself, but I'll humor you this one time."

It burned, waiting to ask Travis what his problem was, but now was not the time to let everyone in the room know that he was being a total jerk to her. Everyone was focused on Damon as they should be.

The fact that Travis didn't face her or even acknowledge her arrival made it that much more difficult to hold on to the appropriate bedside manner. She had so much to say, but it was all for his ears only.

Wes turned to her. "Keena, Sarah and I are going to head back to Prospect. My parents are on their way. Do you want to ride back with us? Grant will also be with us, but I'll make him promise to be on his best behavior."

Grant sighed. "You never let me have any fun."

She shook her head immediately. She wanted to make sure that Damon got everything he needed. It wasn't time for her to go.

Before she could say that part, Travis interrupted. "That's a good suggestion." He didn't say her name but stared directly at her. What was that about? "I mean, Prospect doesn't have a doctor while you're here. We don't know what the next day or two looks like, but there will be plenty of family here with Damon and the hospital staff here won't want to let steady Dr. Murphy down. You've made it clear that Damon is your patient. You can go back to Prospect. We'll be okay."

Keena was vaguely aware of Wes and Sarah shooting glances at each other as if they were surprised by this comment. Grant muttered under his breath, but she couldn't make out what he was saying.

And Travis returned to staring at Damon's breakfast tray.

So she addressed Damon. "What do you

think? You're my patient, not him. Want me to stay?"

Damon took the glass Travis held out and finished the juice before answering. "I'd feel better if you were in Prospect, since that's where Micah is. He was so pale when we left. What if he's sick and you aren't there?"

Keena studied Damon's dark eyes and some of the hot anger Travis had inspired drained away. Their reasoning was not that far apart, but the way Damon said it meant something. There was a person he cared about in Prospect, so he would make the sacrifice and send her back.

Whereas Travis had turned into some weird robot who appeared to care very little about where Keena was.

"Okay," Keena said reluctantly, "I'll take the offer of the ride. That will give me extra time to get home and start on those cookies I owe you, but don't you think for a minute I'll let anyone here forget they owe me big-time favors and I'm calling them all in for you. If they don't have you out of here by to-morrow, I'll come back and get you myself."

Damon solemnly nodded. "I doubt any of them will cross you, Steady Murphy."

His snort of laughter tickled Keena so she giggled in response. "I'm never going to live that nickname down now, am I? I had a shot of enjoying life as a free woman in Prospect where no one had ever heard it, but you're going to fix that."

Damon grinned. "No way, but I told Grant and you know how he is."

"Hey," Grant said before he shook his finger. "That's a valid critique of my character. I believe you may have fully integrated into the Armstrong fold, kid. That didn't take much time at all."

Wes sighed. "Damon, I sure hope you're on the side of good. We need all the help we can get with the other side as it relates to this family."

"We'll go pull the SUV up to the Emergency entrance downstairs, Keena," Sarah said. She hugged Damon and then gripped Travis's arm to pull him out in the hallway. Keena glanced at both of the Armstrong brothers left in the room to see if they knew what she might be saying. Both men shrugged.

So Keena squeezed Damon's hand.

Travis stepped back inside the room and

she moved to leave but Damon said, "Hey, Keena, if I'm not home tonight, the three of us, you, me and Micah could have a video call. We can both make sure he's okay." She agreed. He added, "And I'd like chocolate chip. The ones you made before were really good."

"You got it." Keena locked eyes with Travis and said, "I'll be calling you for updates. I'll also be asking my friends to come through to check on Damon's progress. You can send me away, but I'll be following up on my patient." Then she leaned closer to say, "And don't think we're done with this conversation. When you get back to Prospect, you better have a good explanation or an excellent apology."

Grant whistled dramatically but Wes towed him down the hallway.

Proud of her exit line, Keena followed but stopped in the restroom to wash her face with cold water, a guaranteed wake-me-up. The woman staring back at her was worn out; her hair was tangled into one large knot, and her eyes were bright with anger still, but Keena wasn't giving up. She headed directly for the emergency department. Annoyance had her hitting top speed. It was like she'd never missed a night on duty. Angie Washington was coming in for her shift and they met at the nurses' station. "Dr. Murphy, what are you doing here? Are you back?"

Keena rubbed her forehead because she was so tired. The question stopped her in her tracks, but the answer was easier than she expected. "Honestly, Angie, I believe I'll be making the move to Prospect permanently. Dr. Singh offered me a partnership in his clinic, and I've never felt more at home any other place, but at this moment, I can't even explain why I feel that because cowboys are so annoying, you know?"

The nurse pursed her lips as she considered the question and laughed when Keena waved it away. "Don't answer that. I've been running on fumes for too long."

"Some things haven't changed, I see," Angie murmured. "What can I do, Dr. Murphy?"

"I came in with a friend...a patient, rather. His name is Damon. He's in an exam room waiting for test results after a fall. There's some concern about numbness and pain in his leg. Dr. Shane is aware he's a friend of mine. Could you check in on him and his dad now and then? I'd sure appreciate it."

Angie nodded. "I'll text you with any updates I get. How is that?"

Keena sagged against the desk. "Perfect. I don't know what I would have done without you, Angie."

She smiled. "You seem different, Dr. Murphy. Hard to put my finger on exactly what that is, but there's something more… alive? Is that the right word?" She tilted her head back. "Does this friend or his father have anything to do with that or your decision to change temporary to permanent?"

Keena returned the nurse's smile. "I'm afraid so and I don't know what to do about it." She suddenly remembered Wes and the others. "I'm sorry. It has been a long night and my ride is out front waiting. Hope it's an easy shift."

She was happy stepping out into the afternoon sunshine and sliding into the back seat next to Sarah. Wes and Grant turned around to stare at her when she slammed the door. "Everything okay?" Sarah asked.

"Yeah," Keena said before she leaned her head back against the seat and took a deep breath. "I finally figure out the answer to one important question and something else unravels right before my eyes, but I guess I should get used to that."

Sarah squeezed her arm and mouthed, "Hardheaded Armstrongs," so broadly that Keena had no trouble reading her lips. The laughter that escaped was a relief.

Wes and Grant seemed to realize this was something they weren't a part of so they turned around and faced the front. She waited until her traveling companions successfully agreed on a fast-food stop and they were soon on the road. "Could one of you help me with something?"

Grant turned to stare at her. "Anything. You know that. You're one of us now and you always will be, even if Travis is aiming to take over my claim to fame as the problem in this family." He frowned. "I guess I'll have to be the hero for the moment, at least."

Keena felt the sting of tears well up but she forced them back. "Give me your mother's phone number."

Grant reared back and looked to Wes for direction. He had not expected that.

Before reasonable Wes could try to dig

around for more information, Sarah pulled up Prue's number on her own phone and handed it to Keena. "Calling in the big guns is an interesting strategy." She smiled extra hard and extra bright at Wes and Grant as if to reassure them that everything in the back seat was fully under control. "In this case, I approve."

Keena quickly punched in the number before she could chicken out. When Prue answered, Keena blurted, "Prue, it's Keena. Do you remember telling me that you were on my side? We were standing in Handmade, talking about how falling in love with a man's children creates these ties that you can never be free of." She stared hard out the window. She didn't want to watch anyone's reaction to her admission, not yet. "Well, I messed up. I've gone and done it and Travis is being a…" She wanted a good word, one that Sadie Hearst might have tossed in there, but none would come to mind.

"Oh, hon, you don't have to fill in the blank. I've lived this conversation more often than I'd like. Sometimes these fellas can't tell skunks from house cats, and when they fall in love, all reason flies out the window." Whatever Walt said in response to that was shushed loudly by Prue. "Tell me, what can I do?"

Keena sighed. "I'm not sure, but I think Travis expects me to walk away from Prospect, so he started shoving me out the door."

"And you ain't goin'? Is that what you're sayin' here?" Prue asked.

Keena waited for panic to take over, for her pulse to race or some kind of physical reaction to betray her anticipated anxiety, but none came. "I believe that's exactly what I'm saying. Dr. Singh is looking for a partner. I know now how much I can bring to this practice. I'm going to accept."

Prue's victory yell made Keena pull the phone away from her ear. Everyone else in the car with her heard it, too.

"This is a challenge worthy of my skill, sweet girl. You give me today and tomorrow, and Travis will work all his confusion out. You can count on me." Prue's wicked laughter settled over Keena like a promise.

She knew where she belonged.

It was time Travis figured it out, too.

CHAPTER SEVENTEEN

WHEN HIS MOTHER and father arrived at the hospital, Travis had been cornered by an efficient nurse named Angie. Instead of asking him questions or introducing herself, she walked up to the bed and said, "Damon, we have a good friend in common. Her name is Keena and she asked me to make sure you get VIP treatment." Then she'd peered over her shoulder at Travis and sniffed. "You must be the cowboy."

He couldn't put his finger on why that sounded like an insult, but Angie was unimpressed with him. "And the father. Yeah."

She pursed her lips. "Dr. Shane's got a consult with a neurologist first thing." Her finger made determined taps as she paged through Damon's chart on the tablet in her hand. "It's just a precaution, but it looks like you'll be enjoying the dinner they serve in this fine establishment. I would apologize in advance, but it's chicken finger night in the cafeteria and those are pretty good." She picked up his cup and shook it. "He needs water." Then she handed it to Travis and pointed toward the hallway. "You'll find an ice and water machine next to the nurses' station, cowboy."

Travis was ready to stretch his legs anyway, so he held the cup up to his parents in the doorway. "Be right back."

His mother's disapproving expression made him wonder if he was somehow in trouble as he followed the nurse's orders, but then he realized he was a fully grown adult and straightened his shoulders before he walked in the room. His mother and the nurse stopped mid-whisper and shot him nearly identical looks of judgment.

Whatever Keena wanted to say to him, she'd already lined up her support group. Getting to his mother before he had a chance to get her on his side was smart.

He shouldn't have been surprised.

"Thanks, Travis," Damon said, taking the water and sipping it. "Angie says she's known Keena for years. Someday we'll have more funny stories about her to share, won't we?"

The three adults in the room turned to watch him closely.

He was beginning to understand that he'd messed up by assuming he knew what Keena was thinking.

"Since she told me she was about to become Dr. Singh's partner in the clinic, it would not surprise me a bit, Damon." Prue raised her eyebrows at Travis and hmphed when he sat down with a thump.

His phone rang and he saw Keena's name on the screen. She'd requested a video call so he swiped up and felt the wash of relief when she and Micah appeared together. It looked like they were in the kitchen at the Rocking A. "Hey, Travis," Micah said loudly as if he hadn't quite got the concept of the video call, "how is Damon?"

Travis did his best to memorize the way they looked before he said, "He's good. Talk to him."

After he handed the phone to Damon, he met his mother's stare and they stepped outside, his father trailing after them. "She turned my own mother against me. I admire that. I really do."

Prue rolled her eyes. "Get a grip, Travis. No

one is against you. We are all for you. All of us. Me, your daddy, Wes, Clay, Grant, Matt, Sarah, Jordan and the entire town of Prospect. Have been since you first landed in our living room, scared of every shadow. You're brave enough to join the army, travel wherever they sent you and come back home alive, *and* take on fostering on your own, but you can't tell a woman how you feel?" His mother poked her finger in his father's chest. "Who does that remind me of?"

Then she stomped back inside and closed the door abruptly.

Walt scratched his head. "Now, when we left Prospect, I was on her good side. You've gone and messed that up for me, son."

Travis massaged his temples, critically aware of how little sleep he was running on at that point. "Got any advice on how to fix it?"

Walt shoved his hands in his pockets. "I've tried quite a few different things in my time. Fancy dinner invitations, flirting, arguing, agreeing with everything she says, and most recently finding the cash for a fancy pot filler in the kitchen she always dreamed of."

"None of them have worked with Mom," Travis said.

Walt grunted.

"Guess I could try the one thing I didn't hear on that list." Travis nodded. "An apology."

CHAPTER EIGHTEEN

ON THE SUNDAY before Thanksgiving, Prue and Keena finished arranging the Majestic Prospect Lodge's restaurant while they listened to Sarah and Jordan Hearst dissect each decision they'd made regarding the setup for the community's holiday dinner.

While the sisters bickered over whether or not to do full place settings or something more casual, Keena draped the last crisply pressed tablecloth over the table where she and Prue had been stacking the linens. The tiny red-and-white gingham check was cheerful yet smart enough to say this was an occasion.

"No one will miss Sadie Hearst's influence here," Prue said with clear satisfaction. "I love that Jordan is using so much of the stuff Sadie left in storage. It's a nice touch."

Keena agreed as she picked up the bouquet of silk mums in deep oranges and burgundies that Sarah and Jordan had bought yesterday. The duo had been struck with the floral inspiration as they were digging in the magic closet for anything they might use for centerpieces and "absolutely had to go" in search of the pretty decorations. Prue and Keena had been elbow-deep in soapy dishwater at the time, making sure all the plates, silverware and glasses were clean and ready to go.

"Do you think they do this to get out of work or…" Prue crossed her arms and frowned at Sarah and Jordan who were pacing off steps like they were about to turn and duel.

Keena laughed as she stared down at the bouquet. "I don't know if it's a choice they make, but it seems to happen that way."

Prue nodded and took the bouquet from Keena before she marched right between Sarah and Jordan and plopped the flowers down on the table. "Enough. It's a family dinner. Food will be served buffet-style. Put the plates down at the end, silverware on the table, and quit the yammering." She pointed at the mums. "Keena and I are out of here."

Keena didn't wait around to see what the reaction would be. Prue urged her to lead the way through the lobby and out the front door, so Keena managed to hold back her giggles until they were safely in the parking lot.

"Those girls will wear an old woman out, I tell you." Prue placed her hand dramatically on her brow as if she'd been through battle.

"Old woman?" Keena said doubtfully. "You were running rings around all of us, Prue." She'd been busy calling the shots, so she'd had to stay one step ahead. But Keena didn't see any value in saying that part aloud.

"I have five boys. My physical conditioning is superior." She pulled her phone out and sent a text. "Good thing yours is too, Doc." Then she raised her eyebrow. "Travis has been waiting on Damon hand and foot since they got home, but if he doesn't fix all this between you today, I'll do something drastic."

"Nothing drastic, Prue, please." Keena pulled her own phone out to check for texts but it was blank. "There is always the possibility that Travis is looking for someone else, even if I do plan to be right here in Prospect." She exhaled slowly. "And that's okay."

Prue's snort startled a crow from one of the pines at the edge of the parking lot. "No way. That man is gone, has been ever since he told that social worker that teeny little lie, remember?" She patted Keena's shoulder. "I've been working, never you doubt that. This is all under control."

"Prue, I..." Keena had been trying to find the right words for Prue Armstrong for days, but they wouldn't come. She would have to stumble her way through and hope Prue could hear her message. "Thank you. Whatever happens this week or next year or whenever, it's hard to find the right words to say how much I admire the way you make such a big, wonderful family wherever you go. I appreciate how everyone feels loved when they're around you."

Prue covered her mouth with her hand and blinked rapidly. "Well." She cleared her throat. "I don't have the right words, either." She squeezed Keena tight and held her there for a moment. "Keena, I spent a lot of time telling my boys they need to find good partners, but this ol' world has exceeded my expectations when it comes to you." Keena started to remind her the universe hadn't done anything in her case yet, but Prue spoke first. "I've always wanted some kind, smart, caring daughters to go with this mess of sons. And however I get 'em, I'm gonna keep 'em, you hear?"

That reminded her of how Travis had been certain Prue would go to war for all of her kids, not only her sons. It was sweet to be included in that number, no matter what.

Keena nodded. "All right. I'm going to head home and attempt my third apple pie. Faye's has some kind of secret ingredient I can't quite figure out." Something in the back of her mind made her wonder if she should try vanilla.

"If Jordan calls, ignore your phone. You know she wants those beams stained and I don't trust the girl not to get a wild notion in the middle of the night to go for it before the holiday. You can start answering the phone again in December. We will need to drop hints for extravagant gifts they can wrap up and leave us under the tree." Prue waved and Keena was still laughing as she drove onto the highway, headed for home.

It had been a good day. She was running through the list of dishes she was planning to master before Thursday when she stopped in her front yard and saw Travis sitting on her porch steps.

She got out and slowly crossed the yard, her hands in her back pockets.

"Hi," he said and stood. "My mother told me you were on your way here, so I decided to wait."

"The déjà vu is hitting. At least you don't have an axe this time." Keena scuffed her sneaker in the crunchy grass. "Thank you for the texts about Damon's prognosis. I'm glad the numbness is improving. Deep bruises like that can take a while to clear."

Travis took a small step forward. "Seems he's being tormented by being able to look at horses but not get on one. He's grounded anyway, but he and Micah have brushed every horse in the barn until they shine like show ponies."

Keena laughed. His tone was "overwhelmed single parent who wished his kids could be outdoors doing what they love."

"Sometimes the punishment is harder for you than it is for them."

Travis grinned. "That's what my father said."

Both of their phones dinged with incoming messages.

Travis held up his phone. "When my mother

hears someone talk about how Dr. Murphy helped a student with the flu or rescued the newest Armstrong or toiled to resurrect the Majestic…that was from Jordan Hearst… My mother passes it along to me. Prospect's hero. How did I ever think I could let you go so easily?" He rubbed his forehead. "I tried to do it because…I love you. I want everything you dream of for yourself to come true."

Keena moved closer to him. "Your mother warned me about falling in love with a man and his children. It was already too late for me. Whether I'm in Prospect or Denver, my heart belongs at the Rocking A."

Travis tipped his head back, blinking rapidly, before he pulled her into his arms. "We aren't going to make the same mistakes my parents did, Keena. I promise."

Keena pressed her forehead to his chest, content to listen to his heart beating. "We won't. I don't think they'll let us."

His chuckle filled her with the bubbly certainty that she was absolutely where she belonged.

"My text is from your father." Keena's lips were twitching. "Would you know anything about that?"

Travis sighed. "When I realized how badly I'd messed up, my dad tried to help."

Keena read, "'One—make sure Travis apologizes. He means it. He knows he's lost without you.'" She paused to check that she had his attention. "'Two—ask him what he's learned. It's important.'"

He ran his finger over her brows and down her cheek. "We belong here. We belong together. Whatever else life throws at you or me, nothing comes between us."

Keena was certain Travis Armstrong was the only man who could make her believe those words. That bone-deep honor she'd put her faith in early on was so easy to see when she stood there in his arms.

He'd made her the promise she'd hoped for but never expected to find. As she repeated the words, Keena knew she was home. "I love you, Travis Armstrong. Nothing comes between us."

EPILOGUE

It was Thanksgiving. Travis settled his best hat firmly on his head and hopped out of the truck. He took the stack of containers Keena had handed him with firm orders to "Be careful. There's a pie in there," and moved around the truck to meet her in front. Micah was holding her hand and Damon was leaning heavily on the crutch that made it easier to walk on uneven ground. He'd only need the aid for a few more days.

"Which one are the cookies in, Keena?" Micah asked as he ran a finger down the stack of containers.

"Red. It's your favorite color. That makes it easier to remember," Keena said as she bent down and added, "but I saved you a few at home, too." Her wink and fist bump reassured Micah so he zoomed ahead of Damon to the front door of the lodge and yanked it open for them.

"First official outing. You ready for this,

Steady Murphy?" Travis drawled. He loved to see the spark of annoyance that lit in her eyes, but she was onto him.

"That's it. The one time you get to say that today. You promised." She waggled her finger at him.

Travis was nodding as he dropped a quick kiss on her lips. "Yes, ma'am. You can trust me."

"I do." She slipped her arm through his and proceeded to the lodge. Inside, there was a crowd milling and Travis was impressed all over again at what the Hearsts had managed with some elbow grease and the assistance of their friends. The lobby was still sparsely decorated, but the restaurant appeared ready for business. After he set Keena's desserts down where his mother indicated, he stepped back to join the rest of the crowd. Everyone appeared to be forming a loose line in preparation for the ringing of the dinner bell.

Jordan Hearst raised her voice to get their attention. "I want to say a quick word…" She gestured to her sister. "Yes, Sarah, it'll be very quick, about how much we appreciate everyone coming here today. The Hearsts have so much to be grateful for, thanks to Prospect. We loved Sadie more than life, and we can't thank her enough for bringing us home, but we can thank you for making us family."

The sentiment captured exactly all the jumbled up words in his head as he stared at Keena. "I couldn't have said it any better."

When he realized everyone was staring at them, Travis cleared his throat.

"You were saying," Prue prompted him.

The happiness in Keena's eyes reassured him. From the very beginning, she'd understood him like no one ever had before. That hadn't changed. Somehow, they were connected and he knew in his heart that was only going to get stronger.

"Words aren't always easy for us," Keena whispered, "but you know what we're very good at?"

Travis traced his thumb over her cheek before he pressed his lips to hers. Their audience's wild whoops and applause confirmed that they were very good at kissing.

And with a lifetime ahead of them, they would only get better.

* * * * *

*For more great romances in
The Fortunes of Prospect miniseries
from Cheryl Harper and
Harlequin Heartwarming,
visit www.Harlequin.com today!*